# PRAISE FOR ALISSA BAXTER

"Romance and intrigue make a heady combination in this story about a young lady who knows her own mind and a dashing gentleman determined to change it. Filled with fascinating details about the Regency, this sweet romance is sure to delight any true fan of the period." ~ award-winning author Regina Scott

"Alissa Baxter's writing is period perfect." ~ Mimi Matthews, USA Today bestselling author of *The Matrimonial Advertisement*

"A truly traditional Regency romance, with lots of witty banter, very reminiscent of Georgette Heyer. Recommended for anyone who likes a completely clean traditional Regency, with strongly authentic writing, historical accuracy and a satisfying romance." ~ Mary Kingswood, author of traditional Regency romances

# OTHER TITLES BY ALISSA BAXTER

*The Earl's Lady Geologist*

*The Viscount's Lady Novelist*

*Send and Receive*
(republished as The Truth About Clicking Send and Receive)

*The Blog Affair*
(republished as The Truth About Cats and Bees)

# The Baronet's Lady Biologist

## Biologist

ALISSA BAXTER

For Jem and Tony, the original entomologist couple

# CHAPTER ONE

Georgiana Linfield frowned at her illustration of the life cycle of a butterfly. Had she known she would want to sketch insects one day, she would have paid more attention during her drawing and painting classes at the select ladies' seminary she had attended in Bath.

But copying pieces of fruit in a bowl or bunches of flowers artistically arranged in a vase had been deadly dull, and she had consequently paid scant attention to her drawing master. Now she was paying the price for her inattention.

Fortunately, her cousin Cassy—an excellent scientific illustrator—had given Georgiana advice on how to draw precisely from nature. Indeed, Georgiana's water-colour drawings were of an adequate standard. But her work was not, by any stretch of the imagination, in the same class as her cousin's. When she travelled to London next year, she was determined to ask Cassy for more lessons—that was, if her mother allowed it.

She heaved a sigh. Mama had been delighted when Georgiana informed her that she planned to spend more time drawing and painting after so many years of neglect. But when she discovered Georgiana intended to sketch beetles, butterflies, and other insects instead of the more conventional subject matter generally favoured by young ladies, she had read her yet another lecture about her shocking lack of feminine accomplishments.

Fortunately, Georgiana was proficient at playing the pianoforte, so at least Mama could find no fault there. She loved music and had found it easy to pay attention during those classes at the seminary.

Georgiana also tolerated her weekly dancing lessons, as the physical activity was an excellent outlet for her boundless energy. But the other tiresome accomplishments expected of a young lady about to make her come-out in London were the bane of her existence. At least once a day, she consigned Cousin Agnes, who insisted that she work on her needlework every afternoon, to Jericho.

What made it even more painful was that her twin brother, Stephen, wasn't forced to stay indoors, working on mindless activities. No, he was afforded a great deal more freedom than she and roamed the Linfield estate at will, unencumbered by the tiresome restrictions placed on Georgiana. She sighed again as she laid the drawing aside and returned her attention to the work she had been engaged in earlier.

Seated at a table in her father's natural history museum, she was compiling a chronological account of the yearly additions to his collections. Due to their size and variety, she had created several sections, each representing a separate class of the Animal Kingdom.

The door of the converted stable creaked, and Georgiana glanced up. She set her pencil on the table as Papa entered the museum, accompanied by two gentlemen.

The man just behind her father drew her attention. Tall and lean, he wore biscuit-coloured pantaloons, Hessian boots, and a many-caped greatcoat that fell to the stone floor in dramatic folds.

The gentleman who entered the airy chamber behind him was built on smaller lines. Instead of a traditional neckcloth, he sported a neckerchief of spotted cotton, a bright contrast to the beautifully folded cravat of the other man.

Georgiana stared at that pristine white neckcloth. Stephen would be entranced. Her brother spent hours in front of the mirror every day, trying to improve his cravat-tying skills. This man was clearly an expert at the art.

She lifted her gaze to the stranger's face and flushed at his raised eyebrows. His dark hair and faintly bronzed skin contrasted with light blue eyes.

"Ah, Georgiana," her father said. "Here you are. Your mother is searching for you, you know." He smiled and nodded in the direction of the taller man and then at his companion. "Allow me to present Sir Giles Tavistock and Viscount Hanssen, both renowned natural historians."

The two gentlemen bowed. Georgiana rose and curtseyed, her cheeks warming at Sir Giles's rather sceptical expression.

"Sir Giles recently returned from a trip to South America with a collection of butterflies. He has brought them to show me," her father said.

Georgiana resumed her seat. Papa had mentioned the baronet's proposed visit yesterday, but for some reason, she had envisioned a dusty old man—not this handsome young gentleman. She cleared her throat. "My father told me that you collect butterflies, Sir Giles. How fascinating it must have been to travel to South America."

Sir Giles met her gaze, and his lips curled into a faint smile that stopped just short of a sneer.

"We are fortunate Lord Hanssen accompanied Sir Giles today as he is a famous ornithologist and can have a look at our Black Stork," her father continued. He turned towards that gentleman. "It was captured by means of a shot-wound in the wing while migrating."

"A rare bird indeed," Lord Hanssen said. "I have only seen one other in England. In 1814, a Black Stork was shot on a moor in West Sedgemoor, in Somersetshire."

Her father pressed his lips together suddenly, his brow lowering. "Sir Giles, I meant to bring your butterfly collection to compare it with mine. Let me return to the house to fetch it." He sent Georgiana a meaningful look before leading the way out. "If you and Lord Hanssen would care to walk in the grounds, Sir Giles, I shall return directly."

The gentlemen bowed politely in her direction and followed her father outside. Georgiana let out the breath she had been holding. Her mama would be furious when she discovered her daughter had been here all afternoon instead of working on her embroidery.

She waited a few minutes, then crept around the table and made her way to the old stable door. Finding it slightly ajar, she was about to push it open when an amused masculine voice caught her attention: "Hounded, even here, Giles. The ladies flock to you, even in the depths of the country."

"It's a damned nuisance."

"I was quite taken aback at that vision of loveliness in a natural history museum, of all places. She's a real little beauty—are you sure you're not tempted?"

"Not at all." The baronet's voice was bored. "I have no desire to be caught in parson's mousetrap. Least of all with a disingenuous young lady feigning interest in natural history."

Lord Hanssen laughed. "A rather obvious ploy to place herself in your path. But you must admire her bravery. Did you see that bird-catching spider in the case behind her? My younger sister would have run screaming if she'd set eyes on it. But Miss Linfield sat composedly in front of it, as cool as you please."

"Let us walk in the grounds. I don't wish to be trapped in conversation should she emerge from the museum."

The men's voices faded away as they moved off, and Georgiana stood still, quivering with rage. How dare he? She jerked the door open and raced outside, her heart pounding in her ears. As if she would ever sink to such depths to attract a gentleman's attention. Who did he think he was?

She turned and stuck her tongue out at the men's retreating backs. The childish action relieved her agitated feelings somewhat as she strode up to the house, ignoring Cousin Agnes's advice to take dainty steps when she was out walking. Her father's elderly cousin pursed her lips nearly every day and said: "Georgiana, you must at least *attempt* to move with a feminine gait. You appear quite boyish, striding about as if you have no skirts to consider."

What a pity she had skirts to consider. They were a huge impediment when she was out on the estate, engaging in fieldwork. And when she knelt to examine a particularly interesting insect or frog, she often soiled her muslin gown, much to the dismay of her old nursemaid, Annie.

Annie had looked after her since she had been in the nursery. However, Mama had stated yesterday that she would be hiring a proper lady's maid to take care of her daughter's sartorial and personal needs in preparation for their journey to London next month. Georgiana only hoped she wouldn't be anything like Padgett, her mother's martial dresser, who had a stiff, imposing manner and viewed Georgiana with distinct disapproval.

She entered the house to find Benson, the butler, in the vestibule, his hands behind his back and his head bent slightly forward in a somewhat meditative stance.

"Lady Linfield asked me to inform you, Miss Georgiana, that she wishes to see you immediately you return to the house. Her ladyship is in the drawing room." He paused for a moment and then lowered his voice: "I advise you not to keep her waiting."

Georgiana grimaced. "Thank you, Benson."

She handed her old friend her cloak and bonnet and then hurried past him into the large, airy hall. Several doors led off from it, and she crossed the black and white chequerboard marble floor to a pair of double doors where a footman stood at attention. Walking past him, she entered the recently redecorated drawing room.

Her mother was seated on a chaise longue in front of a roaring fire. Georgiana hesitated a moment before approaching her. Why had she not examined her appearance in the mirror before bearding the lioness in her den?

Mama turned her head, a slight crease between her brows. "And where have you been, Georgiana?"

"Um… In the museum."

"Cousin Agnes told me that she left you working in the parlour on your embroidery, but when she returned, you had disappeared. And that was hours ago. It is not well done of you, Georgiana." Mama pursed her lips together. "If I have told you once, I have told you countless times, if you fail to refine your accomplishments, you will not be a success in London, no matter how beautiful you are. A gentleman wants a wife he can be proud of, one who will be able to hold her own in Society."

"But I hate embroidery!"

"It is not about the embroidery, my dear, but what the embroidery represents. Your lack of application to a skill which is an essential accomplishment for a young lady shows a deplorable lack of duty."

Georgiana frowned at the patterned Aubusson carpet. "Papa asked me to compile a chronological account of the yearly additions to his collections." She raised her eyes to meet her mother's censorious gaze. "If I am meant to work on my needlework, languages, and music all day, when will I be able to assist him?"

"I shall have a word with Papa. Now that we are getting closer to removing to London, you will need to stop working in the museum—or at least severely limit the time you spend there."

Her mouth dropped open. "Stop working there? Oh, no, Mama! I couldn't abide that."

"You know very well that one day you will need to focus your attention on a husband and children. Your passion for natural history will necessarily fade into the background. I am not saying that you must give up your interest in this subject as I know you enjoy the work. But while it may be a small part of your life, it must not represent the whole." She picked up a book from the table beside her. "I gave this to your sister before she married, and she told me she benefited greatly from its wisdom. I recommend you read it, as well."

Georgiana took the volume from her mother's hand. *Letters To A Young Lady: On A Variety Of Useful And Interesting Subjects, Calculated To Improve The Heart, To Form The Manners And Enlighten The Understanding* by Rev. John Bennett.

"You might be surprised at its content," her mother continued. "Mr Bennett speaks positively of young women who take an interest in natural history. But he also makes it clear that it should be only one of many interests a lady should cultivate."

Georgiana replied only with a brief jerk of her head.

"And now…on to the reason I have been looking for you, my love. Sir Giles Tavistock and Lord Hanssen stopped here on their way to Beverton Manor, where they will be staying with Oliver and Harriet. I wanted you to meet them, but you were nowhere to be found."

Georgiana knew her father was on friendly terms with Sir Giles, but she had not realised her brother-in-law, Oliver, was also acquainted with him. Her surprise must have shown as her mother continued: "I believe Sir Giles and Lord Hanssen were in the same year as Oliver at Eton and Oxford. Your sister came over to inform me that they will be making up a party to attend the Clifton Assembly tomorrow night. She wants you to join it."

"Oh."

Her mother frowned. "Is that all you have to say?"

"Oh, dear?"

"Don't be facetious, Georgiana. Most young ladies would be

delighted to be thrown in the path of Sir Giles. He is quite the matrimonial prize, I would have you know. He is very wealthy and is from an excellent family—connected to both the Earls of Fenmore and Rothbury."

Georgiana's brows drew together. Her half-brother, Edward, the Earl of Rothbury, was her mother's only child from her first marriage. Widowed young, she had remarried when Edward was a young boy, and then had four more children—James, Harriet, Stephen, and Georgiana. Theirs was a confusing family tree at times.

"How is Rothbury connected to Sir Giles? Am I also related to him?"

"No, no. Sir Giles is Rothbury's cousin on his father's side, so no relation of yours."

"That's a relief. He appears arrogant."

Her mother knit her brows. "You met Sir Giles at the museum?"

"Yes, and I found him proud and disdainful. Not an agreeable man at all."

"What did you do to set his back up?" Her mother's resigned tone stung, igniting Georgiana's ire.

"What did *I* do?" She narrowed her eyes. "It is more what *he* did to set up *my* back."

Her mother let out a long sigh. "I hope you haven't taken one of your unreasonable dislikes to him."

Georgiana was about to reply when her sister, Harriet, stepped into the room. "I left my reticule here and only realised it when I reached Beverton. Oh, there you are, Georgie! I was hoping to see you earlier, but you weren't here. Has Mama told you about the party we are making up for the Clifton Assembly?"

Georgiana nodded but made no reply.

"I am sure it will be delightful." Harriet smiled happily. "Be sure to wear that ball gown with the silver lama flowers, dearest. You look beautiful in it." She picked up her beaded reticule off the sofa. "I had better head back to Beverton. I should be there in time to welcome Sir Giles and Lord Hanssen."

"You don't need to make haste on their account, Harriet." Georgiana grudgingly supplied the information. "Papa is showing them around the museum."

"You met them there?"

"Papa presented them to me."

"I am sure you will have a great deal in common with Sir Giles, in particular, Georgie. He shares your fascination for butterflies." A fine line appeared between her brows. "I must go… I told Oliver I wouldn't be long. He must be wondering what has become of me."

Harriet bid Mama farewell and clasped Georgiana lightly on the arm as she left the room.

Georgiana gripped the book in her hand as her mother spoke again: "It will do you good to mingle in a more formal environment, my love."

"Yes, Mama." Her voice was wooden. Arguing with her mother about the ball would be pointless. Clearly, she was set on the idea. "If I may be excused…"

With her mother's nod of dismissal, Georgiana hurried out of the room. She would do her best to avoid Sir Giles tomorrow evening. In the ordinary course of events, she would love to discuss natural history with a fellow enthusiast. But not with him. Never with him. The baronet's condescending comments at the museum echoed in her mind, heating her blood to the boiling point again. He was detestable.

# CHAPTER TWO

Georgiana reached her room, flung herself onto her bed, and stared up at the canopy. After a few moments, she turned over, opened the book her mother had given her, and paged through it, stopping at a passage near the beginning of the volume of letters: "They, who talk degradingly of women, do not know the value of the treasure they despise... The sedentariness of your life, naturally followed with low spirits or *ennui*, whilst we are seeking health and pleasure in the field... will expose you to a number of peculiar sorrows."

She jerked upright as she reread the passage. How odd that a man had put her frustrations into a nutshell. Her mama and Cousin Agnes acted as if they did not exist and tried to brush them aside.

Reading on, she grimaced when she saw that the author believed domestic qualifications were the highest point of usefulness for females. But this must only be because, like most men, he considered his comfort of paramount importance, and only women could provide for it.

Still, he had summed up the essence of her dissatisfaction with her lot in life, and it was reassuring to have it acknowledged in black and white. She wished to work in a scientific field rather than be confined to a dull, inactive life. That ladies were kept from such activities was the height of unfairness.

She frowned at the pale blue silk counterpane. Why had her sister invited her to join her party? She knew Georgiana had no interest in attending public assemblies.

Although Harriet did not lecture her as Mama and Cousin Agnes were prone to do, she made it clear that she was concerned about Georgiana's lacklustre attitude towards her upcoming Season. Perhaps she was trying to pique her interest by throwing her in the path of two eligible males.

She sighed. What a pity that Harriet had married Oliver so shortly after meeting him. The plan had been that she'd be presented in London next year, and Georgiana would have her Season the year after.

However, Harriet and Oliver had met and wed this year, and Harriet no longer needed Mama's chaperonage during the upcoming Season. Therefore, Mama decided to bring out Georgiana in her sister's stead, effectively removing her extra year of precious freedom.

As Papa had obtained a seat in the House of Commons during the general election, they would be travelling to London for the Opening of Parliament in January. Georgiana would be trapped in London from then on.

At a tap on the door, she rolled off the bed. "Come in."

Her twin brother poked his head inside. "Papa wishes to speak to you in his study."

Her mouth turned downwards. "I suppose I am in trouble again."

"He didn't look angry when he asked me to call you."

She gave a slight shrug and moved towards the door. "Did you meet Papa's guests?"

His face lit up. "Yes, indeed. They are ever so knowledgeable about natural history. I am inclined to accept Harriet's invitation to the Assembly tomorrow. I want to speak to Sir Giles about my beetle collection. He has written several papers about insects for the Linnean Society, you know."

"Oh?"

He raised his brows. "I thought you would be more enthusiastic, Georgie. Sir Giles has a particular interest in butterflies."

"So Papa said. I met Sir Giles at the museum earlier. But I found him rather high in the instep."

"You did? I did not find him so. He seemed a very agreeable sort of chap, as a matter of fact. He was interested to learn of my discovery of the *Ctesias serra*."

She shook her head, a smile playing about her mouth. "You would find a dead bore agreeable if they shared your interest in rare woodland beetles." She glanced at the clock on the wall. "I'd better not keep Papa waiting."

She hastened down the corridor towards the curved oak staircase but slowed as she descended the stairs. No need to bring more censure upon herself should her mother discover her walking at such an unladylike pace.

She knocked on the study door and entered the room. Seated behind his mahogany desk, with its green leather top, her father perused one page of a multi-leafed letter. He glanced up at Georgiana's approach and waved at the upright chair in front of the writing-table. "Sit down, my dear. Sit down."

She took her seat and gazed at him expectantly, but his gaze had fallen once again to the letter he held. Eventually, he looked up. "Well, well… My cousin Howard has written to me. When I made that brief trip to the Capital a fortnight ago, I told him about the work you've been doing for me in the museum. He has written to ask my permission for you to perform the same task for him when we travel to London. Cousin Howard has an impressive natural history collection in his home in Grosvenor Square, but it needs to be organised."

Georgiana sat frozen in her chair before leaning forward to place her clasped hands on the desk. "That would be delightful, Papa. But will Mama allow me to work there?"

"I am certain she will. She has been concerned that you will not have enough to absorb your energy in London in the months leading up to the Season." His smile was somewhat rueful. "She has always been confounded by your tirelessness, my dear."

Georgiana's eyebrows snapped together. "But Mama just told me that I need to spend more time refining my accomplishments."

"I am sure there will be enough hours in the day for you to assist Cousin Howard and also perform the tasks your mama requires of you."

"I sincerely hope so." Her voice was fierce. "The work will make my time in London more tolerable."

"Try not to speak like that, my love. It distresses your mama when you show so little interest in your London Season." He steepled his fingers together as he studied her intently. "I have reassured her that you are still very young and that you will develop an interest in marriage when the time is right. You are not yet turned eighteen, after all, so I cannot understand the hurry. But try not to behave as if it is a curse to be coming out. Most young ladies would be overjoyed at the opportunity."

She pressed her lips together. "Yes, Papa."

"It is a pity that you did not see Sir Giles's butterfly collection before he left, my dear. It is truly magnificent. He has taken it to Beverton to show Wentford. Perhaps you could ask to see it when you visit your sister next."

Her brother-in-law, Oliver, Viscount Wentford, was married to Harriet. The Wentfords, who were currently staying at Beverton Manor, the small estate bordering Linfield Court, were in the process of transforming the manor into an orphan house for young girls.

"How long will Sir Giles be staying at Beverton?"

"A sennight, I believe. You really should try to see it."

She rose to her feet. "If you would excuse me, Papa, I need to dress for dinner."

At his nod, she turned and left the room. Even though she would love to see those butterflies, she wouldn't visit Harriet until Sir Giles had left Beverton Manor. If she did pay a morning call on her sister, the man would doubtless say she was hounding him, such was his conceit. When she saw him at the Assembly tomorrow, she would ensure she left him in no doubt that he held no attraction for her.

The next evening, she examined herself critically in the glass as Padgett put the final touches to her hair. Her mama had insisted that her own personal maid assist Georgiana to dress before the ball, and she had submitted to the woman's ministrations without protest. No use in complaining, after all.

And in truth, although Padgett wasn't in the least amiable, she was very good at her job. Georgiana wore the elegant white gown, embroidered at the hem with silver lama flowers, which Harriet had suggested. Her dark hair had a natural wave, and Padgett had teased out a few curls to frame her face before crowning the arrangement with a wreath of white rosebuds and pearls that matched her simple pearl necklace and earrings.

The maid stood back to examine her and then gave a brief nod. "Now mind, Miss Georgiana, not to soil your dress."

Georgiana bit back a terse reply. Padgett, like her old nurse-maid Annie, treated her as if she were still in the schoolroom. Perhaps it wasn't such a bad thing that Mama was hiring a lady's maid for her. Being surrounded by family retainers who had known her since the cradle, made it hard to feel like a grown woman.

A few minutes later, she left her bedchamber and made her way down the stairs. Stephen awaited her in the hall, and John-coachman would drive them to Beverton Manor. From there, they would travel on to the ball in the Wentford carriage.

Her mother and father would not attend the gathering tonight because Harriet, now a married lady, was considered a suitable chaperon for Georgiana. She found the arrangement quite a relief. Harriet did not criticise her every move or assume she was on the verge of making a *faux pas* at any moment, as her mother and Cousin Agnes were wont to do.

The Wentford family coach awaited them when they arrived at Beverton Manor. Her brother-in-law, attired in elegant evening wear, greeted her warmly before assisting her inside, where her sister was already seated.

"Sir Giles and Lord Hanssen will follow us," Harriet said as Oliver and Stephen took their seats. Her sister smiled as the carriage lurched forward a few moments later. "I hope you will enjoy your evening, Georgie. I remember being overwhelmed when I attended my first public ball at the Lyme Assembly Rooms. It is quite a different experience from dancing in the ballroom at home."

"I suppose it is a good opportunity for me to practise my dance steps in a more formal setting." She turned to her brother. "It will be good for you too. You always step on my toes."

Stephen shook his head adamantly. "I don't intend to dance. After I've spoken to Sir Giles, I'll steal away to the card room."

"Would that I was you," Georgiana said gloomily and then felt churlish at Harriet's downcast expression, visible in the dim light from the carriage lamp.

The Clifton Assembly Rooms were situated in The Clifton

Hotel in the Mall, a grand building with rooms of the first description. Their party entered the cloakroom, where a large group of ladies and gentlemen had already assembled. Georgiana wrapped her paisley shawl more tightly around her shoulders, trying not to shiver. A chill laced the evening, but dancing should warm her up.

The assemblies were held every alternate Tuesday during the winter season under the superintendence of the master of ceremonies, Mr Madden, who had greeted them upon their arrival. Georgiana looked around at the crowd of ball-goers. Most of the younger ladies wore white, while the older women dressed in darker hues. Some men donned military costume, but most of the gentlemen were attired in formal wear, sombre moths amongst their bright butterfly ladies.

The ballroom doors opened, and they had turned to make their way inside when Sir Giles and Lord Hanssen joined them.

Georgiana nodded stiffly as the two men bowed and murmured greetings, their unkind words of the previous day still ringing in her ears. She turned away, grateful that Stephen was at her side. She need not accept an invitation from either of them to escort her into the room.

Her relief was short-lived, however. Just after they entered the spacious chamber, where musicians were striking up for the first dance of the evening, the baronet spoke quietly in her sister's ear.

"Yes, of course, Sir Giles," Harriet said with a warm smile. "I am sure my sister will be delighted to dance with you."

⁓

Giles bowed in Miss Linfield's direction and then proffered his arm. She held her head at a stiff angle, not looking in the least as if she wanted to dance with him. But after a moment's hesitation, she curtseyed and placed her hand on his arm.

He led her into the middle of the ballroom, where she took her place opposite him. As they waited for the rest of the set to form, he said, "Lady Wentford told me that this is your first public assembly."

She inclined her head but made no reply.

He frowned slightly, studying her impassive features. Only her eyes were expressive, flashing daggers at him. What had he done to set her back up? Or perhaps she was merely nervous about dancing with a strange man.

"Your father showed me around the museum yesterday, and he said that you organised and categorised all his specimens. You enjoy such work?"

She opened her eyes very wide. "Oh no, Sir Giles. I only *feign* an interest to throw myself in the path of unsuspecting males."

He snapped his brows together. "You overheard me."

She gave a tiny shrug as the dance started, and then conversation became impossible as they progressed down the set.

Giles took her hands in his as they danced down the centre of the line, and then they separated and came to a standstill when they reached the bottom of the set. As they awaited their turn to dance again, he murmured, "Eavesdroppers never hear any good of themselves, Miss Linfield."

Her eyes narrowed. "I was *not* eavesdropping. I was about to leave the museum to return to the house when I overheard your conversation. Do young ladies really pursue you so fervently?"

"I cannot answer that question without sounding ungentlemanly."

She gave him a brittle smile. "As I already consider you so, it should make no difference."

He stiffened. "Are you always so outspoken?"

"It is my besetting sin, according to Mama."

They began to progress down the set again, and Giles contemplated the top of her head as they came together to complete a figure. When they paused, once again, in the movement of the dance, he said, "I regret that you overheard my conversation with Lord Hanssen, Miss Linfield, and as a *gentleman,* I offer you my apology. However, a word of advice…" He waited until she raised her defiant green eyes to his. "If you wish to have a successful Season in London, it would be wise to cultivate a few social graces."

The colour rose in her cheeks, staining alabaster skin. A vision of beauty, she stood in obvious defiance, staring up at him, and Giles ignored an unmistakable tug of attraction.

Miss Georgiana Linfield was not for him.

Georgiana wrenched her gaze away from Sir Giles's and reproached herself for allowing her sense of outrage to get the better of her. Now she had committed the cardinal sin of behaving in an unladylike manner. Why could she never curb her tongue? She spoke without care of any possible consequences, and time and time again, it landed her in trouble.

They did not speak for the rest of the dance, and when Sir Giles returned her to her sister's side, Lord Hanssen requested that she stand up with him. And from then on, she was never without a partner.

She enjoyed the physical outlet that dancing provided, but attending a ball was not merely about pleasure and exercise. Young women were, in essence, being critically measured as potential marriage partners in this complicated social ritual. Georgiana found that aspect of an assembly profoundly distasteful, as it reinforced the role that Society expected of women—one of decorativeness and compliance.

Even the act of dancing reinforced the submissive role of women—the gentleman always took the lead, after all. If only there were some way she could take charge of her own life.

But although her portion was respectable, she was no heiress. She needed to marry well to avoid ending up alone and dependent on various family members for a roof over her head. Her independent nature shied away from the dreadful thought, but its truth could not be denied. She had limited choices, and she needed to face that fact.

The best thing she could do was find an indulgent husband who would not impose his will on her but rather give her the liberty to pursue her interests. An image of Sir Giles's handsome face flashed into her mind, and she dismissed it with a toss of her head. The baronet was the last man she would ever consider marrying. He would no doubt rule his household with a rod of iron. She planned to wed someone so besotted with her that he would give her free rein to do whatever she wanted.

# CHAPTER THREE

They arrived in London on a cold, inclement morning in January. When their coach drew up in front of Linfield House in Berkeley Square, Georgiana gazed at the dripping plane trees in the garden. What a gloomy prospect. She already felt trapped.

She descended from the carriage and followed her mother inside. Her father, Stephen, and Cousin Agnes had made the journey in another coach and would arrive soon if they encountered no travel mishaps.

Georgiana made her way upstairs to her bedchamber. Decorated in delicate shades of blue and gold, it was warm and cosy, with a fire burning merrily in the grate. She stretched her hands out to the dancing flames long enough to feel their warmth and then walked over to the window. She smiled wistfully at the view below—an oblong, shrub-filled garden enclosed by an iron balustrade in the centre of the Square.

Her mother had allowed her to collect worms from the garden in boxes when she was a child. But now that she was about to make her come-out, it was doubtful that Mama would consent to such activities. She let out a deep sigh before turning around when the door opened. Kirby, the lady's maid her mother had hired for her in Bristol, entered the room.

Kirby directed Peter, the footman, where to place Georgiana's trunks, and when he left the room, she bobbed a curtsey. "Her ladyship requests that you join her in the drawing room, ma'am."

After the maid assisted her into another gown and tidied her somewhat rumpled curls, Georgiana made her way to the airy reception room. She came to an abrupt halt when she crossed the threshold. If she could beat a retreat, she would… Her brother, Rothbury, spoke to her mother, and standing beside him near the fireplace was Sir Giles Tavistock.

The baronet bowed when he saw her, and she dropped a curtsey in return before hurrying over to Rothbury. He took her outstretched hands and smiled. "How are you, brat?"

"All the better for seeing you." She squeezed his fingers. "How is Cassy?"

"Very well. She plans to visit later today. Sir Giles and I were just passing on our way to White's." He turned towards the baronet. "I believe you have already met my cousin, Georgie?"

"We met at Linfield." Stepping away from Rothbury, she inclined her head. "How do you do, sir?"

Her mother, seated on the chintz sofa, said in a bright voice: "Georgiana, I have been telling Sir Giles all about your great love for butterflies. He has promised to bring his collection for you to view. Whyever didn't you make the time to see it when Sir Giles was staying at Beverton? Your father was amazed that you did not jump at the opportunity."

Georgiana met the baronet's eyes and flushed. "Yes, well, I was fully occupied in completing my work in the museum before we left for London."

"Such conscientiousness," Sir Giles murmured.

She smiled coolly. "Nothing holds a greater attraction for me than my work, Sir Giles."

"Nothing, Miss Linfield?" His blue eyes glinted.

"Nothing at all." She turned to speak to her brother. "How was your wedding trip? Did Cassy enjoy travelling to the Continent?"

"Very much so. I am sure she will tell you all about it when she sees you."

Georgiana pressed the palms of her hands together. "I am delighted you have come to London, particularly as I have been hoping Cassy will assist me with my scientific illustrations."

Her mother's brow creased. "I am sure Cassandra will give you some useful advice regarding her technique, my love. But I trust you plan to draw such things as flowers and landscapes as well?"

"An excellent notion, Mama. It is a fine idea to place insects among flowers in their natural environment."

"I thought you could perhaps...er...occasionally leave the insects out?" She cleared her throat. "They do not have to be present in *all* your drawings and paintings, my love."

"No?" Georgiana's mouth tilted up at the corners.

"No!" Her mother shook her head when Georgiana let out a peal of laughter. "You persist in teasing me, my love."

Rothbury chuckled. "Well, you do rise so beautifully to the bait, Mama." He turned to Sir Giles. "We should be off."

The two men took their leave. However, a few moments later, Sir Giles stepped back inside. "I shall bring my butterfly collection to show you tomorrow if that suits you, Miss Linfield?"

"Oh, yes. Thank you, sir. I look forward to seeing it."

He studied her thoughtfully. "Would you consider drawing the various specimens for me if Lady Linfield has no objection? I am seeking an artist to sketch each butterfly."

He glanced at her mother, who nodded and smiled. "An excellent plan, Sir Giles. It will put my daughter's talents to good purpose. She is always seeking out opportunities for scientific illustration."

"Miss Linfield?" Sir Giles spoke quietly, but there was a thread of laughter in his voice.

Georgiana clenched her jaw. He was studying her very much as she imagined a stoat would examine a rabbit. But she was not so easily intimidated.

"I would be pleased to assist you," she said in a calm voice. "It sounds like the sort of collection that would be dear to any natural historian's heart. I want to do your butterflies justice, but I imagine you will need the collection when you write your paper?"

"I have a duplicate of each specimen, so I will keep the one collection with me while you work on the other." He bowed. "Thank you, Miss Linfield. And *au revoir*."

He left the room, and Georgiana stared at the door, which the footman closed after him. "*Au revoir?*"

"Sir Giles's mother is French."

"Ah."

"I am glad you appear to be warming to him, my love. He would be an excellent match for you, you know. Your father and

I would welcome it."

Her eyes narrowed. "I am not warming to him at all, Mama. I was merely trying to be civil."

"But he would be an ideal suitor! I would think you would find him most appealing as he shares your love of entomology. I have been so relieved that we need not hide your interests from him, as we shall need to do with other suitors, at least in the beginning..." She dabbed at the corners of her eyes with her handkerchief. "It greatly concerns me that your peculiar pursuits could make you the laughingstock of Polite Society."

Georgiana stepped closer to her mother. "Forgive me, Mama. I did not mean to distress you."

"It is merely that I am troubled about your future. If you do not conform to Society's expectations, you may become an outcast, and I couldn't bear that." She crumpled the linen square in her hands. "That is why I was so delighted when your papa told me Sir Giles was coming to Linfield. As he shares your interests, he won't think you strange."

"No," she said slowly. "But shared interests are not the only basis for marriage."

"Indeed, my love. And if you cannot see him as a potential suitor, I shall say no more." She placed her head on one side. "Although, I am somewhat surprised at your indifference towards him. Sir Giles is a very handsome man."

"Handsome men are not always agreeable."

"He does not seem *dis*agreeable."

"He thinks far too highly of himself."

Her mother sighed. "Well, if you cannot like him, I shan't attempt to change your mind."

"Thank you."

Her mama regarded her with a contemplative expression on her face. "So, what kind of man *would* you like to marry?"

Georgiana tilted her chin up. "Someone as unlike Sir Giles as possible."

～

Giles walked beside his cousin as they made their way to White's, a slight frown marring his brow. That Miss Linfield had consented to illustrate his butterfly collection for him was a boon. He had, in all truth, doubted she would be agreeable to the idea. Her love for insects, however, had clearly won out over her dislike for him.

It intrigued him that she had such an interest in natural history. And not just an interest…from what he could ascertain, she appeared to be fascinated by the subject—unlike his sisters, who screamed whenever he tried to show them any of the insects he collected. He had assumed all young ladies were cast in a similar mould…thus his unkind assessment of Miss Linfield's presence in her father's natural history museum.

Having grown accustomed to any number of ploys used by scheming mamas seeking to throw their daughters in his path, he had immediately assumed the worst of Miss Linfield and had voiced his scepticism to Hanssen. And now, she appeared to detest him for his dismissive words, which was understandable. However, after being pursued as a matrimonial prize for many years, he found Miss Linfield's dislike of him a novel experience.

He travelled abroad frequently on entomological expeditions. When he returned to England, he avoided the Marriage Mart in Town as he was not yet ready to stop his travels and settle down, no matter how much his sisters plagued him.

His mother was more discreet about her concern for his single state, but even she had studied him searchingly when he visited her on his way to the Capital. "Will you remain for the Season, *mon cher*?" she had said.

She looked relieved when he told her of his plans to write a scientific paper for the Linnean Society, which necessitated a journey to London. Giles had been planning to ask his cousin's new wife to illustrate his article. However, he had been reluctant to impose on her time as she was in the process of assisting Rothbury with his latest geological paper after their recent return from Germany.

Therefore, Miss Linfield's being agreeable to represent his specimens artistically came as a relief.

Miss Linfield… His lips twisted into a wry smile. Perhaps she would thaw over the next few weeks as she collaborated with him. Although, maybe not. She had been at pains to show him that her interest lay in his butterflies and not in him. Which should be a relief. The last thing he wanted was to raise any expectations in the breast of a young lady about to make her come-out.

However, despite his logical assessment of the situation, he couldn't deny that her indifference rankled. Miss Linfield's complete dismissal of him as a potential suitor put him on his mettle, igniting in him a strong desire to pick up the gauntlet she had so defiantly flung down when she had informed him that nothing held a greater attraction for her than her work.

But it would not be wise to do so. Embarking on a game of flirtation with a gently-bred young lady was the first step to becoming leg-shackled. And that was something he was determined to avoid until he had fulfilled his wanderlust. His restless spirit precluded him from marrying before he was ready, and he did not plan to settle down for a couple of years at least.

He must resist the temptation to flirt with the beautiful Miss Linfield. Somehow, he knew it wouldn't be easy.

# CHAPTER FOUR

As promised, Sir Giles brought his butterflies the next day. When the door opened, Georgiana was seated in the drawing room with Cousin Agnes, trying to untangle some embroidery threads. She rose from her chair and curtseyed in response to his bow, and then her gaze flew to the large book he held.

After Sir Giles exchanged polite greetings with her elderly cousin, he walked over to Georgiana and presented the tome. But Georgiana's attempts to open it showed the "tome" wasn't a book at all, but a store-box designed to look like a leather-bound volume.

The scent of camphor tickled her nostrils as she studied the exotic specimens pinned inside on paper-lined cork. One butterfly, with significant green markings on its black forewings and red spots on the outer edge of its hindwings, caught her attention. "What splendid colours, Sir Giles! That is a beautiful shade of green."

"Emerald," he murmured. "Like your eyes."

As she met his intent gaze, heat rushed into her face, but she did not look away. She wasn't some simpering female, easily thrown into a flutter when a man made an audacious comment. If only she could wipe that hovering little smile from his lips with a sharp set-down, but it was probably best to ignore his remark, especially with Cousin Agnes listening in.

She cleared her throat. "What species is it?"

"A *Parides sesostris*. From Caracas."

"How fascinating it must have been to travel to that part of the world. Papa has a bird-catching spider from South America."

"Indeed. I saw it in his museum. You were sitting in front of it as calmly as can be. Lord Hanssen was most impressed at your imperturbability."

She raised her brows. "Was he expecting me to cower in terror?"

"Let us just say that most young ladies do not have your...er...intrepidity."

"Indeed. My sister is quite terrified of spiders. I like all living creatures, though. Even the large and hairy ones."

Sir Giles's lips twitched. "I am pleased to hear that."

"I meant the large and hairy *spiders*."

"Of course you did." His voice was annoyingly soothing.

Georgiana glared down at the butterflies. "I will start drawing these as soon as I can. However, I will be sorting out my father's cousin's insect collection during the next few weeks, so I may take some time to complete the illustrations. Do you need them by a specific date?"

"Would you be able to complete them within the next couple of months?"

Georgiana placed the store-box on a side table and resumed her seat. "I shall do my best to finish the work by then. Pray be seated, sir."

Cousin Agnes cleared her throat as the baronet sat on the sofa. "I am pleased dear Georgiana has such a feminine subject to draw on this occasion. Perhaps after she has painted your butterflies, Sir Giles, she should embroider them on cloth. I shall assist her, of course. She is still gaining proficiency in all the accomplishments required of a young lady, are you not, my dear?"

Before Georgiana could respond, her cousin continued: "I thank God for small mercies that her interest lies with butterflies and not with those beetles her brother favours." She wrinkled her nose in distaste. "Imagine embroidering *those* ugly creatures on cloth."

"They are not ugly at all, Cousin Agnes. In fact, if you study them closely, you will see how beautiful they are."

As the elderly lady shook her head vehemently back and forth, Georgiana sighed. "Insects are much-maligned creatures. In fact,

I would go so far as to say that they are viewed in very much the same way as women in our society."

Her cousin's eyes widened, and then her gaze darted nervously to Sir Giles. "What do you mean, my dear? Of all the nonsensical things to say."

"No, it is not nonsensical. Insects aren't appreciated at all by most people but are seen as fit only to be trodden underfoot and crushed. As William Burke states in his *Introduction to Entomology* we need to remove from our minds deeply rooted, long-standing prejudices against insects."

"Who, precisely, is crushing you underfoot, Miss Linfield?" Sir Giles leaned against the back of the sofa, folding his arms.

She shrugged. "I'm afraid society crushes all women underfoot. As a result, I cannot pursue my interest in science as a man can. Instead, I must focus my attention on finding a husband."

"So you are looking for a husband?" His eyes gleamed. "I thought nothing held a greater attraction for you than your work."

"Nothing does," she said sweetly. "Which is why I plan to make a very wise choice in my husband."

"Seeking to rule the roost, Miss Linfield?" he drawled.

She smiled but made no reply, merely folding her hands neatly in her lap.

"Be careful what you wish for, *mon papillon.* A henpecked husband could become somewhat dull after a while." He rose to his feet and glanced across at Cousin Agnes. "Your servant, ma'am. Miss Linfield."

And with a glinting smile and a bow, he left the room.

～

The next day, Georgiana and Cousin Agnes walked the short distance from Berkeley Square to Grosvenor Square, where Cousin Howard resided with his sister. When they entered the stately house, a footman led them towards the library. As Georgiana stepped over the threshold, she gazed around the wood-panelled room, with its gallery above, and then turned to greet her father's cousin, who had been a frequent visitor at Linfield Court before a stroke confined him to a wheelchair the previous year.

"My dear, how you have grown up!" He still had the same twinkle in his eye, but he was a shadow of the robust man he had once been. "Do you still soil your gowns and invoke your mama's wrath upon every possible occasion?"

She dropped a curtsey. "I am afraid so, Cousin Howard."

He chuckled. "You have a knack for going against the grain, my dear. Quite refreshing, I must say." His jovial smile faded somewhat as he nodded at her companion. "Cousin Agnes."

The door opened at that moment, and his sister, Cousin Theodosia, entered the room. "My dear cousins, how delightful to see you again." Her gaze rested exclusively on Cousin Agnes. "I have asked Peterson to bring our tea to the library so we may have a comfortable cose while our young cousin receives instructions about the work my brother wishes her to do." She turned her head to view Georgiana critically. "I must say, I was surprised when I was informed that a girl not yet turned eighteen would be organising his collection. My brother assures me, however, that Cousin Georgiana is quite up to the task."

"Indeed, she is," Cousin Howard said. "Our young cousin is skilled in categorising specimens and has done wonderful work in Barnaby's museum."

Georgiana had only met Cousin Howard's sister on one occasion when she accompanied him on a visit to Linfield Court. She hadn't warmed to the older lady at all as she tended to speak as if she had a very pungent smell under her nose. However, she smiled and curtseyed in response to Cousin Theodosia's greeting. Still, she let out a breath of relief when the woman led Cousin Agnes towards a sofa at the far end of the spacious chamber, where they settled down and began a low, earnest conversation.

Georgiana gazed at the leather tomes which lined the shelves of the wall. "What a splendid collection of books, Cousin Howard."

He glanced at the shelves. "Oh, those aren't books, my dear. They have been designed to look like a stack of leather-bound volumes, but they are, in fact, store-boxes for my insects."

"Of course." Georgiana nodded. "I saw such a box yesterday. Sir Giles Tavistock has stored his South American butterfly collection in something very similar."

He raised bushy grey brows. "Giles is in town? I hope the boy comes to see me soon. He enjoys pottering around my library, although he has told me on numerous occasions that it needs better organisation. Which is where *you* come in, my dear." He beamed at her.

Georgiana's eyes widened. "You are acquainted with Sir Giles?"

"He is my godson."

"Oh."

"I taught him all I know about entomology, and now his knowledge surpasses mine. His travels take him all around the world, and I look forward to seeing his exotic discoveries whenever he returns home. Is it a good collection of Flies?"

"Very much so. And expertly pinned."

"Indeed, I showed Giles the correct way to pin an insect as a boy. He is also most particular with his storage techniques, and although it isn't common practice, we both agree on the necessity of labelling each item. Unfortunately, too many collections lack any identifying system." He nodded at a nearby chair. "Please be seated, my dear."

"What sort of system do you have?" she asked as she took her seat.

"I have kept a written record over the years of all the insects I have collected, with an account of the place I found each specimen, the food it ate, and the time of day it appeared. In addition, each insect was assigned a number corresponding to a description in one of my journals." He waved at the shelves across the room. "But as you can see, I have a large number of collection boxes, and it is frequently difficult to locate what I am looking for."

"So my task is to arrange everything into a more accessible system?"

"Indeed. I need you to transcribe all of my descriptions into one journal. A tedious task, I'm afraid, but I trust you will find some pleasure in viewing my collection."

"I can assure you I won't find it tedious at all."

He smiled. "I am pleased to hear that, my dear. As much as I have enjoyed my work as a collector over the years, my attention of late has shifted to biology—the theory of living organisms as opposed to their mere classification."

"Oh!" She leaned forward eagerly. "I have a great interest in the different forms of life and how they come into being. I like to study the anatomy of invertebrate animals under a microscope."

"You are a biologist then as well, my dear, and not merely a natural historian. There is a distinction, you know."

"A lady biologist… if only I could be that."

"And why shouldn't you be?" He raised his brows. "Your father tells me you have an extensive knowledge of living creatures."

"I am afraid I need to marry. My life has been planned out for me. Marriage, children, and perhaps a little dabbling in natural history on the side, when time allows." Her voice crackled a bit, faintly bitter.

"You are still very young, my dear. You need not marry for a while. And hopefully, you will find someone who shares your interests, as your brother did."

"Yes." The corners of her mouth tilted up. "Rothbury and Cassy are ideally suited, and Cassy illustrates all Rothbury's specimens for him. Perhaps I should aim to be a wife-assistant to a man of science as well."

"I would suggest my godson as a possible suitor, my dear, but I doubt he will marry for a while yet. Passionate butterfly hunters are notoriously difficult to pin down." He chuckled at his own joke.

Georgiana pressed her lips together. "I have no interest in attracting Sir Giles's attention."

"Wise young lady."

She inclined her head towards a corner of the room, where a mahogany table held a stack of journals and a variety of writing materials. "Is that where I am to work, Cousin?"

"Indeed. I have left everything you may need for your task on that desk. I must thank you for giving up your time, my dear. Most young ladies would not wish to be confined to a library upon first arriving in London."

"It is my pleasure," she murmured as she stood up. She had taken only a single step towards the mahogany desk when the door opened. The butler's stentorian voice announced: "Sir Giles Tavistock."

# CHAPTER FIVE

Giles advanced into the room and halted, surprised to see Miss Linfield standing next to his godfather, seated in his wheelchair. The older man looked up, and a smile lit his face as Giles greeted him.

"Ah, Giles, my boy. We were just speaking of you. Georgiana was telling me about your South American butterfly collection." His godfather's gaze rested on the leather box he carried. "Is that it?"

"It is."

"Splendid, my boy. Splendid."

Giles bowed in Miss Linfield's direction and murmured a greeting before walking over to the older man. "I trust you are well, sir?"

"Never been better…especially since my young cousin has agreed to organise my insect collection." He rubbed his hands together, looking pleased.

Giles studied Miss Linfield. "I did not realise it was my godfather's collection you planned to organise."

"Indeed." Her smile seemed a trifle forced. "It would appear we live in a surprisingly small world."

"A trifle too small for you, Miss Linfield?"

She opened her eyes wide. "If I agree with you, sir, I will appear terribly rude."

He laughed before turning back to his godfather. "It appears we have both called upon Miss Linfield for aid. She has agreed to illustrate these butterflies for me."

"A most talented young lady, is she not? We must keep her skills to ourselves, though. Otherwise, all the gentlemen in the Linnean Society will be asking for her assistance."

Giles studied Miss Linfield's face carefully. She really was very lovely. If gentlemen from the Linnean Society sought an introduction to her, it was doubtful they would approach her only for her entomology skills. She was tall and slim, with dark hair that contrasted strikingly with a creamy complexion. But her eyes were her most remarkable feature—brilliant green with thickly fringed lashes, sure to stop any man dead in his tracks.

Her cheeks pinked slightly under his inspection, and then she moved swiftly away to sit at a nearby table. "If you would excuse me, sir, I need to start my work."

Giles looked down the length of the room to where his god-father's sister conversed with Mrs Linfield. Handing the box of butterflies over to his mentor, he walked across to greet the older ladies before returning a few minutes later.

Miss Linfield was paging through one of the journals and did not look up when he passed the table. He rested his gaze on her bowed head for a moment, a crease between his brows, but then his godfather began firing questions at him in rapid succession.

Out of the corner of his eye, he noticed when Miss Linfield glanced up from her work. And soon, she abandoned all pretence of reading his godfather's journals as she leaned back in her chair, listening openly to their conversation.

"I wish I were still fit enough to travel the world." The older man sighed. "But, alas, my hunting days are behind me. At least you can bring me back your finds, Giles, and I can live vicariously through your experiences." He glanced across at Miss Linfield. "I am sure my young cousin envies you your freedom as well. She was just saying that she won't be able to pursue her interest in biology once she marries due to the limitations society places on females."

Miss Linfield opened her mouth to speak but then clamped her lips together again when Mrs Linfield approached her with their hostess in tow.

"I have just informed Cousin Theodosia that we must leave," Mrs Linfield said as she came to a halt. "Your mama wants you to work on your needlework this afternoon, Georgiana."

Miss Linfield gave a wry smile as she stacked the books neatly in front of her. "I shall return tomorrow morning, Cousin Howard."

"Thank you, my dear."

Miss Linfield rose to her feet and murmured her farewells before following her female relatives out of the library.

Giles studied the door, which closed softly behind her. "An unusual young woman."

"Refreshingly so. She was always grubbing around in the dirt as a young girl, looking for insects. I hope she can sort out my collection for me."

"I am sure she will. The museum at Linfield Court is very well organised. And it is mostly due to Miss Linfield's efforts, her father tells me."

His godfather settled back more comfortably in his chair. "Then it is a good thing that I secured her assistance before the Season starts. She won't remain unmarried for long. Not with that face."

~

When Georgiana returned to Berkeley Square, Rothbury and his wife, Cassy, were in the drawing room. Georgiana darted a look at Cousin Agnes as she sat across from them on the chaise longue. Thank goodness her older brother's visit gave her an excuse not to work on her embroidery.

Cassy sat on the sofa beside her. "How are you, dearest?" Her face lit up in a warm smile. "Edward tells me you have agreed to illustrate and paint Sir Giles's butterfly collection."

"Indeed. I hope I can do it justice." She paused for a moment, staring straight ahead, and then turned to look at Cassy. "It would be wonderful if I could bring the butterflies to Rothbury House tomorrow morning for you to oversee my first illustration. I shall be working at Cousin Howard's house later in the morning, organising his insect collection. His house is a mere stone's throw from yours, so would it be possible for me to come to you first?"

"What a good idea." Cassy's gaze rested on Cousin Agnes for a moment, and then she cleared her throat. "In fact, why don't you come every morning, Georgie, if Mama agrees? Your maid could accompany you, as it is a very short walk to Rothbury House, and then she could escort you on to Cousin Howard's. Or you could travel in the coach if the weather isn't fine."

Cousin Agnes's lips tightened. "I am not sure it is at all the thing for Georgiana to visit Cousin Howard without me."

"But Cousin Theodosia should be there at that hour. It is not as if it is a bachelor's establishment. I am sure it will be unexceptionable. And it will free you from a very dull task, Cousin Agnes."

"Yes, indeed." Georgiana smiled at her elderly relation. "It will be so tedious for you to accompany me every morning."

"I think it is an excellent idea, Cassandra," Mama said. "As long as you don't mind seeing so much of Georgiana?"

"I shall enjoy it. Besides, I promised Georgie I would assist her in developing her drawing skills, and this will provide an excellent opportunity to do so."

The next morning, Georgiana rose early with a sense of lightness. It was as if she had been freed from prison—the prison of being in Cousin Agnes's keeping. Her strict presence weighed on Georgiana's spirits, very much like a lead boulder, truth be told. How wonderful to have it lifted away.

Dear Cassy... She, of all people, knew how chafing it was to submit to Cousin Agnes's constant supervision. Their elderly relation had been her sister-in-law's companion before her marriage to Rothbury.

After a light breakfast in her bedchamber, Georgiana made her way downstairs, the box of butterflies clutched carefully in her kid-gloved hands.

They left the house quietly, and Georgiana took a deep breath as she walked along. Kirby followed a few steps behind, carrying her drawing materials. The hour was not advanced enough for many people to be about, but Cassy was an early riser and had suggested Georgiana visit her before the day became too busy.

When she reached Rothbury House, a footman led her to the library. Cassy was comfortably ensconced in a window seat but rose immediately and indicated a nearby mahogany table. "Good morning, Georgie. I thought it would be best to work here, as the light is so good."

"I cannot thank you enough for offering to help me, Cassy, and for rescuing me from Cousin Agnes."

"Cousin Agnes isn't the easiest of companions for a young girl, as I can well attest." Her wry expression spoke volumes.

"Indeed. But Mama insists that I spend the vast majority of my time with her every day. Cousin Agnes is, after all, an expert needlewoman and can teach me all the other accomplishments I fail so dismally at."

Cassy touched her arm. "Don't be so hard on yourself, dearest. Your mama was saying just the other day that your embroidery is much improved. And at least it is unexceptionable that I assist you with your drawing and painting, as those are feminine accomplishments too."

They sat at the table, and Cassy drew a sheet of paper towards her as Georgiana opened the box of butterflies. "The best advice my mother ever gave me when I was learning about scientific illustration was that I should only draw what I could see," she said as she picked up a pencil. "I know it sounds obvious, but it is truly the best thing you can do to give an accurate representation of a specimen. Never embellish or include something you *think* should be there but isn't. Sometimes our minds can play tricks on us, and we can draw what we expect to see rather than what is there."

Georgiana drew a piece of paper towards her. "Let me try… although I still believe you cast my drawings into the shade."

Cassy laughed. "Was that an intentional pun?"

"No!" She chuckled. "I suppose shading is on my mind."

They worked quietly together for a while, and then Cassy placed her pencil on the table and leaned back in her chair. "Are you looking forward to your Season, dearest?"

Georgiana shook her head. "Not really. I had hoped for a year of freedom before being launched into the Marriage Mart."

"Perhaps you could still have that freedom…You do not need to accept an offer of marriage this Season, and as the acknowledged beauty of the family, I am sure you will have a vast array of suitors to choose from, both this year and next."

Georgiana drew her brows together. "I think Mama hopes to marry me off this year as she wants me off her hands as soon as possible. She lives in constant dread that I will disgrace her at any moment."

"I am sure she only wants what is best for you, dearest. Rushing into an early marriage is not always advisable. You must know your heart and your mind before you commit your hand."

"I have always known my mind. It is far better to rely on that than on your heart."

Cassy smiled. "You have no desire to form a *tendre* for someone?"

"I aim to find a husband who will be amenable to my wishes. That is far more important for a woman than silly notions of love. If I have to be trapped in marriage, I hope it will be with someone who is accommodating."

"As long as you don't choose a weak man, Georgie. The tyranny of the weak is often underestimated, as it can be so well-disguised."

Georgiana opened her mouth to respond, but then the door swung open, and Sir Giles Tavistock entered the library. She stared at him with a narrowed gaze. The dreadful man seemed to lurk around literally every corner.

The baronet bowed. "Good morning. I saw Rothbury at White's last night, and he told me you would be working on your illustrations here this morning."

Cassy's expression was welcoming as she stood up. "Have you come to check on our progress, Sir Giles?"

"I confess to some curiosity. But please don't stop on my account."

After a muttered greeting, Georgiana returned her attention to the butterfly she was sketching. How vexing that the baronet thought it necessary to check up on her efforts.

"Fine work, Miss Linfield." His deep voice rattled her nerves from somewhere above her shoulder.

She set her pencil down and twisted around in her chair. "Thank you, sir. My sister-in-law is an excellent teacher."

"I cannot take the credit," Cassy protested. "You are a quick learner and have abundant natural talent."

"Indeed," Sir Giles said. "I am in full agreement." He stepped away from the table, his eyes crinkling at the corners. "I have left my horses standing in the street, Miss Linfield, so I cannot stop for long. Would you care to drive with me to the Park? I require further illustrations for my paper, separate from these, which I should like to discuss with you if you are amenable to the idea."

"Do go, Georgie," Cassy urged. "You have been cooped up

indoors ever since you arrived in London. The fresh air will do you good."

Georgiana hesitated. She had the strangest notion she was about to step into a spider's web. Perhaps the best way to escape the silken threads was to push straight through them. "I hope a short drive will suffice to relay the necessary information, Sir Giles?" she said coolly. "Unfortunately, I am working at Cousin Howard's later this morning, and I cannot spare the time."

He raised his brows. "It is a good thing then that I am driving my bays. They go at a spanking pace."

As Georgiana rose to her feet, she met his amused gaze. He didn't seem at all deflated by her thinly veiled set-down. She turned to Cassy. "I shall leave everything here if it isn't an imposition, but I'll take the store-box home tomorrow as I would like to examine the butterflies more closely."

"Should I take you to my godfather's house after our drive?" Sir Giles asked.

"Yes, please."

"Georgie dear, I believe your maid is in the kitchens, having a cup of tea," Cassy said. "I'll ask her to walk on ahead to Cousin Howard's house and await you there."

Georgiana smiled her thanks as she placed her hand on the baronet's outstretched arm. Outside, some splendid-looking bays were being walked up and down the cobblestones by a young groom. Georgiana drew to a halt and studied the well-matched pair before the baronet helped her up into his curricle. He nodded at the youth, who sprang up onto his perch behind his master, and then Sir Giles set the horses in motion.

Georgiana stared straight ahead as he drove the short distance from Grosvenor Square to Hyde Park. However, as they entered the Park, she took a deep breath of the cold, crisp air and raised her eyes to the sky. The sun was shining today, although it appeared to be playing a game of hide-and-seek, popping out to shine a bit and then peeping from behind scudding clouds as if to tease the humans, desperate for light and warmth below.

"In January, the sun is a fickle friend, Miss Linfield. She will elude you if you seem too eager for her appearance."

"I hope it doesn't rain today. London is a miserable place in winter." She folded her hands in her lap and sighed. "I wish I were back at Linfield."

"I don't wish it."

Georgiana turned her head and met his lazy blue gaze. "Well, of course, you don't. You wouldn't have an artist then."

"No, I wouldn't, would I?"

Her gaze faltered. "How can I assist you, sir?"

"I have some preserved caterpillars and the plant species upon which I found them. I plan to display them along with the adult specimens. Would you be able to illustrate them for me as well?"

"Yes, of course. I am familiar with sketching the life cycle of a butterfly. It is a particular interest of mine."

"Excellent." He turned his team around at the end of Rotten Row, and they started trotting back along the bridle path. "Do you have any other particular interests?"

"I love the countryside. If I had the choice, I would spend all my time out of doors." She bit down hard on her lip. Why had she told him that? She had no desire for a *tête-à-tête* with this man, no matter how innocent the topic of conversation.

"Your brother accompanies you on these excursions?"

"He does. But now that we are in London, I haven't seen much of him. He spends his days in the British Museum, studying the natural history collections."

"I must tell Rothbury to bring him to my home one day. I am sure he would like to see my collection of tropical beetles."

"Thank you. He would be delighted."

They left the Park then, and the baronet drove the short distance to Cousin Howard's house. After he helped Georgiana down from the curricle, he studied her with a quizzical expression. "You see, we *can* have a civil conversation, Miss Linfield."

She stared up at him for a fraught moment. The problem was she didn't wish to engage in any conversation with Sir Giles, civil or not. She wanted to avoid him like the plague. But unfortunately, he had something to offer her, something it was impossible to refuse—the opportunity of doing the work she loved in a socially sanctioned way.

Her mother had raised no objections to the baronet's request for her assistance. She no doubt nursed hopes that Georgiana and Sir Giles would eventually make a match of it, despite her avowed dislike of the man—and dislike him she did. Especially as he managed to make her feel very young at times with his odious habit of humouring her whenever she attempted to put him in his place.

So it was that her response came with a somewhat forced smile. "Well, sir, I decided to take your advice."

He tucked her hand in his arm as he drew towards the front door. "Oh?"

"I have cultivated some social graces in order to have a successful London Season. Just as you suggested… In fact, your rather scathing denunciation of my conduct that evening alerted me to the fact that I needed to master the art of appearing to be polite, even when I don't feel like it." And if that wasn't a masterful setdown, she didn't know what was.

Sir Giles rubbed his jaw, his smile somewhat rueful as he knocked on the door. "I am delighted you pay such heed to what I say, *mon papillon*."

"I am not a butterfly."

"Perhaps not yet… but butterflies do not come into the world fully formed."

"I am not a caterpillar either." Her voice was frigid.

"Aren't you?" He grinned. "A caterpillar contains all the parts that will one day transform into a butterfly, even though they may have prickles—and some are dangerous to the touch."

She found herself trapped by his gaze. Trapped and drowning. Then the porter opened the door, and she hurried across the threshold. Away from him.

As far away as possible.

# CHAPTER SIX

Georgiana settled into a routine where every morning, depending on the weather, she would either walk or take the carriage to Rothbury House and sketch Sir Giles's butterfly collection in the library. He had delivered the other plant species and the preserved caterpillars to Linfield House, but she decided to draw those only after completing her initial task.

Cassy worked beside her, illustrating the numerous fossils she and Edward had collected abroad. She freely answered Georgiana's many queries about the delicate process she employed to represent each specimen accurately. Cassy proved a far better teacher than the drawing master from the seminary, and Georgiana progressed in leaps and bounds under her tuition.

After her spell at Rothbury House, Georgiana would spend a few hours at Cousin Howard's home, organising his collection. One morning, he informed her that his godson had been called away to his country estate in Wiltshire and Georgiana received the information with relief. Now there was no chance of Sir Giles visiting unexpectedly and distracting her from her work.

Cousin Theodosia usually sat on the far end of the spacious apartment, working on her embroidery, while Cousin Howard popped in frequently to observe Georgiana's progress. She put the experience she had gained in her father's museum to good use as she began the slow process of entering the various species into the leather-bound journal Cousin Howard had given her.

Her elderly cousin frequently spoke about his expeditions

abroad, reminiscing about the insects in the boxes she sorted. Georgiana would set aside her pencil to listen with rapt attention on these occasions, interspersing the odd question.

After one such discussion, about a month after she had begun her task, he leaned back in his chair and smiled broadly. "My dear, I am amazed at your thirst for knowledge. If you had been born a man, you would have become an expert in your field."

"I know of a woman who made a name for herself in the field of entomology."

His brow creased for a moment before clearing. "Ah yes, you must be speaking of Maria Sibylla Merian."

She nodded eagerly. "Papa told me all about Maria's expedition to Dutch Surinam, where she discovered new plant and animal species. He gave me her two-volume series on caterpillars for my sixteenth birthday. It ignited my love for butterflies."

"She was an extraordinary woman indeed. I have one of her Surinam watercolours hanging in my study if you would care to see it."

Georgiana tapped her fingers on the leather armrest of her chair, staring into space. "If only I could lead the unconventional life she did. Somehow, she managed to throw off the shackles of the society in which she lived." She sighed. "If I had even a tenth of her talent for drawing and painting, I would attempt to earn my living. But although I am a competent artist, my work will never compare to hers."

"Come, my dear. A girl of your station should not even be thinking about earning her living."

Georgiana bit her bottom lip. "I am well aware of that."

"Hmmm." He studied her meditatively for a few minutes and then spoke with great deliberation. "After seeing your dedication to your work, I am fully cognizant of the sincerity of your desire to map a different path for yourself." He puffed out his cheeks. "I have an idea…a rather unconventional one, which may solve some of your problems."

She glanced towards the end of the room when Cousin Theodosia rose to her feet, then returned her gaze to her elderly relative. "Pray tell me."

"As you know, my health is deteriorating. My physician has informed me that I do not have much time left—maybe a year or two, if I am fortunate. I have no relatives besides your father's family, and although I have left the bulk of my estate to my godson, I do not see why I should not leave you an independence. Then, should you decide not to marry, you can follow in the footsteps of your heroine."

Georgiana's mouth dropped open. "I could not accept such generosity from you, Cousin Howard."

"And why not? I never had children, but I would have wished for a daughter just like you if I had. Besides, you are my relation. Therefore, it is perfectly acceptable for me to leave you a bequest in my Will."

She stared at him in silence—and then Cousin Theodosia was upon them, looking down her long nose at Georgiana. Feeling the constraint of the woman's presence, she swallowed the knot in her throat. "Thank you, sir. I am much obliged."

Cousin Theodosia's gaze veered from Georgiana to her brother and then back to Georgiana again. "I do believe it is past time that you returned home."

Georgiana glanced at the clock on the opposite wall. "Yes, of course." She closed the boxes in front of her and placed her pencil neatly beside the journal. "I shall see you tomorrow." Her smile encompassed them both as she rose to her feet. Cousin Howard beamed back at her, but Cousin Theodosia's face seemed set in stone. Georgiana walked past her, and near-palpable hostility radiated from her every pore.

Georgiana shivered. The elderly woman didn't like her very much.

～

As Giles knocked on his godfather's front door, he could not repress the hope that Georgiana Linfield was there, working in the library. He'd failed to put her from his mind the entire time he had been away, his attempts to convince himself he was indifferent to her proving utterly futile. Indeed, he was halfway to falling in love with her.

He wasn't yet quite sure what he would do about it. She still appeared to dislike him. But the prospect of matrimony, once so intolerable, seemed ever more attractive to Giles. If he married, he could take his wife abroad with him just as Rothbury had done.

Marriage no longer seemed a dreaded domestic cage but rather a way in which he could have the best of both worlds. Of course, he enjoyed his travels abroad, but it was often a solitary existence, though the excitement of his discoveries usually overrode any sense of loneliness. Still, he found the thought of having someone as beautiful and spirited as Georgiana Linfield at his side, sharing his adventures, quite exhilarating.

The door opened, and he smiled at the porter, who informed him, in a lowered voice, that the master was indisposed.

"Is Miss Linfield here?"

"No, sir."

Giles was about to depart when his godfather's sister entered the hall. "Ah, Sir Giles," she said, drawing to a halt. "How fortuitous that you have called. I am desirous of a word with you."

He bowed. "Good morning, ma'am. I trust that my godfather is not seriously unwell?"

"I believe he is merely fatigued. His attorney called this morning, and he was exhausted after the meeting."

Giles stepped inside and handed his hat and cloak to the porter before following his hostess into the drawing room. As she lowered herself onto an upright chair, she waved at a nearby sofa. However, Giles strolled to the fireplace and leaned his arm on the stone mantelpiece before turning to face her.

He had never particularly liked the older woman, vividly recalling strident lectures as a young boy when he had traipsed dirt into the spotless hallway at Crossings, his godfather's country estate in Berkshire. However, she seemed to be in some distress, so he smiled at her. "How may I be of assistance, ma'am?"

She shuddered as she drew her shawl tighter around her shoulders. "You will not believe what that hussy has managed to persuade my brother to do. I was never so shocked."

"Which hussy?" His brows drew together.

"That odious girl, Georgiana Linfield. I knew she represented trouble the minute Howard told me he had asked her to organise his collection."

"What exactly has Miss Linfield done?"

She fiddled with the edge of the shawl. "I suspected something was afoot a few days ago when I interrupted the two of them having a cosy *tête-à-tête*. No matter how much that girl protests her interest in insects, I am highly sceptical of her assertion. What normal girl has any real interest in such creatures? It was all a pretence, a plot, and I suspected it from the very first, which was why I was careful never to leave her alone with my brother in case of any impropriety. But despite my care, she still managed to get her claws into him. And although I tried my best to act as a strict duenna, the sofa at the end of the library where I sit is a fair distance from the table where she works. It has been possible for them to have many private conversations as my hearing is not good."

She drew in a breath, evidently in a great deal of distress, and Giles waited impatiently for her to continue. *What the deuce is the woman on about?*

"A few days ago, they seemed to be on exceptionally cosy terms…and then today, my brother ordered Mr Richards, his attorney, to attend him in his study. I just…er…happened to be in the hallway outside the room when I overheard part of their conversation." Her eyes bulged, very much like an owl he once came upon unexpectedly while out walking in the woods. "They were discussing his Will. My brother is planning to leave that girl this house, his insect collection, and a very handsome fortune! I was never so shocked. To trap a sick, elderly widower into marriage like this is beyond the pale."

Giles did not speak for a full minute. "You are certain of this, madam?"

She sniffed. "There is no reason for me to make up such a terrible tale—of that, I can assure you. I wish it were not so."

He stared grimly ahead. "Rest assured, ma'am. Miss Linfield will not marry my godfather."

"Thank you, Sir Giles. You have put my mind at rest." She dabbed at the corners of her eyes with a handkerchief. "My nerves have been quite overset by all of this, as you can imagine. But I am confident you will put an end to that harpy's machinations."

He took his leave of her then and strode towards his home in Upper Grosvenor Street. After only a few steps, however, he came to an abrupt halt and turned around. He should confront Miss Linfield as soon as possible.

As luck would have it, his quarry was leaving her home just as he entered Berkeley Square. Miss Linfield came to a halt in front of the garden gate, waiting for the footman who accompanied her to unlock it. She glanced up as he came towards her, and the smile which lit her face brought him to a standstill. However, she swiftly rearranged her features into a more neutral expression and responded to his bow with a stiff curtsey.

"Good afternoon, Miss Linfield."

"Sir Giles."

He moved closer. "May I walk with you in the garden?"

She hesitated a moment, glancing at the footman.

"Your manservant will accompany us, of course. I must speak to you. Urgently."

She lifted an elegant shoulder. "Very well."

Giles escorted her through the gate, and they walked in silence along a path under some enormous plane trees, the footman following at a discreet distance behind. Giles glanced over his shoulder. The servant was out of earshot, at least. He did not wish for his conversation with Miss Linfield to become fodder for the rumour mill below stairs. That was a sure way for it to spread all over London within a matter of days.

He drew to a halt before a statue of King George III on horseback, in the character of Marcus Aurelius. After giving it a cursory glance, he returned his gaze to Miss Linfield. "Congratulations, madam." He deliberately made his voice cold. "It appears you have accomplished your aim of finding a man you can easily manipulate."

"What?"

Her confusion was so convincing that Giles frowned. "I have just come from my godfather's house."

Enlightenment dawned on her face. "Oh…" She bit her lip. "You are angry about the change in Cousin Howard's Will. I know you are his heir, but surely you cannot begrudge me a small portion of his estate?"

"I not only begrudge it, but I am also determined it won't come to pass."

She gripped her hands together. "It is Cousin Howard's fortune to do with as he wills, Sir Giles. You have no say in the matter."

"I beg to differ. I shall do everything in my power to foil your plans."

Her finely winged brows drew together. "*My* plans? I would have you know it was entirely Cousin Howard's suggestion."

"Of course it was. An old man is often a fool for love." He laughed harshly. "Theodosia Linfield has told me all the details of the proposed marriage settlement, so don't try and gammon me it was my godfather's idea. You even requested the inclusion of his insect collection." His jaw tightened as he stared down at her impossibly beautiful face. "To wed a man who is virtually on his deathbed is the act of a cunning, calculating baggage. I had thought better of you, Miss Linfield."

Georgiana stared up at him. "Did you indeed?"

"Yes, fool that I am. But you won't get away with this. I intend to reveal to my godfather how ruthlessly he has been tricked."

The blood pounded in her head. *How dare he?* "You are the most loathsome man I have ever met."

He smiled, a mocking little smile. "Perhaps I am the only man to ever see through your wiles."

She glared at him and then spun on her heel, stalking away at such a rapid pace that Peter, the footman who had been idling some distance away, needed to run to catch up with her. She barely glanced at him as he opened the garden gate, and then she hurried ahead to Linfield House and the sanctuary of her bedchamber.

She threw herself onto her bed, her chest rising and falling in anger. To think she had been pleased when Sir Giles walked into the Square earlier, even experienced an unmistakable tug of attraction. But not anymore. His words and actions had destroyed any budding wish to know him better.

She couldn't believe he had accepted as true Cousin Theodosia's delusions. She must have listened at a keyhole to her brother's conversation with his attorney and grossly misunderstood. Georgiana sat up in indignation. Sir Giles must have a very low opinion of her to think she would even consider marrying an elderly, unwell man…one old enough to be her grandfather!

Well, the baronet was in for a nasty surprise. When he confronted his godfather, the older man would be quick to enlighten

him as to the actual terms of his new Will. She hoped Sir Giles
would feel like an utter fool.

# CHAPTER SEVEN

Giles headed straight back to Grosvenor Square. The sooner he could speak to his godfather, the better. He would take care not to cause the older man offence—it was evident he was under Miss Linfield's spell—but he needed to present him with the truth of the matter before an official announcement was made.

The butler led him to the library, where his godfather sat at the table at which Miss Linfield usually worked. He was paging through a leather-bound journal but set it aside with a smile as Giles crossed the room. "There you are, my boy! Georgiana has done an excellent job, I must say. I am most pleased with her efforts."

Giles gave the book a cursory glance. "Miss Linfield has completed the task you set her?"

"Indeed. She works very efficiently."

Giles frowned. "I have just seen her... We had an...er...enlightening conversation about her future."

"So that's why you look like thunder. I was hoping to tell you the news in person, which was why I asked you to see me immediately you returned to London."

"I did call earlier, but you were resting."

A crease appeared between his godfather's brows. "Forgive me, my boy. It must have come as a shock to hear about this from Georgiana. I am surprised she mentioned it to you, as we decided not to say anything about it, at least not yet."

Giles's eyes narrowed. "Why the secrecy?"

"I have discussed the matter with her father, of course, but an announcement may cause unwanted attention." He chuckled. "Don't want people to start numbering my days, you know."

"I can imagine the attention it will bring, sir! Are you certain this is a wise decision, particularly at this stage of your life? You haven't been well…"

"Indeed. But that is precisely why I acted as quickly as I did. I don't have a great deal of time left, and I want to ensure Georgiana's future." He shook his head. "In truth, I am surprised you are so perturbed. I have only bequeathed this house and a fairly small portion of my fortune to her. The rest of the estate is still yours." He wiggled his grey eyebrows. "Or is it the loss of my insect collection that has you in the suds? I know you've always coveted it, but you have such a vast collection of your own that I thought it only fair to leave mine to Georgiana. I have told her that you are to have the first choice of any specimens you may wish for, however."

"I am much obliged to you, sir." Giles's voice was dry.

"Speaking of specimens…" He leaned back in his chair and folded his arms. "An odd character by the name of Tom Johnson called here the other day, looking for you. Shady-looking Irish fellow. He said he'd heard of your South American butterfly collection and that he wanted to buy it from you. I told him you weren't in Town."

Giles frowned. "Captain Tom Johnson? He's been in and out of prison for years. A scoundrel, if ever there was one. If he's decided to trade in rare butterflies, I won't put it past him to draw unusual markings on a specimen in order to be credited with discovering a new species."

"He informed me that he is willing to pay whatever price you ask for your collection."

"It isn't for sale."

His godfather nodded. "I told him that."

Giles looked at the clock on the wall. "If you would excuse me, sir, I have a meeting with my man of business." He paused and then said deliberately, "I am thankful you haven't made an announcement as yet. A great deal of thought should go into such an important decision."

"I won't change my mind," his godfather stated placidly.

Giles raised his brows but said nothing. If he played his cards correctly, Miss Georgiana Linfield would soon be the one changing her mind.

Theodosia Linfield was slowly making her way down the stairs as he left the library. She inclined her head in the direction of the library. "Have you managed to speak some sense to him?"

Giles glanced around the entrance hall. It was empty. "My godfather's mind is made up. But the engagement is to be kept quiet for now, so I have some time in which to effect a change. I would advise you not to speak about this to anyone."

She sniffed. "You can be sure I won't. I have no desire to acknowledge something that will only bring shame and embarrassment to our name. Especially with my brother's unfortunate history."

"Indeed."

The butler walked into the hallway at that moment, and Giles took his leave and headed home, staring grimly ahead. At six-and-twenty, he was no green youth to be taken in by a beautiful face, yet somehow he had utterly misjudged Miss Linfield. By choosing to tie herself to an ill man to secure a fortune upon his death, she had made it clear that her future independent existence truly was her only ambition in life.

He should have taken her at her word when she told him nothing held a greater attraction for her than her work. But, instead, he had imagined a warm heart beat beneath her frosty exterior.

His old nanny used to say that it was important to listen to how people described themselves, as they knew themselves best. Unfortunately, to his detriment, he had disregarded this wise piece of advice.

Giles turned into Upper Grosvenor Street and spotted a slim, fashionably dressed gentleman of medium height at the entrance to his four-storeyed house. The set of the man's shoulders was familiar, and Giles stopped, frowning a little. "Alphonse," he said, walking up the shallow, stone stairs which led to the front door.

The man spun about to face him. "Tavistock! How excellent to find you at home. It is a convenient time?"

"I am afraid not. I have a meeting now… Good morning, Marston." Giles nodded at his man of business, who was approaching the house.

The Frenchman glanced at the newcomer and frowned. "I assure you my business will not take long."

The porter swung open the front door. After requesting Marston to wait, Giles handed his hat and cloak to the man-servant before leading the way to his book-room.

Nodding towards one of the leather armchairs in front of the fire, Giles stood in front of the fireplace.

"I trust you are well?" Alphonse lowered himself into the chair Giles had indicated. "I haven't seen you since your return from South America. Your paper is due to be read at the Linnean Society, I believe?"

"Yes. I have just completed it."

The other man leaned forward. "Is it about the butterflies you discovered there?"

"News travels fast in entomological circles, it would seem."

"Word is that it is a beautiful collection. It is for sale?"

"I'm afraid not."

The Frenchman sighed before rising slowly to his feet. "I suspected so… Let me not keep you from your meeting."

"You are in London for the Season?"

"Indeed." Alphonse's lips curled. "I must ask after your *chère maman* and your so charming sisters...?"

"They are all in good health."

He gave a flourishing bow *"Bien.* Thank you for your time."

*"De rien,"* Giles murmured, escorting the other man to the door.

"I am delighted you are still able to speak a few words in your mother tongue, *mon vieux,*" he said softly. "So very English as you are…"

Giles's gaze was steady. "As I have said before, Alphonse, I was brought up an Englishman."

The Frenchman merely smiled and then, with another bow, left the room, closing the door behind him with a soft click.

Giles stared at the shut door, a line between his brows. Pierre Alphonse had been his *bête noire* at Eton, frequently taunting him about his dual heritage. Having French blood while England was at war with France had not made boarding school easy. His relations were not supporters of Napoleon, being staunch royalists, but that made no difference to a couple of boys at school who had taunted him endlessly about being a Boney supporter.

Pierre Alphonse was the son of exiled French aristocrats who had lived in England for many years. However, even more than the English boys, he had bullied Giles. He spoke to him in his mother tongue at every opportunity, drawing unwanted attention to him. Giles had always responded in English, which enraged the older child, and so the stage had been set for hostilities throughout their school years.

As a boy, Giles had been small for his age, only growing to his present height after he left school. Yet, somehow, when he was with Pierre Alphonse, who was now a head shorter than him, he still felt like that small, helpless boy at the mercy of older children who'd had nothing better to do than taunt anyone who appeared even vaguely different from them.

He set his mouth in a straight line as the door opened once again, and Marston entered the room. How strange that childhood hurts still had the power to affect one years down the line when the insecurities and vulnerabilities of youth had long since disappeared. He needed to remember that Pierre Alphonse no longer had any power over him.

# CHAPTER EIGHT

Georgiana submitted to her maid's fussing as she dressed for her very first evening party of the Season. This would be an informal affair arranged by one of her mother's friends, Lady Aldwell, who was also bringing her daughter out this year.

Stephen would be accompanying them tonight at his mother's insistence. However, he had not needed much persuasion to join their party as he was a particular friend of Lady Aldwell's younger son, Henry, who was also in London at the moment.

Georgiana set her head on one side as she studied her appearance in the glass. She wore a round dress composed of book muslin over a white silk slip, trimmed at the edge with pale pink satin and Provence roses that matched the flowers in her hair. Pearl earrings, white satin slippers, and white kid gloves completed the ensemble, and Georgiana smiled her thanks as Kirby handed her an elegant shawl of Norwich silk.

Venturing out tonight would do her good. Although she had enjoyed organising Cousin Howard's insect collection over the past six weeks, she had grown tired of staring at the same four walls every day and was desperate for a change in scene. She hadn't even been able to escape to Rothbury House this past week as Cassy had accompanied Rothbury on a short visit to one of his estates.

The party also served as a welcome distraction from thinking about her recent encounter with Sir Giles. She hadn't seen him since leaving him in the garden in Berkeley Square three days ago.

He had, no doubt, already discovered his mistake and would be desirous of begging her pardon. But although her white-hot rage had subsided to a more manageable simmer, she was still furious with him.

When their party arrived at Lady Aldwell's home in Portman Square, they were led upstairs to a grand saloon. As she stepped inside, Georgiana glanced surreptitiously around the brightly lit apartment, but Sir Giles was not present.

Her hostess smiled kindly as Georgiana dipped into a curtsey. "How charming you look, my dear."

She murmured her thanks as Lady Aldwell turned to Mama, a rueful expression on her face. "My son and daughter have prevailed upon me to clear the room for some dancing. I told them they might stand up for a few country dances."

"I think it is an excellent idea." Her mother glanced around the room. "Particularly as the majority of your guests are very young."

Their hostess sighed. "I imagine many of the older, more eligible gentlemen who accepted my invitation will only look in later. However, my eldest son has promised to bring his friends, for which I am grateful, as there are more young ladies here than gentlemen at present. I will feel dreadful if anyone needs to sit out a dance for want of a partner." Her lips curved upwards again as her gaze rested on Georgiana. "Somehow, I doubt *you* will ever suffer such a fate, my dear."

Henry Aldwell came up to them at that moment and bowed. After engaging Georgiana's mother in polite conversation for a few minutes, he turned to Georgiana and stuttered: "I...I am delighted to renew our acquaintance, Miss Linfield."

Stephen rolled his eyes and strolled away, leaving her alone with his friend as Mama turned to speak to an acquaintance.

The young man asked if she wanted some refreshment. At her nod, he secured a glass of lemonade from a passing footman before begging the honour of leading her into the first set.

Georgiana placed her untouched drink to one side and accepted his invitation. Within moments, she was going down the dance with him, listening with one ear to his shy remarks while she concentrated on her steps. This event was an excellent opportunity to practise, truth be told, as she had been so busy since her arrival in London that she hadn't danced at all.

Soon she would be attending assemblies and balls. If she stumbled over her feet tonight, Mama would no doubt hire a London dancing master and insist that she spend the majority of her time with him instead of completing Sir Giles's sketches.

She'd been tempted to stop working on them after his dastardly behaviour. But after careful consideration, she had decided to complete the illustrations. Having her work on display at the Linnean Society was her first step to garnering some sort of recognition in her chosen scientific field. Besides, she hated unfinished tasks.

When the dance ended, Mr Aldwell delivered her back to her mother, who stood in conversation with a fashionably dressed gentleman of middle height.

"Georgiana, my love!" she said with a smile. "Do you remember Monsieur Alphonse? He came last year to Linfield to visit Papa, but I cannot recall if you were at home at the time."

Georgiana curtseyed. "Yes, indeed, Mama. We met when Papa showed Monsieur Alphonse the museum. How do you do, *monsieur*?"

The Frenchman bowed with a flourish. "I am charmed to encounter you again, Miss Linfield. The last time I saw you, you were covered in dust after clearing out an old cabinet."

Her mama grimaced. "Oh, dear! My daughter does tend to tackle the tasks my husband sets her with a deal of enthusiasm."

"But this passion for natural history is enchanting!" His teeth gleamed bright against a sallow complexion. "May I request the next dance with you, *mademoiselle*?"

"Yes, indeed." She smiled at Mr Aldwell, who still stood beside her, before placing her hand on Monsieur Alphonse's arm and allowing him to lead her into the centre of the room.

"You are enjoying your Season?" His dark eyes were as bright as a robin's.

"I am, although I haven't been out to many social events as yet. Mama says London is still very thin of company."

"Not for much longer. Soon you will receive a veritable stream of invitations, and you will be able to pick and choose the *soirées* you wish to attend."

Georgiana made no response as the musicians played the

opening chords, and they began moving down the line.

"I imagine you were pleased to leave your father's dusty museum behind?" he said when the movement of the dance brought them together again.

"No, indeed. I enjoy working there."

"You are somewhat unusual in your choice of entertainments, *mademoiselle*."

"It is my work, *monsieur*. Not my entertainment."

He laughed. "How delightfully refreshing you are."

Georgiana was about to respond when she spotted Sir Giles entering the room. She looked hastily away. "Do you frequently travel abroad on expeditions, *monsieur*?"

"As frequently as I can. My particular interest is in butterflies and moths."

Georgiana smiled. "As is mine."

"*Vraiment*? You are an Aurelian as well?"

"Yes. In fact, I am sketching some South American butterflies at present."

The Frenchman's eyes narrowed. "Those are not Sir Giles Tavistock's butterflies, by any chance?"

She nodded just as the movement of the dance separated them. When they reached the bottom of the set, he said: "How fascinating. I plan to attend the reading of Sir Giles's paper at the Linnean Society."

Georgiana bit her bottom lip. "I wish I could attend. If only women weren't excluded from such gatherings."

"You are excluded with good reason, *mademoiselle*."

Georgiana straightened her spine as she met his laughing eyes. "Indeed?"

"Your beauty would cause a riot and distract the so-sober Englishmen from their so-solemn discussions. Therefore, to maintain order, the gentlemen of the Society *cannot* allow you in."

"You flatter me, *monsieur*."

"I merely speak the truth. You must know that you are very beautiful, Mademoiselle Linfield."

Georgiana was grateful for the movement of the dance, which separated them once again. She was accustomed to receiving compliments from the young men of her acquaintance, but their tributes tended to be more restrained. Monsieur Alphonse lacked the reserve common to Englishmen, however, and his conversation was both intriguing and somewhat unnerving. She did not know what to make of him.

When they reunited further down the line, he began to speak about his most recent expedition to Italy and the various species of butterflies he had collected there. Georgiana listened attentively to his knowledgeable descriptions, interspersing the odd comment here and there, and was so caught up in their discussion that she glanced around in confusion when the last strains of the music sounded. It was time to return to her chaperon.

Sir Giles stood in the corner of the room in conversation with her mother, his head bent at an attentive angle as he listened to her. Georgiana tilted her chin up as she came to a halt in front of them. Getting this meeting over and done with would probably be best, no matter how much she wanted to avoid it.

"I bring your so-charming daughter back to you, *madame*," Monsieur Alphonse said with a bow. "She dances beautifully. But it is her knowledge of Lepidoptera which impresses me most. Such an interest is most unusual in a young lady." He nodded at Sir Giles. "Tavistock. Mademoiselle Linfield tells me that she has been illustrating your South American butterflies. You are fortunate."

"Indeed. Miss Linfield is an accomplished artist." He bowed. "Shall we join the next set, ma'am?"

She would appear rude if she turned him down, as she had already danced with two other gentlemen. So, stepping away from Monsieur Alphonse, Georgiana inclined her head and gave a small curtsey before placing her hand on the baronet's outstretched arm.

As he led her into the newly forming set, she met his gaze and took an involuntary step backwards. She had been expecting an apology from Sir Giles, but he did not look in the least conciliatory. Instead, he seemed coldly angry.

Georgiana stood in frozen silence as they waited for the rest of the set to form, staring fixedly ahead. When the musicians struck up once again and the leading couple began to dance, she curtseyed stiffly and began to move down the line.

They stepped towards one another to complete a figure, and Sir Giles took her hands in his as they progressed down the centre.

Georgiana took in a sharp breath. Although she was wearing gloves, the pressure of his hands seemed to burn straight through the flimsy garments, and her heart pounded rapidly.

"I would like to speak privately with you tomorrow, Miss Linfield. If it is convenient, I shall call on you in the morning and take you for a drive in the Park."

Georgiana tilted her head, feeling somewhat dazed. "Very well."

They moved to their respective sides of the line again before leading off as they reached the top. She was a little less stunned now that the movement of the dance had separated them, and when they reached the bottom of the set, she stole a look at him as they awaited their turn again.

His expression was formidable, and she regretted accepting his invitation. But somehow, trapped by his gaze, she had felt compelled to comply.

Sir Giles turned his head. "You are acquainted with Pierre Alphonse?"

She gave a tiny shrug. "I met him when he came to Linfield last year."

He frowned, but it was time to move down the set again, and no further opportunity presented itself for private conversation. When the dance ended, he led her back to her mother, engaged in a *tête-à-tête* with another matron, and, bowing briefly, walked away.

"My love," her mother said, smiling. "Lady Sefton has kindly promised us vouchers for Almack's."

Georgiana thanked the Patroness of the exclusive Assembly Rooms and answered her kind questions about how she was enjoying her come-out. But when Lady Sefton turned to speak to her mother again, Georgiana glanced around the room and spotted Sir Giles in conversation with Monsieur Alphonse. Somehow, it did not seem like a friendly exchange. The baronet glanced up at that moment, and she shivered as their gazes clashed.

She should never have agreed to see him again.

# CHAPTER NINE

When Sir Giles arrived the next morning, Georgiana was seated in the drawing room, working on her embroidery. Her mother had been pleased when she had told her about his invitation, and she saw them off now with a beaming smile. No doubt she still hoped her daughter and the baronet would make a match of it one day.

When they left the house, the baronet gave Georgiana his hand to assist her into the passenger seat and then moved around the vehicle to retrieve the reins and his whip from his groom. "You may walk home now, James," he said quietly.

The groom stepped away at once, and Sir Giles climbed into the curricle and set his horses in motion. Guiding them out of the Square in the direction of Hyde Park, he drove along in silence. After one glance at his stern profile, Georgiana folded her hands in her lap and stared straight ahead. *She* wasn't going to be the one to initiate any conversation.

When they entered the gates a short while later, he turned his head. "You seemed on very easy terms with Pierre Alphonse last night. Setting up a flirt already, Miss Linfield?"

Her mouth dropped open. "I think you are mad. Or else, you *enjoy* adding insult to injury. Either way, you are entirely objectionable. I wish to return home."

"Rest assured, madam, I shan't keep you out a moment longer than is necessary. This interview is as distasteful to me as it is to you." He tipped his hat to a passing acquaintance. "My godfather is so much in love with you that he refuses to listen to reason."

Georgiana's mind raced. Clearly, he was still under the misapprehension that she was betrothed to Cousin Howard. She was about to enlighten him as to the true state of affairs when he continued. "I have a proposition for you. I trust you will agree to it, although it goes very much against the grain with me to offer you anything. But I am prepared to do it in order to protect my godfather's good name. He will not become the laughingstock of Society in his old age as he once was in his youth."

She drew her brows together. "What are you talking about?"

"His wife ran off with her lover when he was a young man and lived abroad for several years before dying of consumption." He glanced at her. "You are not aware of this?"

Georgiana shook her head.

"I suppose it isn't a tale fit for a young girl's ears." He dropped his hands, and the bays raced forward. He allowed them their heads for a few moments before reining them in to a trot. "Should he marry you, Miss Linfield, people will believe him a fool for love for a second time, and that old story will become grist for the rumour mill again. I refuse to allow that. Which is why I am prepared to offer you the monetary equivalent of what my godfather is leaving you in his Will if you agree to call off the betrothal."

Georgiana let out a gasp. "You wish to *pay me off*?"

"I see no alternative."

Stars exploded in her head as she gripped her hands together. He was the most detestable, odious, insolent man alive. How could he think her such a grasping creature? She closed her eyes for a long moment. Sir Giles Tavistock deserved to be paid back in his own coin. Fully. To the very last penny. And she knew exactly how to exact compensation.

Swallowing the knot in her throat, she said in a falsely bright voice: "But you don't understand, Sir Giles. I am just as much in need of a suitable husband as I am of a suitable fortune. I need the respectability of matrimony if I wish to travel abroad on entomological expeditions. This freedom will not be granted if I remain unwed. So it is with regret that I must turn down your extremely generous offer."

"How can you believe my godfather is a suitable husband, ma'am?" His voice was harsh. "If you marry him, you will soon become a widow."

"But think," she said softly. "That will suit me even better. As a widow, I will be even more at liberty to pursue my scientific ambitions."

A muscle clenched in his jaw. "Have you no conscience?"

"It appears not." She raised her chin in the air. "And now, if you would be so kind, I would like you to take me home."

"Nothing would give me greater pleasure, madam."

Georgiana stared unseeingly at the passing scenery as he drove along the road and out of the gates. Just before they drew up in Berkeley Square, she prepared to descend from the carriage. "As you have sent your groom away, Sir Giles, I shall climb down on my own. Goodbye."

She alighted as he came to a halt, and when she turned around to look up at him, he raised his hat. "Miss Linfield." His lips tightened. "I hope you will think carefully about your future…and reconsider."

She smiled brilliantly. "But I *have* been thinking carefully about it, Sir Giles, and my plans are coming beautifully to fruition."

"You have no heart."

She gave a tinkling laugh. "When did a caterpillar ever have a heart?"

Turning on her heel, she dashed towards the house, not looking back.

Giles stared after her before giving his horses the office to start and guiding them out of the Square. Somehow he would get her to change her mind. But he needed to think carefully about his next move. He'd been mistaken to place all his cards on the table and appeal to her sense of decency. She was a heartless, mercenary little baggage who cared for nothing except her own ambitions. He would do well to remember that.

When he returned home, it was to the news that a visitor awaited him in his book-room. His butler, Sydney, spread his hands wide and said in an apologetic voice, "I did not wish to admit him, Sir Giles, as he seems a rough sort, but he told me he had come to see you on butterfly business. He goes by the name of Captain Johnson."

He gave a quick frown. "I see. You did well to admit him. Thank you, Sydney."

When Sir Giles entered the room, Captain Johnson was studying the bookshelves, his hands clasped behind his back. He turned and gave a brief bow. "How do you do, Sir Giles? It's been some time."

"Indeed. When did you become interested in butterflies, Johnson? It isn't quite your usual line of business." His voice was dry.

"I dabble in many things."

"So you do." Giles sat behind his desk and waved at the leather armchair in front of it. "Please be seated."

Johnson lowered himself onto the chair, his lips curling into a smile as he tugged at long side-whiskers. "Did Mr Linfield inform you of my visit?"

"He did. I'm afraid my South American butterfly collection is not for sale."

"I would pay handsomely for it."

Giles shook his head. "I don't travel abroad on entomological expeditions to trade in butterflies. I value my collections' scientific importance rather than their monetary worth."

"You keep your collections here?" He nodded at the mahogany display cabinets on the other side of the room, near the bay windows.

"Some of them."

Johnson rubbed his hands together. "If I may at least see your South American Flies?"

"My collection will be on display at the Linnean Society next month when my paper is read. If you attend the meeting, you'll be able to see it."

"Ah." Johnson lowered his chin onto the stock tied around his neck. "Of course." He rose to his feet. "Thank you kindly."

Giles pulled the bell, and Sydney opened the library door. "If you would see Captain Johnson out," he murmured.

Johnson crossed the room and went through the door before popping his head back in. "If you change your mind, you have only to let me know." He touched the brim of his rather battered hat and left.

Giles studied the door contemplatively. Beautiful butterflies could be found all over England, yet many collectors overlooked them, seeking exotic specimens from around the world instead. What a shame when there were entomological treasures to be found on their doorstep.

He had spent numerous holidays as a young boy with his god-father, searching for Flies in the fields and meadows around his estate near Eton. Indeed, Giles's English specimens vastly out-numbered his collections from abroad. But some people could find no value in what was right under their noses, seeking instead only that which was unattainable…

His thoughts turned to Georgiana Linfield, and his mouth hardened. He had been a fool to think he could share his life with her, but he had her measure now. He would not allow her to ruin his godfather's last few years.

# CHAPTER TEN

The next few weeks passed in a blur for Georgiana. Sir Giles Tavistock was nowhere to be seen after their last disastrous encounter. To her immense relief, when she visited Cassy one morning, she discovered that the baronet had been called away from London again. However, The Linnean Society meeting where his paper would be read was fast approaching, and he would have to return for that.

After his insulting proposition, she had considered throwing his sketches in the fire. But they were the finest illustrations she had ever done, and she was loath to surrender the opportunity of submitting them to the Society. Besides, both her father and Stephen planned to attend the reading, and they could tell her what kind of reception her work received.

As Monsieur Alphonse had predicted, a deluge of invitations descended on Linfield House after the Aldwell gathering. Georgiana began attending routs, *al fresco* parties, and musical evenings, while her mama promised her attendance at numerous coming-out balls, which would occur later in the Season.

Her own ball would be held in the ballroom at Rothbury House. Their London townhouse did not boast a room large enough to cater for the hundreds of people her mother predicted would respond to the gilt-edged invitations she had sent out. And indeed, despite her mother and Cousin Agnes's reservations, Georgiana had become a success.

Gentlemen flocked to ask her to drive with them in the Park, and whenever she attended an evening party, suitors—including some younger sons—thronged about her. As her dowry was no more than adequate and no one outside of her family circle knew of the inheritance she would one day receive from Cousin Howard, this overwhelming success puzzled Georgiana.

One morning the riddle of her extreme popularity was solved. Her mother informed her that Cousin Agnes had let the cat out of the bag about her promised inheritance. Her elderly relation had visited an old school friend at the beginning of the Season and told her in the strictest confidence about Georgiana's improved financial prospects.

The friend went on to inform her daughter about it, who in turn mentioned it to her son, who had, according to Rothbury, spread the word around the various gentlemen's clubs. As a result, Georgiana was now known to have excellent expectations, which understandably contributed to her newfound status as the toast of the town.

Pierre Alphonse was one of the gentlemen who regularly clustered around her skirts, and, at a rout one evening, he presented himself with a smile and bow. "You see, I was correct, *mademoiselle*. Your beauty has drawn all the Englishmen to your side as well as one particular Frenchman."

Georgiana tilted her head. "As I said once before, *monsieur*, you flatter me."

"*Mais non*, as *I* said once before, I merely speak the truth. May I take you driving in the Park tomorrow? I wish to converse with you in more depth about our shared love of butterflies. It is difficult to make scientific observations at *soirées* such as these."

Georgiana's lips curved into a smile. "Thank you. I should like that."

"You have completed your sketches for Sir Giles?"

"I have."

"I confess to some curiosity about them. May I see them when I call on you on the morrow?"

"My sketches?"

"*Bien sûr*...and the specimens, if you would be so kind."

"I should be delighted to show them to you. You will be able to tell me if my illustrations pass muster."

"I am convinced they will more than pass muster." He

delivered another of his elaborate bows.

When he arrived at Linfield House the following day, Georgiana awaited him in the drawing room. The butterfly store-box rested on a mahogany occasional table beside the sofa where she sat while her illustrations lay on the table in front of her. Cousin Agnes, seated near the window, worked on her embroidery.

After Monsieur Alphonse greeted them, he sat across from Georgiana and picked up her illustrations, studying them closely. "But these are excellent." He glanced across at the store-box. "Those are the specimens, *mademoiselle*?"

"Indeed."

She handed him the box, and when he opened the lid, he shook his head. "*Ils sont magnifiques! Ces belles couleurs.*"

"I am afraid it is hard to do them justice."

"But you have done so, *mademoiselle*, indeed you have…" He studied them carefully. "It must be difficult to find time to do such fine work when you have so many social obligations."

"Fortunately, I finished illustrating these butterflies just after the Season began."

"My congratulations. I am sure they will be well-received by the members of The Linnean Society."

She leaned forward. "Do you truly think so?"

"*Mais oui.* You have an eye for detail. And your drawings are true to life."

"That is a great compliment. Thank you."

He flashed his teeth. "You are far more open to receiving compliments about your work than your so-charming appearance."

Georgiana shrugged. "I prefer the former kind, truth be told."

"Indeed." He glanced around. "Do you draw in this room, Mademoiselle Linfield? I see the light is very good."

"Actually, I prefer to work in my bedchamber. The light is even better there."

"Ah." He closed the box and handed it back to her. "If I may drive you to the Park now?"

"Thank you, *monsieur*." Georgiana rose to her feet and turned to her chaperon. "I shall see you later, Cousin Agnes."

She left the room with Monsieur Alphonse and listened with interest as he told her about his most recent expedition to the eastern French Pyrénées, where he had collected the rare and exquisite Violet Copper butterfly.

Finally, after he had given her a detailed description of the mountain scenery, she sighed. "I would so love to travel."

"Perhaps you will one day, *mademoiselle*," he murmured as they entered the gates of Hyde Park.

"Not many ladies of my acquaintance have travelled abroad."

"*Non*. But there are a few. I met one such English lady when I was in France on an *expédition*. Her name was Mrs Murchison, and she was travelling on horseback with her husband, who was exploring the *Région* on foot. She had a great interest in the wildflowers unique to particular rocks and altitudes."

"That type of travel sounds like a marvellous dream."

"Sometimes, dreams come true, *mademoiselle*," he softly replied.

She met his dark gaze before glancing away. "Oh, there is Miss Aldwell in the carriage with her mama…pray, stop."

She conversed politely with the ladies for a few minutes, grateful for the opportunity to regain her composure. Monsieur Alphonse appeared to be pursuing her seriously, and she found it somewhat disconcerting as she wasn't quite sure what to make of him. He was always very charming, of course. Still, his Continental air was so unlike the manner of the English gentlemen of her acquaintance. She found his flattering comments difficult to interpret. Perhaps all French gentlemen spoke in that manner.

When they drove on, she cleared her throat. "Have you lived for long in England, *monsieur*?"

He shrugged. "My parents moved here during the Revolution. I was born here."

"Oh!"

He turned to look at her. "You seem surprised."

"It is just that you seem…so French."

"I am French. I moved to France after the war and lived there for a number of years. It is more my home than England has ever been."

"You plan on returning there?"

"One day. And perhaps I shall take a bride back with me." His teeth gleamed white in his face as he smiled at her.

Georgiana looked away. He was all but declaring himself. Spotting one of Stephen's friends, she smiled, inclined her head, and then stared straight ahead. Could she contemplate a life with a man like Monsieur Alphonse? He certainly fit her criteria for a husband. He was affable, agreeable, and eager to please. And he was a man of science who shared her interest in butterflies.

He could take her abroad, and she would be free to live the unconventional life she craved, just like the Mrs Murchison of whom he had spoken. She nibbled her bottom lip. It was a tempting thought. But marriage was not an institution to be entered into lightly, and she must take care not to rush into any commitment, for no matter how charming Monsieur Alphonse was, he still somehow seemed a stranger.

She turned the conversation to more general matters, speaking lightheartedly about the various evening entertainments she had recently attended. No further opportunity should present itself for any topic of a more personal nature to come to the fore.

They were about to leave the Park when Georgiana's gaze alighted on a pair of matched bays coming through the gates. She raised her eyes very slowly to encounter the cold, hard stare of Sir Giles Tavistock. He nodded curtly before urging his horses on at a brisk pace. Georgiana held her breath for a moment and then gradually let it out.

The baronet was back in Town.

# CHAPTER ELEVEN

Giles frowned as he left the Park and drove his curricle to Upper Grosvenor Street. Miss Linfield had behaved with a distinct lack of discretion by accompanying Alphonse to Hyde Park at the fashionable hour. He left his horses in his groom's care before heading to Rothbury House on foot. Fortunately, his cousin was at home, reading in the library. "You're back," he said as Giles entered the room.

"I arrived yesterday."

"Cassy was sorry you missed our dinner party last week."

"I hoped to return sooner, but my bailiff kept finding urgent matters for my attention." He strolled across to the window and looked out. "I stopped at Fenmore Park for a few days on my way back. Julian asked me to look in on Lady Fenmore, as all the children have succumbed to the measles."

"He mentioned it to me when I saw him at White's last night. Is Lady Fenmore well?"

He turned around. "My young cousins are a handful at the best of times, but Lady Fenmore appears to be managing. She is planning her summer house party."

"Ah, yes. Cassy and I received our invitation this morning. You'll be there too?"

"Yes. Lady Fenmore is concerned more ladies than gentlemen will be in attendance, so she extracted my promise to come."

"It is good butterfly-hunting country, Giles."

"It is not the butterfly hunting I'm concerned about." His

voice was grim.

Rothbury laughed. "All those matchmaking mamas."

"Indeed. They are relentless." He paused for a moment, then spoke with the utmost deliberation. "I saw Pierre Alphonse driving in the Park this afternoon with your sister."

"He is only one of the many suitors swarming around her."

Giles raised his brows. "One of many?"

"My sister has become all the rage, it seems." His cousin shrugged. "Word got out at the beginning of the Season that she will receive a generous bequest from Howard Linfield upon his death."

"My godfather told me he had included her in his Will. But I thought…" His eyes narrowed. "You say it is merely a bequest?"

"A substantial bequest. He has apparently developed a fondness for Georgiana since she sorted out his insect collection. He told my stepfather that she is like the daughter he never had."

Giles stared at Rothbury as everything fell clangingly into place. Theodosia Linfield must have misunderstood the conversation she had overheard and assumed her brother was discussing a marriage settlement with his attorney instead of a bequest to a distant family member. He suppressed a groan. What a complete mull he'd made of things.

～

Georgiana returned home, retrieved her butterfly sketches from her bedchamber, and requested Peter to deliver the sheaf of papers to Sir Giles Tavistock's address in Upper Grosvenor Street.

She did not, however, hand over the store-box to the footman. Stephen had been invited to view Sir Giles's tropical beetles before he unexpectedly left Town. Her brother had eagerly anticipated the baronet's return and would no doubt proceed hot-foot to see the rare beetle specimens. She would ask him to deliver the valuable butterfly collection into Sir Giles's hands.

Even though she had been sorely tempted, she had not told her twin about Sir Giles's offensive proposition. If Stephen knew how the baronet had insulted her, he would refuse to visit him, and she did not have the heart to spoil his much-anticipated treat.

That evening, Georgiana was to attend her first subscription ball at Almack's. Stephen had agreed to accompany them to the

Assembly Rooms as their father preferred to spend the evenings at his club or at home rather than at balls and dances. Papa would, of course, be at her coming-out ball, but the Season's frenetic social activity was not to his taste.

Stephen, somewhat unexpectedly, appeared to be enjoying the parties his mother insisted he attend, probably because many of his friends formed the coterie of Georgiana's admirers. Although he seemed incredulous that his cronies were so susceptible to his sister, he was glad of their convivial company and frequently persuaded them to retreat to the card room with him instead of dancing, much to his mother's exasperation.

For her introduction to the haut monde, Georgiana donned a silk gown with flower cup sleeves layered with pink and gauze petals. The bodice was very short, and when Kirby settled the folds of the dress into place, Georgiana studied her reflection in the glass, a fine line between her brows. "Do you think this bodice is too revealing, Kirby?"

Her maid shook her head vehemently. "No, no, Miss. Not at all. You look like a fairy tale princess. Indeed, you do!"

Kirby handed her a silk shawl, and Georgiana took it with a word of thanks before giving her image one last glance. She gave a fatalistic shrug. It was what it was…

When they arrived at Almack's, Georgiana looked around in surprise. The rooms were far less imposing than she had imagined. The grandiosity of the Lady Patronesses had led her to expect something more splendid. But these were, after all, public assembly rooms where, according to Cassy, the tea was weak and the bread and butter stale. However, as her sister-in-law pointed out when she asked why the ton bothered to attend, people did not come here to eat and drink, but rather to see and be seen.

Georgiana turned down a couple of suitors who requested a waltz later in the evening, as she had not yet received permission from one of the Patronesses to accept such invitations. Fortunately, however, all her other dances were claimed.

Georgiana was dancing the quadrille with Henry Aldwell and listening to a rather stilted account of his recent excursion to Richmond Park when Sir Giles Tavistock entered the room.

Their eyes met for a frozen second, and then she tore her gaze away and began responding to Mr Aldwell's remarks with such animation that by the end of the dance, he beamed and asked if she wanted to drive with him in the Park the next day. She turned him down gently, explaining that she already had an engagement, and winced as he walked away. Hopefully, she hadn't given him undue encouragement.

Her next partner came up to her then, and Georgiana carefully refrained from looking around the crowded room as she performed her dance steps. Afterwards, when the first melodic strains of the waltz sounded, she immediately returned to her mother's side.

She was congratulating herself on her success at avoiding Sir Giles's penetrating gaze when Lady Jersey, one of the Patronesses of Almack's, approached them with Sir Giles at her side. "Good evening, Lady Linfield," she said with a smile before turning to Georgiana. "May I present Sir Giles Tavistock as a suitable partner for the waltz, Miss Linfield?" She cast the baronet a roguish look. "I am sure you will be the envy of every female present, my dear, as Sir Giles rarely graces us with his presence."

Georgiana stared at the older lady and then, dipping into a curtsey, murmured a somewhat disjointed thanks. She placed her hand on Sir Giles's arm and allowed him to lead her into the growing circle. Her pulse raced madly as he took her hand in his, and she took a step back. She couldn't do this…she had to get away.

But before she could retreat, he spoke softly. "Please don't."

She blinked a few times as she gazed around at the other couples. If she left him alone in the middle of the dance floor, she would create a scandal of such massive proportions that she would never live it down.

Somehow she had to get through this.

After a tiny pause, she inclined her head, and then they were waltzing around the room together. The whirling motion of the dance and the bright lights made her feel quite giddy. She fixed her gaze on the baronet's waistcoat, breathing in his subtle scent. Balance. She must strive for balance. Never before had she waltzed with a man who was not her dancing instructor. Doing so with Sir Giles was slightly shocking.

"I suppose you are wondering why I wanted to dance with you," he said as the tempo of the music slowed.

She jerked her head up but remained silent as he searched her face.

"Rothbury has told me the truth about my godfather's Will. I accused you most unfairly, Miss Linfield. I hope you will accept my sincere apology."

Her eyes narrowed. "This is the second time you've apologised to me on the dance floor, Sir Giles."

"So it is." He gave a faint sigh. "I've blundered rather badly since we met."

"You were very quick to believe Cousin Theodosia's story. What a low opinion you must have of me."

"You told me nothing held a greater attraction for you than your work and that you would choose a husband with that in mind. So you cannot entirely blame me for believing you had settled for a marriage of convenience."

She lifted her chin. "I do blame you, sir. You made some very insulting comments when you confronted me, but no less insulting than the remarks you made upon our first meeting."

"It's a pity we got off on the wrong foot."

"That's a unique way of describing our quarrels on the dance floor."

A smile tugged at his lips. "Will you not give me the chance to make amends, Miss Linfield?"

"I don't know."

"Think about it."

She nodded slightly and then almost stumbled as he drew her closer into his embrace. Closer to the brink... She caught her breath as the final strains of the waltz sounded, and he brought her to a halt.

She needed to watch her step.

# CHAPTER TWELVE

When Georgiana returned home, she bid her mother and Stephen goodnight before walking up the stairs to her bedchamber, holding her candle aloft. She wasn't sure what to make of her conversation with Sir Giles. His apology had been sincere, and he seemed genuinely remorseful about his behaviour, but she had no desire to get on better terms with him.

She pushed open her door and frowned as she stepped inside. Bright moonlight shining through the open curtains showed her bedchamber in a state of complete disarray. Kirby was usually very tidy, so it was surprising that she would leave the room in such a dreadful condition.

Someone gave a sharp intake of breath, and Georgiana turned to face the door. Her maid had just stepped inside and was looking around in horror. "What happened, Miss?"

"I was about to ask you the same question." Georgiana handed Kirby the candle and picked up the lamp from the bedside table so she could better view the chaos.

"When I left your bedchamber, Miss, I assure you the curtains were closed, and everything was as neat as a new pin."

Her brow furrowed. "A burglary then?"

"Oh, no, Miss!"

"Do you know if my father is at home, Kirby?"

"Sir Barnaby is in the library, Miss."

Georgiana hurried down the stairs once again, carrying the lamp. She burst into the oak-panelled room, where her father sat in a leather armchair, reading by candlelight. "Papa! Thank goodness you are here. There has been a burglary."

He set his book to one side and frowned. "Where?"

"In my bedchamber."

"But how is that possible?" He rose, picked up the candle from the table beside him, and strode into the hall to find the porter. "Please tell Taylor to come upstairs at once."

Georgiana followed her father up the stairs, standing in the doorway as he searched her room. "The windows are closed, so he did not enter or leave that way." He frowned. "Has anything been taken, my dear?"

Georgiana glanced at her maid, who shook her head. "Nothing seems to have been stolen, Miss, but I will need to do a thorough search in the morning."

"I don't keep anything of value here, Papa. All my jewellery is in Mama's strongbox."

"Thank heavens for that." His voice was grim.

Her father glanced across at the butler, who hovered in the doorway. "I need you to search all the rooms in the house, Taylor. There has been a burglary." He frowned, taking in the chaotic condition of the room once again. "And please ensure that all the doors are locked. We need to investigate how a burglar managed to gain entrance."

"Yes, sir."

Her father turned back to her. "It's very late, Georgiana. Try to get some rest. We shall discuss this tomorrow."

He left the room then, and Georgiana submitted to her maid's ministrations before tumbling into bed. She was sure she would lie awake all night thinking about what had happened, but within minutes of her head touching the pillow, slumber began to claim her. However, disturbing dreams troubled her sleep. When she awoke, she gulped down her cup of chocolate and repaired immediately to the library, where her father was writing letters.

He looked up as she entered his sanctuary. "Your room seems to be the only bedchamber that was disturbed, my dear. Taylor told me he saw the new footman we hired coming out of your room after you left for Almack's. The fellow must have realised suspicion would fall on him, as he packed his bags immediately and disappeared into the night. These London registry-offices leave a lot to be desired. Your mother informs me that he came with an excellent character reference."

Georgiana knit her brows. "I can't find anything missing, Papa. Perhaps he was looking for my jewels and couldn't find them? Are you sure the other rooms weren't searched? Have you seen Stephen this morning?"

"Indeed. He left just before you came downstairs. He assures me his room was untouched."

"Oh! Where has he gone at such an early hour?"

"Rothbury came to take him to Sir Giles's house to view his tropical beetle collection. I was surprised to see that on their way out, they were laden down with plant samples, preserved caterpillars, and a store-box."

"Stephen is returning Sir Giles's specimens to him now that I've completed my illustrations."

"I see." Her father waved at a chair. "Pray sit down, my dear. I've been meaning to speak to you. You are enjoying your Season?"

"It is entertaining, I suppose."

"Rothbury informs me that Pierre Alphonse has been paying court to you. He doesn't like the fellow much and asked me to tell you that he isn't a good prospect in the matrimonial stakes."

She frowned. "I find Monsieur Alphonse most affable. He is certainly more agreeable than Sir Giles."

"Alphonse has foreign ways."

"Well, he *is* French, Papa."

Her father peered at her from under his bushy brows. "I would be wary of marrying a foreigner, my dear. He might very well take you abroad, and then we'd see nothing more of you."

"I should like to travel, Papa. I have always wanted to. Besides, I have put your museum in order now."

"What has the museum got to do with anything?" His voice was tetchy.

"I thought you might be concerned that you would not have anyone to assist you once I marry."

He stared at her for a moment before rubbing his balding pate. "Your mama would miss her grandchildren if they lived in France."

"My children are likely to be firebrands, Papa. Just like I was.

I am sure Mama will be relieved not to have them underfoot. Besides, she will have my brothers' children to dote on. And Harriet's. She won't miss mine."

"What an odd thing to say, Georgiana! Of course, your mother would miss your children." He hesitated for a moment. "We are very pleased with how you have adjusted to living in Town, my love. Your mama expected you to resist her social efforts, but you have complied with all her directives. I believe you have matured."

"In order to find a suitable husband, I must comply with Society's rules." Her voice was somewhat brittle. "I can submit to directives when I see their point, Papa. And I do wish to marry."

"There! I told your mother that you would desire to form a connection when the time was right." He pressed his fingertips together. "As long as it isn't that Frenchman."

"I am still making up my mind about him."

"Rothbury would not issue such a warning lightly."

"Oh, Rothbury is far too protective."

"He has your best interests at heart, Georgiana. As do we all."

She gave a slight shrug. "If you would excuse me, Papa, I have some letters to write." Pushing her chair back, she rose to her feet and made her way upstairs to her bedchamber, her temper slightly ruffled. Her father assumed she wanted the traditional life of a married English lady when that was the last thing she desired.

If she married Pierre Alphonse, she could leave England and live a life of relative freedom with him. He would take her along with him on his scientific expeditions. It would be the ideal arrangement, and if and when any children arrived, they could, no doubt, make some sort of arrangement with tutors and governesses.

Pushing aside a vague sense of misgiving at the thought, Georgiana returned to her bedchamber and sat at her writing table. But her mind refused to settle on the letter she was composing to Harriet. Eventually, she shoved the page to one side and picked up the book of letters her mother had given her instead.

Georgiana hadn't bothered to read it since her arrival in the Capital, and she turned the pages quickly now, perusing the Reverend's worthy prose.

She skimmed over his words until she came to a passage about Natural History, which he described as a "particularly feminine" subject for a lady to study. He then went on to say:

"Natural history is divided into three grand parts, as it respects the animal, the mineral, and the vegetable kingdoms. Linnaeus is the great father of this science, and from the Swedish school have issued the works of the most eminent masters. But he is too voluminous and scientific for a female, who wants only a general knowledge of nature, and not to penetrate the minutiae of her plan."

Georgiana threw the book across the room in disgust. Why did men always assume women had no interest in studying science in depth? Or perhaps it was only Englishmen who held such narrow views? After all, Monsieur Alphonse had spoken to her as an equal and took her opinions on Lepidoptera seriously.

A knock sounded on the door, and her brother poked his head inside. "Good morning, Georgie. I have something for you."

"Oh?"

He pushed the door open and strolled into her room, carrying a familiar-looking store-box.

She frowned. "Why didn't you give that back to Sir Giles?"

"I did give it to him. He has sent it back to you with his compliments."

"What?"

"He told me that as he has the collection in duplicate, he would like you to have these butterflies as a token of his appreciation for your illustrations."

Georgiana took the box from him. "I cannot accept such generosity."

"Why not? You worked hard enough on those drawings."

"I know, but…"

"It is a superb collection, Georgie. I'll take 'em if you don't want 'em."

"No, no, Steve… I'll keep them. But—" She stared into the middle distance, frowning. "I never imagined Sir Giles would give these to me."

"He's a splendid chap and generous to a fault. He told me I'm free to visit his home whenever I wish to study his collections."

"Did you examine his tropical beetles?"

He sank onto the armchair in the corner of the room. "I was amazed at their size. Some of them are utterly enormous. He even has a *Dynastes hercules*."

"A rhinoceros beetle?"

"Yes. It must be seven inches in length. Sir Giles told me it is only the males who have those horns—one on the head and one on the thorax—and that he once observed two males engaged in combat to win possession of a female."

"It sounds rather like a duel."

He grinned. "That's exactly what it's like. Apparently these fights can cause considerable injuries. During combat, the male beetles try to pin their rivals between the horns so that they can raise them up and throw them."

She pulled a face. "Rather gruesome."

"No less gruesome than a human swordfight." He headed back towards the door. "I'm meeting Aldwell now…" He turned back. "What on earth have you done to the poor chap? He is be-witched. I can barely get a decent sentence out of him these days."

Georgiana laughed. "I swear I've done nothing."

"Well, I hope you choose a suitor soon so you can put my friends out of their misery. They've all become dead bores since they met you."

After the door shut behind him, Georgiana studied the wooden panels meditatively. That Sir Giles would give her his pre-cious specimens astonished her. Yes, he had collected the butter-flies in duplicate, but he must have done so to replace any insects in his principal collection that might be lost or damaged. And now, he no longer had that protection.

Perhaps it was his way of trying to make peace with her. If it was, it was an admirable gesture that she would accept in the spirit in which he had given it. What concerned her, however, was that she wasn't sure if his actions *could* be described as merely concil-iatory.

Last night, the expression in his eyes had been disturbing, and she would be lying if she denied his effect on her. Her heart raced uncomfortably fast when he held her in his arms, and although she had done her utmost to appear aloof in his presence, she had felt the complete opposite.

The baronet was far too attractive for her peace of mind, and she suspected he knew she wasn't entirely indifferent to him. Hopefully, he would leave her alone from now on, but she had a nasty feeling he did not intend anything of the sort.

*Will you not give me the chance to make amends?* His words flashed into her mind, and she winced. No matter how angry he made her, she could not ignore the fact that he affected her quite differently from the rest of her suitors. Even Pierre Alphonse, who anyone could see was skilled in the art of flirtation, did not make her heart flutter in the same way.

But it would be to her detriment to forget how dreadfully Sir Giles had upset her. She was attracted to him like a moth drawn to a dangerous flame, but everyone knew that the light, so appealing to these unsuspecting creatures, killed them in the end. She would be a fool to forget that.

# CHAPTER THIRTEEN

Giles frowned as he surveyed the gathering in Lady Hanssen's saloon. He had started accepting more invitations to parties of this nature, hoping to encounter Georgiana Linfield at some of the entertainments. Unfortunately, he did not know if she had received an invitation to the rout this evening.

Eventually, he spotted her in the corner of the room, conversing with her brother and some of his friends. Giles willed Georgiana to meet his gaze. However, she failed to turn her head, and his lips twisted wryly. He was well on his way to becoming one of those lovesick puppies he had always pitied.

Hanssen came up to him. "So you accepted my mother's invitation, old boy. Thought this was the kind of evening you despised."

"I do, in general. But I have a particular reason for attending tonight."

His friend followed his gaze. "Ah! So, you've decided Miss Linfield is rather charming, after all."

"Indeed. Along with the rest of London, it appears," he said dryly.

"Yes. She is quite the rage." His eyes narrowed. "Thinking of becoming a tenant for life, old chap?"

Giles shrugged. "I've attended three coming-out balls in the past week hoping to dance with Miss Linfield, but she will have none of me."

"What an unusual chit she must be! Usually, the ladies toss so many handkerchiefs in your direction, you'd think you were coming down with a bad cold."

Giles turned his head to meet his friend's amused gaze. "The trouble is, Miss Linfield overheard our conversation outside her father's museum when we visited Linfield Court."

"Oh." Hanssen gazed meditatively into space. "How very unfortunate." He remained silent for a minute before saying out of the corner of his mouth, "Don't wish to give you false hope, old fellow, but Miss Linfield is looking our way. Perhaps she isn't as averse to your attentions as you think. She did sketch your butterflies, after all."

"She wishes to become a scientific illustrator and is using me as the proverbial stepping stone." Giles bowed as he spotted his cousin's wife on the other end of the room. "I didn't know Lady Fenmore was in Town."

"I saw Fenmore this morning at White's. He told me Lady Fenmore arrived yesterday with the children."

"They have all recovered?"

"I believe so, although Fenmore wants Lady Fenmore to take the air as she is rather fatigued. He suggested a drive to the Place later this week with the Rothburys. I could extend an invitation to young Linfield and his sister if you wish?"

At Giles's encouraging nod, Hanssen went on: "I'll arrange for a picnic to be set up under the old oak tree in the meadow, and we could engage in a butterfly hunting expedition, perhaps?"

"An excellent plan. Thank you, Hansy."

"I'll issue the invitation to Linfield at tomorrow's Society meeting." His friend grinned suddenly. "Never thought to see you at the mercy of a pretty face, old boy!"

The next evening, Giles entered the House of the Linnean Society in Gerrard Street in Soho. The organisation's Secretary planned to read Giles's paper to the assembled members and their guests shortly, and a large crowd had already gathered in the common meeting-room for the event.

A group was clustered around a wooden table in the corner, where Giles's South American butterfly specimens were on display. He was about to join them when Stephen Linfield came up to him with a friendly greeting. Before he could reply to the younger man, the Society's Secretary stopped beside them, looking flustered. "I am most concerned, Sir Giles. It appears that someone has taken your collection. It was on that table just a moment ago, but now it has disappeared. Let me make an announcement. Perhaps someone unfamiliar with the Society's etiquette has carried the box off to another part of the room."

Giles followed the Secretary to the front of the chamber, but before the man garnered the attention of the crowd, the Librarian approached them. "I have found the specimens, sir. They were on a chair at the back of the room. I have returned them to the display table."

The Secretary frowned. "I am relieved! But it is most vexing that they were taken in the first place. Before I read Sir Giles's paper, I shall reiterate to our members that they must not touch the specimens on display." He sniffed. "One would think they would know better by now."

The Secretary hushed the crowd before presenting the paper in his dry, solemn voice, rendering it as dull as ditchwater. But the facts presented in the article must have been of some interest to the assembled gathering as several gentlemen, including Hanssen and the Linfields, clustered around Giles after the reading ended to discuss its contents.

"You're in luck," Hanssen said much later as they left the Society's premises. "Stephen Linfield has expressed an interest in attending the picnic. He says he'll bring his sister along if she hasn't any prior engagements, and subject to Lady Linfield's amenability to the idea, of course."

A ghost of a smile played about Giles's lips as he murmured his thanks. Hopefully, he would soon persuade Georgiana Linfield that he wasn't the ill-mannered boor she believed him to be.

～

Georgiana sat beside Stephen as he tooled his curricle along the turnpike road leading southwest out of London towards the town of Epsom. Breathing in the fresh, crisp air, she gazed at the Surrey scenery gently engulfing them as they left the bustling Metropolis behind.

How wonderful to be in the countryside again after so many months of city living! She had missed being out in the open, free from the restrictions of Society, where nothing mattered except her natural surroundings and the treasures waiting to be discovered behind every leaf and blade of grass.

As they drew closer to their destination, groves of beech and ash trees spread out on either side of them. Fields and meadows, separated by hedgerows, stretched to the hills beyond.

Less than an hour after they clattered over London Bridge, Stephen turned into the gates of Hanssen Place. A groom on horseback awaited them there, and he led them along a twisting road through a park of well-grown elms, poplars, and oaks, where large numbers of deer grazed on the grass.

Eventually, the road led onto open ground. The groom stopped beside a verdant meadow dominated by an enormous oak in its centre. A footman, who stood to one side, assisted Georgiana down from the carriage while another groom took possession of the team of horses.

"Don't forget our nets," Georgiana called to Stephen as Lord Hanssen and another gentleman approached them.

Their host bowed and smiled. "Welcome to my home, Miss Linfield. May I introduce Lord Fenmore to you?"

Georgiana curtseyed and murmured a polite how-do-you-do as Lord Fenmore bowed in her direction. And then Stephen walked around the curricle, and they all strolled towards the oak tree, where a young, elegantly dressed matron was seated on a chair under its extensive branches.

"Lady Fenmore! Pray allow me to present Miss Linfield and Mr Linfield." Lord Hanssen said.

Georgiana curtseyed again as the older lady rose to her feet. "I have heard so much about you, Miss Linfield." Her gaze swept from Georgiana to Stephen. "Rothbury is my husband's cousin, and he speaks of you often." She indicated a fair young lady dressed in an exquisitely embroidered sprigged muslin gown who stood a short distance away. "This is my cousin, Miss Hamilton. She is staying with me at present."

After the introductions, Lady Fenmore smiled. "Let us sit down, my dear, and have a comfortable cose. How are you enjoying your Season? I am afraid I have missed most of it as my children have been laid low with the measles."

Georgiana was answering her question when another curricle drew up at the edge of the meadow. She blinked when she spotted the man in the driving seat. She shouldn't have been surprised to see Sir Giles here as he was a good friend of Lord Hanssen's, but Stephen had made no mention of his attendance today.

After greeting Lady Fenmore and Miss Hamilton, Sir Giles turned to Georgiana. "Your servant, Miss Linfield."

She inclined her head coolly. "Sir Giles."

"I see you brought your nets. If I may, I should like to join you in a hunt."

She made no reply, but Stephen jumped into the awkward silence. "Of course, Sir Giles! We shall welcome your expertise."

Cassy and Rothbury arrived a few moments later, and Georgiana was grateful for the rapid expansion of their party. Perhaps she should remain with the ladies today. While she hated to forfeit this precious opportunity to hunt for Flies, she did not intend to spend any time with Sir Giles if she could avoid it.

Stephen stood in conversation with the baronet, but hurried over to her after a time, his face lit with excitement. "Sir Giles tells me that he's found Purple Emperors here in the past."

Georgiana's eyes widened. The Emperor was the elusive prize every butterfly hunter aspired to collect. The males, with their famous iris sheen, were more sought after than the females. However, they usually fluttered in the tops of trees, defending their territory, and descended only on occasion to drink or feed. Hence, they were notoriously difficult to capture. She frowned suddenly. "Isn't it too early for them to be out?"

"Yes, but we can hunt for their larvae and breed 'em. And Peacocks, Brimstones, and Red Admirals abound at this time of year. Should we go?"

Georgiana looked guiltily at Lady Fenmore and Cassy, who had been listening to their conversation. Her sister-in-law laughed. "Do go, Georgie. I know it will be torture to stay here now that you know what treasures await you."

"I won't be away for long." Georgiana smiled gratefully. She joined Stephen, who held their nets and a jam jar for any possible finds.

"This is an excellent collecting-ground for larvae," Sir Giles said. "Have you reared butterflies in the past, Miss Linfield?"

She met his eyes for a brief moment. "Yes, of course."

Miss Hamilton, who had moved closer to Cassy and Lady

Fenmore, smiled winsomely up at the baronet. "May I join your party, Sir Giles?"

Lady Fenmore frowned. "But your slippers, Caro… they are so delicate. I doubt you will be able to walk very far. Miss Linfield's shoes are much sturdier."

An expression of distaste spread over Miss Hamilton's face as she peered at Georgiana's sensibly shod feet.

"I am wearing my stoutest shoes," Georgiana said cheerfully, following the direction of the young woman's gaze. "They are for country walking and have no pretence to fashion."

"They are certainly very…durable." Miss Hamilton's nose wrinkled.

"I'm afraid if you wish to pursue an interest in insects, you will need to find some practical footwear," Georgiana said. "It is a prerequisite for walking on rough, uneven ground."

Miss Hamilton shook her head. "I do not own any shoes quite like that." Her expression implied that she didn't want to.

"If you would prefer to examine insects that have already been captured, Miss Hamilton, you should visit the British Museum to view Sloane's natural history collections," Sir Giles said quietly.

Lady Fenmore nodded. "An excellent idea, Sir Giles. Perhaps we could make up a party later in the week if you and Mr Linfield would be so obliging as to be our guides?"

The baronet bowed. "Of course. It would be my pleasure."

"I would be delighted to show you the museum's beetles, Miss Hamilton," Stephen said. "That is my particular field of interest."

"Beetles?" Her voice squeaked.

"There are some splendid specimens on display."

Georgiana glanced from Miss Hamilton, who had grown quite pale, to Stephen, who smiled eagerly at the lovely young woman. "I do believe Miss Hamilton might prefer to see the Lepidoptera collections."

"The Lepi-what?" Miss Hamilton sounded quite faint.

"Lepidoptera is the order of insects that includes butterflies and moths," Georgiana explained.

"Oh, yes, yes." Miss Hamilton dipped her head. "My interest lies there… But I only wish to see the butterflies. Moths are eerie."

"Eerie?" Stephen stared at her.

"That odd way they have of fluttering around lights…" She gave a delicate shudder. "I don't like them at all."

Sir Giles picked up his butterfly net and a walking stick. "We should leave now so that we'll be back in time for the picnic."

"Yes, indeed," Lady Fenmore said. "We shall look forward to seeing what you have captured."

Georgiana stole a glance at the baronet, who walked beside her. A pincushion, stuck with pins of varying sizes, was attached to a ribbon around his neck, and he had flung a small leather knapsack over his back.

She leaned down to examine a Brimstone fluttering nearby, and when she caught up to the men a short while later, she positioned herself beside Stephen. Her brother asked Sir Giles a stream of questions, but he ceased speaking when they neared the meadow's edge and entered the wood.

"If we're in luck, we should find the larvae here." Sir Giles walked to a group of poplar trees and carefully searched amongst the branches. Within minutes, he located a brown caterpillar lying in the fork of a sallow branch. After looking in a few more trees, he found a couple more.

Stephen placed the precious creatures into his jam jar while Sir Giles collected food plants for the larvae. Then, he removed his stovepipe hat, lined with white paper, and placed the plants inside.

Georgiana studied the unusual repository. "You have a specially designed hat for insect collecting, Sir Giles?"

The corners of his eyes creased. "Would you care to look at it?" He handed his hat to her. "I got the idea from Abel Ingpen. He lines his hats with cork and paper so that he can transport insects during long excursions. The cavity of the hat also serves well to carry food plants."

"What a unique idea!"

He grinned. "Indeed. It is very convenient."

When they emerged from the wood, Sir Giles began beating the vegetation with his walking stick, dislodging a Great Orange-tip butterfly in the process. "Would you like me to capture this for you, Miss Linfield?" he asked.

She met his inquiring look. "Thank you, but no. I have one in my collection already."

His gaze lingered on her face. "I have been meaning to tell you that your illustrations received high praise at the Society the other night."

"They did? I am so pleased." She clasped her hands together. "Papa and Stephen told me they were well-received, but I confess to some anxiety."

"Anxious? You, Miss Linfield?" His lips curved into a teasing smile. "I can't believe it."

"I am not immune to the occasional qualm, Sir Giles." She raised her chin. "In regard to my work, of course."

"Of course," he said gravely, although his eyes were laughing.

Georgiana looked down and prodded a bush with her net. Stephen had wandered off to look for beetles in the nearby woodland, and she was alone with Sir Giles. Perhaps she should follow her brother back into the wood...

A wasp suddenly flew out of the bush. Georgiana darted away, but it came straight towards her. A burning pain suddenly engulfed her arm, and she cried out as she clutched the sore spot. Within a minute, a swarm of angry attackers emerged from the vegetation. She must have disturbed a nest. Frozen in terror, she flung an arm across her face to protect herself from the swarming creatures.

A pair of strong arms encircled her waist. Georgiana gulped. "Stand completely still, Georgie," Sir Giles said in a low voice. "Don't move your arms at all." He drew her close against him, so very close, and backed slowly away.

Eventually, he halted, and Georgiana, her eyes shut tight, remained motionless in the protective circle of his embrace. She expected to be stung again and again at any moment and braced herself for the onslaught. But nothing happened. And then, after what felt like an eternity, Sir Giles released her and led her some distance away.

"Sensible girl. If you'd moved your hands or tried to swat those wasps, you would have made them even more aggressive."

"My instinct was to do exactly that—or even to run. But I know how dangerous that sort of movement is around wasps."

He examined the welt on her arm. "Have you been stung before?"

"Only once, when I was a young girl." She smiled wryly. "Once was enough."

"You had no adverse reaction?"

"It was only very painful."

He frowned. "Let us return. There is an ice sculpture on one of the picnic tables. A bit of ice on your arm should help with the swelling."

Stephen came out of the woods at that moment, looking very pleased with himself. "I've just found a stag beetle."

Sir Giles glanced at him. "I'm afraid we need to leave straight away." He handed over his net and walking stick. "Take these for me, if you will. Your sister has been stung by a wasp."

"I thought I heard a yelp." Stephen studied her in concern. "Are you all right, Georgie?"

"It hurts a little."

"I am sure it hurts more than a little. Wasp stings are devilishly painful."

She smiled rather wanly at him as she placed her hand on Sir Giles's outstretched arm. She shouldn't accept his help, she really shouldn't, but it was nice to have him to lean on over the rough ground. The pain had reduced somewhat, but her arm still throbbed.

They made their way across the meadow to the great oak tree. When they arrived, Cassy rose to her feet. "You're just in time. We are all getting hungry." Her eyes narrowed as she studied Georgiana's face. "Are you unwell, dearest? You look quite pale."

"I was stung by a wasp."

Cassy winced. "Oh, no!"

Sir Giles released her arm, leaving her suddenly bereft, and she drew in a sharp breath. How silly to feel this way.

The baronet had a brief word with Lord Hanssen before heading to the picnic tables, laden with a vast array of tempting dishes. He picked up the ice sculpture of an eagle from its stand in the centre. It had melted rapidly in the warm weather, but enough remained of the display figure for him to wrap it in a linen napkin. "Place this on your arm, *ma chère*" he said when he returned to her side.

She blinked at him. *Ma chère*... He had just called her his dear. She pressed the ice against her skin, and the pain began to ebb away. Cassy urged her to sit down, and Rothbury brought her a glass of lemonade. Such solicitude from her family members... She looked at Sir Giles out of the corner of her eye. He stood alone, to one side, ceding his position to her nearest and dearest, as was only proper.

She wished him closer and the others far away and found the desire of some concern.

No, indeed, it was of great concern.

# CHAPTER FOURTEEN

Georgiana was in the drawing room chatting with Cassy the following day when Sir Giles was announced. After greeting her sister-in-law, he turned to Georgiana. "I came to find out how you are feeling today, Miss Linfield."

She gave a slight smile. "My arm is quite swollen, but it is not as painful as it was yesterday. Pray be seated."

He lowered his tall frame into a chair. "I trust you are fit enough to join us on our excursion to the British Museum tomorrow?"

"I look forward to it. I haven't had the opportunity to visit the Museum since I arrived in London, and I particularly wish to see John Ross's polar bear. Stephen has described it to me in a wealth of detail."

"It is a sight to behold for any biologist."

"You've seen it?" she asked eagerly.

"I have. There are also Inuit artifacts and zoological specimens on display from the Arctic, which you should find interesting. Ross returned from his expedition with a number of curiosities."

"I would give anything to travel to such a far-flung place."

A smile played about his lips. "I believe we share the same spirit of adventure, Miss Linfield."

His gaze was intent, and after a few moments, she glanced away. "Miss Hamilton and Lady Fenmore will be joining us tomorrow?" she asked after a short pause.

"Yes. I am escorting them to the museum at eleven o'clock."

The door opened again, and Taylor stepped inside to announce Monsieur Alphonse. The Frenchman strolled into the room but came to an exaggerated halt when his gaze rested on Sir Giles. "*Bonjour*, Lady Rothbury. Mademoiselle Linfield." He nodded at the baronet before turning back to Georgiana. "I see Sir Giles is before me, *mademoiselle*. I had hoped to drive with you in the Park this morning."

"I would have liked that, *monsieur*, but I am going out shortly with my mother."

"I shall stay then and speak with you a little, if I may?" Then, without a pause, he proceeded to engage her in lively dialogue. Sir Giles and Cassy began speaking about an upcoming trip Rothbury was planning to the Continent.

The Frenchman glanced across at Cassy. "I imagine your brother and Lady Rothbury must be eager to travel abroad before family responsibilities bind them to their country estates."

Georgiana raised her brows. "Bind them? Rothbury has travelled far and wide since he reached his majority."

"*Oui*. But in these days, English noblemen are tied much more closely to their land than Frenchmen."

She studied him sympathetically. "Your family lost their estates during the Revolution, *monsieur*?"

"*Mais oui.*" He shrugged. "I do not repine, however. The responsibility for vast estates would impinge on my freedoms, and I would detest being unable to travel."

"Englishmen travel."

"When they are young and free from responsibility, perhaps... But once an Englishman marries, he puts his roots down like a solid oak tree and tends to his lands, living the traditional life of his ancestors. *C'est inévitable.*"

She opened her mouth to defend her countrymen and then closed it again. His observation was a little too apt. "You make Englishmen sound rather dull," she said tartly.

His lips curled. "They are merely staid and, at times, lacking in *joie de vivre*. But I believe you have observed that yourself, *mademoiselle*."

She raised startled eyes to his. "I do not understand your meaning, *monsieur*."

"Do you not desire to break free from the rules which bind

you to this so-proper society? I have gained that impression during our many *conversations*."

"Well, yes," Georgiana said. "But it is only a dream."

"It could become a reality," he said softly. "I would liberate you from a life of convention—if I had the opportunity."

She felt the colour rise in her cheeks and looked away, only to encounter Sir Giles's keen gaze, which disconcerted her even more.

Fortunately, Monsieur Alphonse rose to his feet then and took his leave. Sir Giles stayed only a few moments longer before doing the same. "I shall see you at the museum tomorrow," he said curtly before leaving the room.

Cassy gazed pensively at his retreating back before looking at Georgiana. "Is anything the matter, dearest?"

"No, no," Georgiana said. "Nothing at all."

But after her sister-in-law departed, she stared into the distance, awash in a maelstrom of conflicting emotions. She was at a crossroads in her life, and soon she would have to decide the way forward. But which direction should she take?

Marriage might be a bridge to a new life, but it was a frighteningly permanent one. She chewed on her bottom lip, wishing for more information so she could make an informed decision. She needed to understand better how Monsieur Alphonse envisioned their future together. She would pose subtle questions of that gentleman when next she encountered him.

As her husband, he would gain complete direction of her existence. Ultimately, it would be the soundness of his character which determined the quality of her life. The sobering thought gave Georgiana pause. Could she relinquish such control to another human being?

A sigh escaped her lips. She was of marriageable age, yet her ability to pursue an interest in biology remained severely limited by the dictums of propriety. However, if she became an old maid, she could travel the world with Stephen at her side. Cousin Howard had suggested that when he discussed the bequest with her. But she would need to wait several years before that became possible.

Whatever road she took, the choice she made now would affect the rest of her life. She must tread carefully.

The next morning, Georgiana and Stephen arrived at the museum a few minutes early. She accepted a printed account of the museum's contents when she crossed the threshold before entering the hall, where Sir Giles, Lady Fenmore, and Miss Hamilton already awaited them. After a polite exchange of greetings, they made their way towards the gallery of Natural History in the west wing.

Miss Hamilton let out a gasp as she came to a halt in front of an enormous stuffed alligator hanging in the staircase. And when the other girl proceeded to pass a crocodile in its glass case, she leapt into the air and looked around nervously. Georgiana suppressed a grin. Did Miss Hamilton expect a wild animal to jump out at her at any moment?

"It is never a good idea to stop until you have reached the collection you plan to see, Miss Hamilton," Sir Giles said. "As you have expressed an interest in butterflies, Miss Hamilton, it is best to ignore everything else on display. Otherwise, you will be so distracted you will never reach your destination." He turned to Georgiana. "I am sure you will agree, Miss Linfield."

"Oh, yes," Georgiana said. "Whenever I visit the British Museum, I am ruthless in my determination to view only one room at a time."

Miss Hamilton nodded. "Indeed. The curiosities are so numerous they dazzle the mind."

A variety of stuffed birds were on show, including huge vultures and tiny hummingbirds, as were fish and a number of reptiles, all preserved in spirits. Their party passed by them all until they reached the room that housed the Hans Sloane collection of insects.

They split up then as they strolled from case to case, observing the vast array of specimens that included a fascinating walking leaf insect, which looked exactly like its name.

Each glass case bore an inscription indicating its contents. Even though Georgiana had seen the collection before, she never failed to be astonished at the sheer number of spiders, butterflies, and bees on display. She shivered a little when she walked past some wasps before stopping in front of a case of brilliantly coloured beetles. She studied them with interest before stepping back to read the inscription.

"Diamond beetles," Sir Giles said from behind her. "They are native to South America."

"What truly splendid creatures."

"Indeed." He searched her face. "I hope you have given my request some thought?"

"Your request?"

"To give me a chance to make amends."

"Oh, *that* request…" She cleared her throat. "I don't believe it is a feasible idea."

He raised his brows. "And why is that?"

"We have been at outs frequently since we met. It shows we could never be friends."

"Then it is a good thing that I am not seeking your friendship, Miss Linfield."

The blazing light in his blue eyes gave her pause. His gaze made her feel wonderfully alive while also creating a sense of alarm in her, an instinct to dive for cover, to hide from the tide of uncontrolled emotion within her breast.

She drew a steadying breath as warmth immersed her from within, rather like slow-moving lava burning through everything in its path. Desperate to cool the flames, she jerked her gaze away, and it fell upon Miss Hamilton. The young lady stood frozen in the middle of the room, not looking to the left or to the right. She seemed very pale.

Georgiana stepped towards her. "Perhaps we should return to the museum another day. I don't think Miss Hamilton is feeling quite the thing."

Sir Giles frowned as he looked at the other girl. "Are you unwell, ma'am?"

"I cannot bear to see any more insects." Her voice was faint. "Even the butterflies appear strange when you study them too closely…all those dreadful feelers." She gave a delicate shudder.

Lady Fenmore came up to them, a crease upon her brow. "Caro, dearest…are you ill?"

"I'm afraid I cannot abide these insects for much longer. They make me feel quite overcome."

"My sister is the same," Georgiana said quietly. "I used to think it strange that she was so afraid of them, as most insects are perfectly harmless. But she cannot seem to help her response to them."

"Should I escort you home, Lady Fenmore?" Sir Giles asked.

Her ladyship hesitated as she glanced at Georgiana. "I don't like to break up our party…"

"Oh, Stephen and I have visited this museum countless times. We shan't repine, Lady Fenmore. In fact, I am feeling a trifle tired myself and would appreciate the opportunity to return home early."

Georgiana met Sir Giles's eyes for a fleeting moment and flushed at their ironical expression.

"You're tired, Georgie?" Stephen said as he came up to them. "That's a first, I must say."

Her cheeks burned at the knowing little smile curling Sir Giles's lips. The sooner they left, the better.

The baronet offered Miss Hamilton his arm, and after she placed a shaking hand on his coat sleeve, he led the way out of the gallery.

When they reached the entrance to the museum, Georgiana and Stephen bid the others a hasty farewell. Miss Hamilton looked even paler than before, and Lady Fenmore and Sir Giles were distracted in their efforts to assist her.

Back in Berkeley Square, Georgiana hurried upstairs to her bedchamber, her thoughts in a whirl. Within the space of a few days, two gentlemen had intimated that they wished to propose to her.

Monsieur Alphonse promised her freedom, adventure, and travel should she marry him, whereas Sir Giles…

She gazed out of the window and sighed.

# CHAPTER FIFTEEN

Georgiana's coming-out ball loomed ever closer on the horizon, and her mother consulted with Cassy on an almost daily basis about the myriad details. As the acceptances continued to roll in, it became clear that the ball was destined to become one of the crushes of the Season.

Georgiana dutifully participated in numerous discussions amongst her female relatives about the grand occasion. Still, more often than not, her mind wandered when they began talking about the flowers, the chalking of the floors, or the various refreshments that would be on offer.

However, although she had never bothered much about her clothes, it was impossible to react with indifference towards the ball gown her mother had ordered for her from Madame Bouchet, London's most exclusive *modiste*.

The white gauze overdress was brocaded with white silken flowers and worn over a pink satin slip. Tulle, blond lace, and garlands of roses trimmed the hem, exactly matching the wreath *à-la-Flore* made for Georgiana's hair.

When the evening of the ball arrived, Georgiana dressed with a sense of anticipation. Her father had turned down three unsuitable candidates for her hand this week. Surely the news had come to Monsieur Alphonse's ears by now. That bit of information might well prompt him to pay his addresses to her sooner rather than later, so it was imperative that she find out more about his prospects for the future when he approached her this evening.

Ignoring the slightly hollow feeling in her stomach at the thought of his proposal, she allowed Kirby to put the finishing touches to hair, arranged in corkscrew ringlets that fell to one side. She stared defiantly at her reflection in the glass. She must stick to her original plan of finding an amenable husband who would do her bidding instead of entertaining silly, romantic thoughts of a blue-eyed baronet who delighted only in provoking her.

After an early dinner at Rothbury House, Georgiana took her place with her mother and father at the top of the sweeping stone staircase leading up from the ground floor. Beautiful arrangements of roses, white azaleas, and white and pink hyacinths had been placed on every available surface. Their perfume lingered in the air, intermingling with the scent of the elegantly dressed ladies and gentlemen arriving at the mansion in ever-increasing numbers.

Georgiana had just greeted the Fenmores, who had moved on and stood a little to one side, conversing with the Rothburys, when Sir Giles approached. He greeted her parents politely before offering her a smile. "I hope I can claim a waltz with you later, Miss Linfield?"

Georgiana's mind raced. No gentleman had asked to waltz as yet. If she turned Sir Giles down, it would look very odd to her parents, who were listening to their conversation. Indeed, even now, her mama was nodding and smiling, obviously expecting her to accept the invitation. So, with a somewhat brittle smile, she murmured, "Thank you, Sir Giles. Perhaps the first waltz?"

"I look forward to dancing it with you." He bowed and moved away, and Georgiana released her breath as she observed his retreating back. After their last dance, she had vowed never to waltz with him again. Yet, here she was, committed to being enclosed once again within the disturbing circle of his embrace.

She straightened her spine. Perhaps it wasn't such a bad thing. She could use the dance as some sort of test. When they had waltzed together the last time, Sir Giles's strange effect on her senses might well have been entirely due to the tension of the moment. They had quarrelled, after all, and she had been overwrought. Of course! That must be why her heart had raced so madly, and she hadn't been able to think.

Upon entering the ballroom a short while later, she spotted

Cousin Howard sitting at the far end of the room and made her way to him immediately. "What a delightful surprise, sir," she said with a smile."

"I wouldn't have missed it for the world, my dear. When Lady Rothbury sent me an invitation and suggested I spend the night here, I accepted immediately. She told me it was to be a surprise for you."

"A lovely surprise! I have missed our conversations since the Season began."

Cousin Theodosia came up to them then, and Georgiana greeted her coolly. The older lady must know by now about the mistake she had made, but her manner was no less unbending. Therefore it was with a sense of relief that Georgiana heard a violinist strike a chord and the lilting notes of a flute filling the air.

Mr. Aldwell partnered her in the first set. After the dance ended, Stephen approached Georgiana to complain bitterly and at length about their mother's insistence that he partner a lady for every single dance this evening.

She shook her head. "I believe Mama just wants you to do your duty, Steve. She told me there is nothing worse than ladies needing to sit out of dances because too many gentlemen have disappeared to the cardroom."

His gaze swept the room. "Well, there's not a dearth of men here tonight. All my friends have come in the hope that you'll favour them with a dance. Have you decided who you're going to marry yet?"

"I am still giving it some thought."

"Sir Giles seems the best of the bunch. I hope you'll choose him."

Georgiana gasped. "He's the last man I'd consider!"

Stephen lifted his shoulder in a half-shrug. "I thought you'd begun to favour him over the rest of your suitors."

"Not at all!" She shook her head. "If you must know, I am considering Monsieur Alphonse's suit."

"Alphonse? Don't like the fellow at all. He seems a slippery customer."

She knit her brows. "Why do you say that?"

"It's just the impression I've received. He's too smooth by half."

Georgiana frowned but made no response. Her brother often made quick assessments of people, but he was quite an astute judge of character. She didn't want to dismiss his opinion of the Frenchman out of hand, but her next partner claimed her before she could question Stephen further.

Monsieur Alphonse arrived much later in the evening and immediately approached her to make his apologies. "I trust I am not too late to claim a dance, Mademoiselle Linfield?"

"I am afraid all my dances have been claimed, *monsieur*."

"I thought it must be so." He sighed heavily. "*Mille pardons.* I was unavoidably detained."

"It is no matter."

"But it is!" He spread out his hands. "I am cast down with regret."

Rothbury appeared beside her then to inform her that their mother desired to speak to her. So, with a nod at Monsieur Alphonse, she allowed her brother to lead her away.

"Are you enjoying your ball, Georgie?"

"Oh, yes! It is quite delightful. Thank you for allowing us to have it here."

"It is my pleasure." He studied her contemplatively. "I need to speak to you about a somewhat urgent matter. Will you be at home tomorrow morning?"

"Yes. Mama hasn't planned any engagements as yet. She is convinced we'll all be exhausted."

"I don't think I've ever seen you tired in my life."

"I find certain things fatiguing." Her lips curved wryly.

"Oh?"

"Mmmm... Polite conversation when the talk is about nothing of substance. It is all so dreadfully dull."

"Is that why you favour Monsieur Alphonse's company?"

She inclined her head. "We speak of his travels and entomology."

"Ah."

Her brow creased. "I know you cautioned Papa about him. Is there a specific reason you dislike him?"

"Let us speak about it tomorrow, Georgie. This is neither the time nor the place to have a serious discussion."

She gave a small sigh. "Very well."

Sir Giles came up to them then to claim Georgiana for his promised waltz. He did not initiate any conversation as he led her away, and when they took their places in the circle and began to whirl around the ballroom, he remained silent.

When Georgiana eventually looked up, the warmth in his eyes caused her skin to heat. Tell-tale warmth crept into her cheeks, and she tried—and failed—to steady her breathing as the blood pounded loudly in her ears, so loudly she was convinced he must hear it.

She wasn't giving a thought to her dance steps. They seemed to move together in total unity without the need to give heed to anything so mundane. She looked away from him, trying to catch her breath.

A powerful physical accord between two people did not necessarily extend to a harmony of mind and spirit. She must not forget that.

No matter how attractive he was, Sir Giles Tavistock was not for her.

# CHAPTER SIXTEEN

Rothbury called the next morning just as Georgiana was settling down to read in the library. He took the seat across from her, and after she had placed her book on a nearby table, she gave him her full attention.

"I believe Mama is still resting in her bedchamber after last night's exertions," he said. "Did she enjoy the evening?"

"She appeared to. It was a lovely party."

"I noticed you didn't dance with Alphonse."

"He arrived very late."

Rothbury studied her thoughtfully. "Would you accept his suit if he proposed, Georgie?"

She hesitated. "I am considering all possibilities at present. Monsieur Alphonse has hinted that he would take me travelling with him should we marry. Travelling has always been one of my treasured dreams."

"I wouldn't say that is a good enough reason to consider matrimony."

She shrugged. "Why not? You and Cassy enjoy travelling together."

"My willingness to take Cassy abroad with me on field trips is not the reason she agreed to marry me, however. Have you fallen in love with Alphonse?"

"Well, no." She bit her lip. "He seems very charming, but I don't know him very well."

He leaned back against the sofa. "I am relieved to hear that.

He isn't to be trusted, Georgie. Last week Alphonse told his tailor, who also happens to make my coats, that he would be able to pay off his debts very shortly as he will be marrying you. Alphonse is looking for a rich wife who will be able to rescue him from his financial embarrassments."

"I'm not rich!"

"Not yet. But you have excellent prospects. Alphonse is well aware of that."

She sat up straighter in her chair. "How presumptuous of him to talk in that manner. And to his tailor!"

Her brother's eyes crinkled at the corners. "He is a very good tailor. I am sure Alphonse would do anything to receive an extension of credit." He paused for a moment. "Have you given him reason to believe you may be open to receiving his addresses?"

"It seems I must have. But I have been at pains not to encourage him as I was unsure if his manner was sincere or merely how gentlemen speak to ladies on the Continent. Now that I know his intentions are purely mercenary, I'll make it clear I don't favour his suit." She looked down at her hands, intertwining her fingers together.

"I need you to wait a while before you do that."

Her head shot up. "What?"

Rothbury frowned as he rested one arm along the edge of the sofa. "Fenmore approached me a few days ago to inform me that the Government has a particular interest in Alphonse. They suspect he may be engaged in a plot to rescue Bonaparte from St Helena."

She stared at him in shock. "How is that even possible?"

"Alphonse has been observed meeting an Irishman, a Dr O'Meara, who was Bonaparte's doctor on St Helena up until last year when he was dismissed from British service. When O'Meara returned to England, he began petitioning for Napoleon's release."

Her brow furrowed. "Monsieur Alphonse has never even hinted that he supports Napoleon."

"Indeed, he has been very discreet. But we believe he is one of the leaders of the scheme."

"Do you have any idea how this plan will be executed?"

"No. But we can hazard a guess. A few years ago, French

refugees in Philadelphia and conspirators in Brazil devised a plot with an American, a Captain Hawkins. Hawkins planned to fit out a couple of ships that were meant to sail to St Helena with a number of small steamboats on board. The aim was to use the steamboats to rescue Bonaparte at night and take him to South America to join the Brazilian nationalists in their revolt against Portugal."

Georgiana's eyes widened. "This is the plot you think Monsieur Alphonse is involved in?"

"We don't know. The attempt was meant to take place in January or February last year. But in August 1817, the British Ambassador in Washington wrote to Lord Castlereagh at the British Foreign Office, enclosing copies of letters detailing the conspiracy."

"It was a real threat?"

His jaw tightened. "Nothing came of it in the end. But with the present unrest in Europe, it would be disastrous for Bonaparte to be liberated from the island, especially as the British Ambassador has stated there is constant communication between French officers in the United States and disaffected people in France and other parts of Europe." He leaned forward. "This is where you come in, Georgie. Fenmore has asked me if you could try to discover if there is a new plan afoot."

Her lips parted in shock. "Lord Fenmore wants me to spy on behalf of the British Government?"

"He merely wants you to relay any information you may discover to me. The Governor of St Helena, Sir Hudson Lowe, intercepted correspondence sent there last year about yet another plot to liberate Bonaparte. The communication made it clear that attempts have been made to bribe some of the troops, and we know Bonaparte is able to draw large sums of money from bankers in Europe to effect an escape." He sighed. "I realise it is asking a lot of you, my dear, but we are extremely concerned about the ramifications should such a scheme succeed."

She pressed her lips together. "Encouraging Monsieur Alphonse to think I am still open to receiving his addresses does not sit well with me."

"You needn't encourage him. You just need to not *dis*courage him for a while."

"Should he pay his addresses to me, I shall have to refuse

him."

A line appeared between his brows. "Perhaps we could let it be known that your father has decreed you cannot accept an offer of marriage until you turn eighteen. I could broach the matter with him if you wish. I am sure he will bring you to London next year for another Season, as that was when you were originally meant to make your come-out. It will give us time to discover any plot which is being formulated."

Georgiana met his direct gaze for a moment, and then she jumped up from her chair and walked across to the window. Suddenly her eyes felt very dry, and she blinked a few times as she stared out into the Square. Although she'd had her doubts about Monsieur Alphonse, she had found his interest in her opinions flattering. He had appeared to respect her as a fellow entomologist. How maddening to know it had merely been a ploy to win her over so he could gain access to her fortune.

She spun around and crossed the room swiftly to her brother.

"Are you very distressed?" He studied her, his brow furrowed.

"A little. I thought Monsieur Alphonse respected my contributions to science. I feel like an utter fool."

"I am sorry to disillusion you, my dear."

"You did well." She straightened her spine. "I will do my best to assist you in finding out if he is involved in any plot."

"Thank you, Georgie."

She tipped her head to one side. "Does Papa know?"

"No. And please don't say anything to anyone—not even to Stephen."

"Why can't Stephen know?"

"Things have a way of getting out." He rose to his feet. "You only have to look at how quickly the news spread about your bequest to understand the inherent danger of taking too many people into your confidence. Your cousin Agnes told only one person, and within a couple of days, the whole of London knew about your inheritance. Discretion is of the utmost importance in matters such as these."

Georgiana let out her breath. "Indeed."

"I sorry to put such a damper on the rest of your Season. To make it up to you, Cassy and I would like to invite you to join us on our next expedition."

Her eyes widened. "You really mean that?"

"Of course I do."

"I would give anything to travel with you! But do you think Mama and Papa will agree?"

"I spoke to your father last night. He said he would grant his permission should you not be betrothed by the end of the Season."

"There is no chance of that happening now." She beamed at him. "This is beyond anything! Thank you."

"I am pleased you are not too cast down about Alphonse. Cassy assured me your affections weren't engaged in that direction. She has her own ideas about where your regards lie."

She studied him narrowly. "What do you mean?"

He laughed as he moved towards the door. "I know better than to wade into a discussion of that nature."

"What precisely did Cassy say, Edward?" She straightened her shoulders. "If you don't tell me, I'll follow you to Rothbury House and ask her myself."

He raised his hands in the air and grinned. "Merely that you are not...er.... entirely indifferent to my cousin."

She glared at him. "I have absolutely no interest in Sir Giles. And you can tell Cassy that with my compliments."

"The lady doth protest too much, methinks."

At her outraged gasp, he chuckled. "I'll say no more, never fear." Then his expression sobered. "You must take great care in your dealings with Alphonse, Georgie. If at any time you feel uncomfortable or unwilling to continue in this endeavour, you must cease from it at once. Your safety and comfort are of primary importance. You understand?"

At her nod, he sighed heavily. "I am inclined to tell Fenmore that we should seek another line of investigation. However, Alphonse's interest in you has provided us with a unique opportunity to discover whether anything is afoot. But you must be discreet in your inquiries. Alphonse is no fool, and if you affect too much of an interest in his activities, he may become suspicious."

"I'll be very careful. And I shall do my best to find out if he is involved in any sort of plot." She swallowed. "I would hate for us to go to war again. Last year, I attended The View of the Battle of

Waterloo at the Panorama in Leicester Square. Did you go?"

"I did and found it very well done."

"I was amazed at how real the painting looked. I actually expected the soldiers to start stirring as they appeared so true to life. But the only moving thing was that smoke puffing out from the artillery wagons." She hugged her middle, staring into the distance. "Seeing the wounded and the dead lying on the ground, even only in painting form, was a terrible sight. I cannot erase the images from my mind."

He bowed his head. "There is a strange sense of pall that lingers after a war. It is as if the nation is slowly recovering from a prolonged illness that brought us very near our deathbed. It takes time to heal from both the financial and the physical toll."

"Like a long convalescence," Georgiana said quietly.

"Indeed. We are not in a state to even contemplate resuming hostilities with France, and that is why we have asked for your assistance. Lord Bathurst, the cabinet minister in charge of Bonaparte's custody, is taking this threat very seriously. He informed me that a body of disgruntled people in France would view Bonaparte's escape as a rallying point. Undoubtedly, his return to the Continent would have dire consequences." He placed his hand on the door handle, preparing to leave.

"I hope I will be able to discover some information for you then."

"Thank you, my dear."

As the door clicked softly behind him, she sank onto a chair. Her vision for the future...altered in one fell swoop. How strange! However, it was better to discover that Monsieur Alphonse was not what he seemed before being tied to him in marriage.

And, to be honest, she had never felt entirely at ease in his company. His manner of speaking led her to suspect he did things a little too brown on occasion.

He had flattered her sensibilities, but had not been in the least sincere, unlike Sir Giles, whose blunt manner precluded her from ever doubting where she stood with *him*.

She let out an impatient breath. Why couldn't she put the blasted baronet from her mind? He crept into her thoughts throughout the day, no matter how hard she tried not to think about him. She had the sneaking suspicion that Sir Giles had guessed this and was playing a waiting game with her, biding his time until they could fight out this thing between them that unsettled her so.

She dismissed the disturbing notion as she walked back to the window and stared outside.

She had work to do.

# Chapter Seventeen

Georgiana was in the drawing room when Monsieur Alphonse called the next morning. She had wondered how to find the opportunity to converse with him in private, so when he asked if she wished to drive with him in the Park, she accepted his invitation with alacrity.

"How delightful that you are not otherwise engaged, Miss Linfield," he said as he directed his horses out of the Square. "I was concerned I was no longer in your good graces after my late arrival at your ball."

"I do not take offence at such things, *monsieur*," she said lightly.

"An excellent characteristic for a lady to have." A gig cut in front of him, and his brow lowered as he calmed his horses. When he had them under control again, he glanced down at her. "I am thinking of taking my younger sister to visit the butterfly collection at the British Museum later this week."

"Oh, it is excellent! My brother and I viewed it recently."

"I am too late then. I had hoped to ask you and Mr Linfield to join us."

Georgiana's mind raced. She needed to use every opportunity to engage him in private conversation. "We would be pleased to revisit it, *monsieur*."

"*Non, non.* That would be too dull for you, as you have seen it already." He paused for a moment. "Have you paid a visit to Bullock's Museum? We could view the natural history collections there instead?"

"Thank you. That would be most agreeable."

"*Superbe*. My sister only arrived in Town recently. She is to make her *début* next year." He gave Georgiana a wry smile and shook his head. "In the meantime, I am seeking ways in which to amuse her."

"Mademoiselle Alphonse is also interested in entomology?"

He laughed. "In truth, she is far more interested in fashion. But she does admire butterflies."

They turned into the Park then, and Monsieur Alphonse began speaking about his upcoming trip to France. Georgiana listened attentively, and waited before delving into questioning him. She did not quite know how to inquire into his views regarding the war or his opinion of the erstwhile French Emperor.

Her brow wrinkled. This was harder than expected. She would have to think of some way of bringing the conversation around to these sensitive subjects. And even if she managed to do so, it was unlikely he would reveal any of his plans to her.

Rothbury's idea was viable in theory, but it wasn't going to be easy to eke out information from the Frenchman. Indeed, she found it difficult to maintain a civil manner with him after his reprehensible behaviour. She felt like giving him the cut direct; instead, she had to pretend she still welcomed his attentions.

She listened to his conversation and politely responded to his remarks. By the time they left Hyde Park, she realised that Alphonse possessed a knack for elaborating at length on a subject while revealing very little about his personal beliefs. She needed to try to lead the conversation into the political realm. "You mentioned once that you were thinking of moving back to France, *monsieur*," she said with a smile.

He glanced down at her. "*Oui*."

"Do you know yet when that might be?"

"It is impossible to predict the future, *mademoiselle*." The timbre of his voice was even.

Georgiana just refrained from wincing. Her need to examine him must necessarily result in asking questions that would seem vulgarly curious—not a role she relished. Monsieur Alphonse had neatly sidestepped her query, and it felt very much like a snub, even while delivered in his usual charming tones.

When they turned into Mount Street, a man dressed in sober

clothes hailed Monsieur Alphonse, who drew the carriage over to the side of the road.

"Forgive me, Mademoiselle Linfield. I will be but a moment. I require urgent speech with this gentleman." He glanced over his shoulder at his groom, who jumped from his perch and took the reins so that Monsieur Alphonse could climb down from the curricle.

He spoke to the stranger in low tones. Georgiana strained to hear, but she couldn't make out what he was saying.

However, the other man's voice proved much more carrying, and she managed to hear the odd word here and there. He had a lilting accent, and she frowned. Could this possibly be Napoleon's Irish doctor? She gazed at a lady's hat in a passing carriage as the word "Blackwall" drifted across to her.

The Irishman took a step closer to the carriage. "Till noon then," he said in his deep tones before hastening away.

Monsieur Alphonse climbed up beside Georgiana and retrieved the reins. "My sincere apologies, *mademoiselle*. My doctor, you understand. I needed to make a *rendez-vous*."

"I trust you are not unwell, *monsieur*," Georgiana said politely.

"*Non, non*, it is for my mother. She has always suffered from delicate health."

"I am sorry to hear that."

He nodded gravely and then began speaking in his usual amicable manner. But it failed to mask a new air of preoccupation, and Georgiana sensed he was in a hurry to deposit her back at her door.

When she entered the hall, she immediately checked the time. Eleven o'clock. Monsieur Alphonse had said he would be taking his mother to see the doctor, but that was most likely made up to deflect attention away from his true intentions. The Irishman had said something about Blackwall. She had heard mention of the place before but couldn't remember where it was.

Taylor stepped into the hall at that moment. After he had taken her cloak, she murmured a word of thanks before saying, "Do you know of a place called Blackwall?"

"Why, yes, Miss. It is a famous shipyard."

"Oh, of course! I thought it sounded familiar. Thank you."

She made her way upstairs, frowning a little. If Monsieur

Alphonse and Dr O'Meara were meeting today at midday, perhaps it was at the shipyard rather than at Madame Alphonse's house. Rothbury had mentioned that one of the earlier conspiracies to rescue Napoleon involved steamboats, so they might very well be working together on something similar. Further investigation was needed. But what could she do?

Reaching the landing, she drew to a halt and stared straight ahead. She *could* do something... Rothbury would undoubtedly consider it too dangerous, but if she didn't act now, she would lose a valuable opportunity to find out what they were doing. And it wasn't as if she could get word to her brother in time for him to make his own plans.

So instead of entering her bedchamber, she went into Stephen's room. She and her twin had visited London on numerous occasions during their school holidays, so some of his old clothes were likely packed away in here. She came upon exactly what she was looking for at the back of his walnut wardrobe.

After taking the clothes to her bedchamber, she hid them in a drawer before going downstairs again. Fortunately, Taylor was still in the hall. Her mother had told her at breakfast that she and Cousin Agnes planned to visit her elderly aunt that morning, but she wanted to make sure. "I believe my mother has gone out, Taylor?"

"Yes, Miss Georgiana. Her ladyship went out with Mrs Linfield some time ago."

"Well, if she should ask for me upon her return, would you inform her that I have an urgent task I need to perform and that I will be occupied with it for some time?"

His eyes twinkled. "Have you smuggled worms into your bedchamber again, Miss?"

The corners of her mouth turned up. "I do have some larvae up there. And I would prefer not to be disturbed today. Lady Linfield will take fright if she comes to my bedchamber."

"I perfectly understand, and I shall ensure that her ladyship is aware of the...er...situation."

"Thank you, Taylor. I knew I could rely on you. Would you send Kirby to me now, please?"

When the maid came upstairs, she assisted Georgiana to undress. However, when Kirby asked which gown she wished to wear, Georgiana shook her head and slipped under the green silk counterpane on her bed. "I don't wish to be disturbed for the rest of the day, Kirby," she said in a wan voice.

"Very well, Miss." The dresser hesitated for a moment. "Would you like me to send up your luncheon on a tray?"

"No, thank you. I only wish to be left alone."

Clearly uneasy, Kirby nevertheless bobbed a curtsey and silently departed.

The minute she closed the door, Georgiana shot out of bed and donned Stephen's old clothes. Unfortunately, the trousers were a little baggy, and the cravat tied around her neck was slightly rumpled. But she wasn't posing as a man of fashion. The only requirement for her raiment today was that it should make her blend into a crowd.

She pinned her hair severely out of sight and crept silently out of her room and back to Stephen's bedchamber, where she located the shabby hat he wore on insect hunting expeditions. Opening the door, she peered to the left and right before hurrying towards the servants' staircase and down the steps.

Fortunately, she encountered not a soul on her way, and when she reached the basement level of the house, she exited quietly via the area.

Safely out of Berkeley Square, Georgiana hailed a hackney and asked the carriage driver to take her to Blackwall Yard. He nodded his assent, and Georgiana smiled in relief as she stepped into the musty-smelling coach. Hopefully, her hunch was correct; otherwise, she was on a wild goose hunt for nothing. *And* she had missed her luncheon.

Weaving through the busy London streets took a fair amount of time, but soon the traffic lessened, and they bowled along at a more rapid pace. The hackney finally drew up outside a shipyard. Georgiana descended from the coach and paid the driver before looking around uncertainly.

Several riverside inns butted one against the other. She walked past The King's Arms, The Coach and Horses, The Britannia, The Plough, and then two more superior-looking establishments called The Artichoke and The George in an attempt to gain her bearings.

She remembered now why the name "Blackwall" had seemed

so familiar to her. Last year, Rothbury mentioned that he was in the habit of attending the famous Whitebait Suppers at The George inn in Blackwall during the Season. This must be where he came with his cronies to dine.

So many hostelries lined up on one street seemed strange. Most likely, however, a great many travellers arrived at the wharf every day. Therefore, a large number of public houses would be needed on this stretch of the river to accommodate them.

She headed back to the shipyard, pulling her hat low over her face as she passed warehouses, a stable, a rigging house, and various other buildings before turning into the yard.

A brick-and-timber structure overlooked the yard, rising to at least one hundred feet. Some sort of machine perched atop the building, and Georgiana studied it with interest. Having grown up in the environs of the port city of Bristol, she had seen shipyards before, but had never set eyes on an apparatus of this sort, where two men on a crane were engaged in installing a mast on a ship.

She stepped carefully around the timber strewn everywhere. The yard was a hive of activity. Workmen milled around the sheds and storehouses while labourers washed the docks and carried away woodchips from ships under construction. A horse, dragging a heavy beam, went past, and Georgiana stepped hastily out of its way.

If Monsieur Alphonse was meeting the doctor here, it was doubtful she would be able to find the two men in such a *mêlée*, particularly if they had something to hide. She removed Stephen's watch, which she had slipped into her pocket, and glanced at it. The time was five minutes before twelve. Perhaps she should walk toward the wet dock and wait there....

Fortunately, no one paid any heed to her as she picked her way around the piles of wood. She bit down on her lip as she gazed around. Had she known Blackwall Yard was so large, she would never have bothered coming here. Seeking a couple of men in such a place was impossible—much like searching for Purple Emperors in winter.

Even making enquiries would draw attention to herself. Georgiana halted. Seeing as how she was a little early, perhaps she should wait near the gatehouse for the gentlemen to arrive. She should have thought of this in the first instance, but she'd wanted to get her bearings.

Turning, she hurried back the way she had come. As she passed the porter's lodge, she drew back suddenly against a wall. Monsieur Alphonse had just entered the yard. He walked straight past her, and after a while, she followed him.

She kept him within sight as he made his way to one of the warehouses, where a tall man with grey hair and a weather-beaten face stepped out of the building to greet him. The Irish doctor joined the two men shortly afterwards, and the trio disappeared into the warehouse together.

Georgiana's eyebrows snapped together. What were they up to?

# CHAPTER EIGHTEEN

The hackney Georgiana hailed bowled along Piccadilly before turning into Park Lane, where the driver set her down on the corner of Mount Street. She had decided to walk home on foot from here and enter the house the same way she had left, using the key she had slipped into her pocket on her way out.

The servants' staircase came out near her bedchamber, so upon entering the house, she would need only to check that the coast was clear before dashing to the stairs.

Gaze lowered, she made her way along Mount Street. She'd been more comfortable at the shipyard than here in her home territory, where she might bump into an acquaintance at any moment.

And did.

Someone tapped her on the shoulder as she passed Park Street. Georgiana leant forward in preparation for sprinting away when a voice said in her ear: "I wouldn't try that, Georgie."

She turned, and found herself at eye level with a familiar broad chest. Tilting her head up, she met Sir Giles's keen gaze for an endless moment. Then, without a word, he grasped her arm and marched her down Park Street. At a house in Upper Grosvenor Street, he placed a key in the front door and swung it open. After glancing around the empty hall, he led Georgiana into a bookroom.

Shutting the door behind him, he placed his hat on a nearby table before looking her up and down. "You have some explaining to do, my dear. Stephen's clothes, I presume?"

She removed her hat, gripping it in her hands. "From a few years ago, yes."

"And?"

"And nothing, Sir Giles. I am not at liberty to tell you why I am dressed like this."

"No?"

She shook her head, holding even tighter onto her hat.

"Your reasons must be urgent for you to risk ruining your reputation in this manner."

"My disguise is excellent." She let out a huffy breath. "I have no idea how you saw through it."

"I don't believe it would be wise for me to answer that."

Warmth flooded her cheeks. "No one else noticed anything."

"I suppose they are not as familiar with your person as I am."

"You are not familiar with my person, Sir Giles."

"But I am. I have danced with you on several occasions." He sounded surprised.

She frowned at the carpet, scuffing the toe of her shoe. "I object to how you said it."

"Said what?"

"The word 'familiar'," she muttered.

"Oh?" He strolled across to her. "How did I say it?"

"With too much..." She paused and cleared her throat. "Well... familiarity, if you must know."

He raised a hand, brushing his fingertips down her cheek. "Is this too familiar, Georgie?"

She caught her breath. She should tell him to go away, yet somehow she swayed forward a little. And then a little more. And then she was in his arms, and he was tilting her chin up. "And this?" he murmured as he lowered his head.

The caress of his lips was gentle at first, but then it wasn't gentle at all, and a curious paralysis spread through her limbs. She dropped her hat and clutched the front of his coat as her knees threatened to buckle.

His powerful arms tightened around her, and the kiss deepened. She was aware of nothing except the need, the overwhelming need, to stay lost in his embrace forever.

She drew back abruptly. "We mustn't."

Resting his chin on the top of her head, he sighed. "Why not?"

"I need to go. I'll be missed..."

He released her, and she drew in a shaking breath as she tried to collect her wits.

"We must have a discussion sometime, Georgie." Giles's voice, while quiet, held a vein of steel.

Georgiana bent to pick up her hat. She couldn't speak to him. Not now... not ever if she could prevent it. She should never have allowed that kiss, especially as she didn't even like the man. Biting down hard on her lip, she winced.

Liking had nothing to do with what had just happened between them.

Sir Giles retrieved his hat from the table. "I'll walk behind you to ensure you return home in one piece. You left via the servants' entrance, I presume?"

"Yes."

He opened the book-room door and had a quiet word with someone in the hall, then spoke curtly to Georgiana. "Let's go."

When they reached the street, Georgiana hurried on ahead, her hat pulled low over her eyes once more. She desperately needed time alone to put her chaotic thoughts in order—something she was quite good at...usually. Somehow she doubted she would be successful on this occasion. Her heart still pounded, her lips tingled, and her mind...would it remain forever a complete and utter blank?

Passion had obliterated all reasonable thought.

～

Giles followed Georgiana home at a discreet distance. She hurried along, looking neither to the left nor right, and when she entered Berkeley Square, she flew down the area steps without a backward glance.

He waited near the garden gate and then turned and strolled back to his house, a smile hovering about his mouth. His simmering relationship with Georgiana had finally come to a boil. Going back from here would not be possible.

As he turned onto Upper Grosvenor Street, he spotted Captain Johnson knocking on his front door. He frowned. The captain had attended the Linnean Society the other evening, but Giles hadn't spoken to him.

"Johnson," he murmured as he came up behind him.

The captain turned. "Sir Giles! I have an offer I believe you won't be able to refuse."

Giles glanced at the store-box in the older man's hands. "Indeed?"

"I had a look at your South American collection the night your paper was read, and it is truly magnificent. But now that you've written the paper, it would be wise to consider a trade. In the name of scientific research, of course." Even the man's half-smile seemed oily at best.

The porter swung the door open at that moment, and Giles motioned the captain to enter before him. Once they reached the book-room, Johnson handed him the store-box. "Have a look. It's a *Morpho menelaus*."

Giles sat behind his desk and raised the lid. An enormous iridescent blue butterfly with a wingspan of about five inches was pinned inside. Eventually, he looked at his visitor. "Have you travelled to the tropical areas of South America, Johnson? I believe this species is only found there."

"I bought it from a collector."

"Ah." Giles studied it carefully. "A magnificent specimen."

The captain bent his head. "I noticed you didn't have one in your collection. Would you be interested in a trade?"

Giles leaned back in his chair, folding his arms. "What's your price?"

"I would prefer a trade."

He raised his brows. "As I've already told you, I don't trade my collections."

"You won't make an exception for a prize such as this?" The man spread his hands wide. "In my mind, this spectacular specimen is worth all the butterflies in your South American collection."

Giles hesitated. In truth, he was tempted. But he didn't trust Captain Johnson and wouldn't be surprised to discover the butterfly was stolen property. Moreover, if the slightest chance existed that the specimen could be of doubtful provenance, he couldn't, in good conscience, add it to his collection.

He shrugged. "Give me the name of the collector you bought

it from, and I shall consider trading it."

The captain's brow creased. "I've forgotten his name, truth be told."

Giles rose to his feet. "I would advise you to remember it if you wish to engage in any trade with me."

The older man stood. "You're a stickler."

"In this field, one has to be. I have no intention of being taken in by a fraudulent butterfly dealer."

Johnson's shoulders stiffened. "You're calling me a fraud?"

"No. I'm merely suggesting that you check the credentials of anyone you trade with."

Captain Johnson shoved his hat back on his head. "I'll hunt the fellow down, never you fear."

"There are other collections out there, you know." Giles stepped around his desk.

"Yours, however, is the prettiest of 'em all. That Librarian at the Society told me off for handling it the other evening. Said I was breaking the rules."

"You've never been one for following them, have you?" Giles said dryly.

Captain Johnson grinned. "Oh, I like to sail close to the wind. Rather like a butterfly, you know." He whistled a merry tune as he sauntered out of the room.

Giles stared thoughtfully at his back. The burly captain was the furthest thing from a butterfly he could imagine.

~

Georgiana sent a message the next morning asking Rothbury to visit her as soon as possible. She was reading a book in the library when he arrived a short while later.

"You're going to be furious with me, Edward," she said, rising to her feet. "But I had to grasp the opportunity."

Rothbury shut the door behind him before turning back to her. "What have you done, Georgie?" His voice was wary.

She took a deep breath and then gave him a brief account of her expedition to Blackwall Yard, concluding: "You must see I needed to go there. Especially after I heard Monsieur Alphonse speaking to that Irish doctor."

"I don't see anything of the sort." Her brother folded his arms as he leaned against the windowsill. "What were you thinking? Your reputation would have been ruined if you'd been discovered."

"That's what Sir Giles said."

"*What?*"

Georgiana's cheeks warmed. "I am afraid I bumped into him on my way home."

"Fortunately, Giles has a discreet tongue in his head, and he happens to be my cousin." Rothbury's brow furrowed. "But what would you have done if it had been anyone else?"

"I know..." She swallowed. "But needs must and all of that."

"No. Needs must *not*. Don't ever place yourself in such danger again. Do you understand, Georgie?"

She nodded.

"Well, thank heavens for that." His voice was stern.

"Will you go to Blackwall Yard to investigate?"

"Yes, of course. It is highly suspicious that Alphonse met O'Meara there—if it was him. I'll make some enquiries." He frowned at her. "In the meanwhile, I hope you will pay heed to what I've said. Had I known you would do such a thing, I would never have enlisted your help."

She raised her chin. "I still think it was worth the risk. If I can play even a small part in preventing England from going to war again, it is my duty to do so."

"Yes, but my duty as your older brother is to protect you, and I forbid you from doing such a thing again. I only meant you to ask Alphonse a few leading questions, not to engage in a crazy escapade such as this." He paused for a moment, rubbing the nape of his neck. "What tale did you spin for Giles? He's no fool. I wouldn't try and gammon him."

She lifted one eyebrow. "I informed your cousin that I wasn't at liberty to tell him anything."

"Hmmm." He frowned. "I imagine he'll want a word with me."

"Will you tell him about the suspected plot?"

"Not now. As I said, the fewer people who know about it, the better. I told Fenmore I wouldn't speak to anyone about this except you." He studied her for a moment. "If you persist in reckless behaviour such as this, Georgie, I shan't be able to take you abroad with Cassy and me."

Her eyes widened. "Has Papa given his permission then?"

"Yes. I spoke to him at White's last night."

"Oh, how wonderful!" She clasped her hands together. "I cannot believe it."

"It is, of course, on the condition that you are not betrothed by the end of the Season."

"That will not happen. And even if the possibility existed, I would do everything in my power to put off an engagement until I return to England. I shall never have an opportunity like this again."

He studied her quizzically. "You're an odd girl, you know. Most young ladies are eager to become betrothed."

"Cassy wasn't."

"*Touché.*" He grinned and took a step towards the door but then turned back. "That reminds me. Lady Fenmore has invited you to Fenmore Park for her summer house party. Cassy and I shall be in attendance, and we'll take you in our coach if Mama agrees. Lady Fenmore has just written to her."

"I should like that very much. Lady Fenmore seems kind."

"She is. But it isn't merely kindness that has prompted the invitation. Fenmore is thinking of asking Alphonse along."

"Then Lady Fenmore is aware of the investigation?"

"I doubt it. But she knows her husband works for the government and facilitates any requests he puts forward. Besides, she likes you." He smiled as he glanced at the clock on the wall. "I need to leave now, my dear. But please take heed of what I've said."

"I'll be as obedient as a lamb."

He wagged his finger at her. "You had better be."

When he left the room, Georgiana sank onto the sofa, her head spinning. Finally, her long-held dreams to travel were about to come true. An image of Sir Giles's face flashed into her mind, but she dismissed it instantly. She refused to think about him. The devastating effect he had on her senses mortified her, especially given her dislike of the man. She went hot and then cold as she recalled the expert manner in which he had kissed her.

She must never be alone with him again.

# CHAPTER NINETEEN

Georgiana and Stephen were waiting for their father's curricle to be brought around a few days later when Taylor opened the drawing room door and announced Sir Giles. Georgiana met the baronet's eyes for a fleeting moment before Stephen turned around from the window where he stood. "Good morning, sir! I meant to call on you this week, but time flew away from me. We are on our way out, I'm afraid."

"So your manservant informed me. However, I have merely called to drop off some leaves for Miss Linfield's caterpillars."

Georgiana stood. "Thank you, Sir Giles. Stephen brought me some leaves from a nearby park the other day, but the caterpillars have such voracious appetites! I am struggling to find enough food for them."

Sir Giles placed a wooden box on a side table. "I'll leave this here for you then. The leaves are from the poplar tree in my garden." He bowed. "Let me not keep you from your engagement."

"We are meeting Monsieur Alphonse and his sister at Bullock's Museum," Stephen said. "Would you care to join us? We plan to look at the butterfly and moth collections."

Sir Giles raised his brows. "I haven't been to Bullock's in an age." His gaze rested on Georgiana briefly, and then he turned back to Stephen. "I should like that. Thank you."

At that moment, Taylor announced the arrival of the curricle outside. The two men discussed William Bullock's natural history collection as they left the house.

Georgiana did not participate in the discussion. She climbed into the curricle in silence, staring in dismay at Sir Giles's back as he walked across to his vehicle.

So much for her plan to avoid the baronet. Could she bear to spend the entire morning with him? Pretending nothing had happened between them would be impossible. And adding Monsieur Alphonse into the mix only complicated matters.

Monsieur Alphonse... She flinched. She did not relish the role she must play today, especially with Sir Giles looking on. He would be justified in thinking she was a heartless hussy if she encouraged another man's attentions straight after she had welcomed his own physical advances. Nor could she pretend she hadn't responded to him—and with eagerness.

She scowled as they turned into Piccadilly. She really shouldn't care about Sir Giles's good opinion. But somehow, she did. What a pity!

Monsieur Alphonse awaited them outside Bullock's Egyptian Hall, a smiling young woman at his side. The Frenchman smiled a greeting before presenting his sister. A dainty, elegant young lady dressed in the height of fashion, Mademoiselle Alphonse chattered away nineteen to the dozen until Sir Giles joined them.

They made their way upstairs to the Pantherion, a display room in the museum's west wing, where light flooded through the domed ceiling. Various exotic, stuffed animals were displayed under some enormous palm trees, and Mademoiselle Alphonse stopped to stare at them, her mouth parted in surprise. "But how peculiar! These animals appear so real."

They lingered near the enclosure for a while before Stephen located a glass case that contained a display of sixty-six foreign butterflies and moths, according to *A Companion to Mr Bullock's London Museum and Pantherion,* which Sir Giles had purchased at the door.

Mademoiselle Alphonse gave the butterflies a cursory glance before saying, with a pout, "I have had enough of these creatures. What I truly wish to see is Napoleon's carriage."

Monsieur Alphonse frowned. "I am not certain it will be of interest to Mademoiselle Linfield."

"Oh, I should like to see it," Georgiana replied. "My brother James came to see it last year and told me all about it. He found it a spectacular vehicle."

"*Certainement*, we shall go if it is your wish," Monsieur Alphonse murmured.

A small crowd had gathered outside the dark blue and gold military carriage, which had been taken at Waterloo. The vehicle was indeed something to behold. Georgiana's eyes widened as she viewed the lamps fixed to each corner of the roof and the Imperial arms adorning the panels of the doors. This certainly was a carriage fit for a king or, more correctly, in this instance, an emperor.

Only three to four people were allowed inside the coach at one time. As they awaited their turn, Georgiana chatted in a desultory fashion to Monsieur Alphonse and Sir Giles. The two men had very little to say to each other. However, when Mademoiselle Alphonse and Stephen rejoined them after wandering off to look at a nearby display case, the young lady more than made up for her brother's lack of conversation.

When their turn came to enter the carriage, Monsieur Alphonse, Georgiana, Mademoiselle Alphonse, and Stephen ascended the steps, leaving Sir Giles waiting outside for them. He had volunteered to do so, having seen the coach when it first went on display in London a few years earlier.

The guide explained that the vehicle's interior had been adapted to fulfil the functions of a kitchen, study, dressing-room, dining-room, and bedchamber.

"I see no bed." Georgiana looked around the space.

Like a magician performing a clever trick, the guide showed them a small box beneath the coachman's seat. The steel bedstead inside could fold out into a bed within minutes.

"How ingenious!" Her lips curved into a smile as the man demonstrated how it worked.

Also on display was a magnificent dinner service, as well as a silver-gilt tea equipage. Cleverly designed, the two shut one into the other. Napoleon's dressing table and desk were also on show. Every item in the carriage was embellished with the Imperial arms and engraved with the letter "N".

"To think the Grand Emperor once sat here." Mademoiselle Alphonse gently stroked the writing table. "It is a wonder, indeed."

"Creature comforts are clearly quite important to him."

Georgiana glanced around. "And he's aware of his own dignity too. His tastes are expensive."

"And why shouldn't they be?" Monsieur Alphonse's chin lifted. "He is the Emperor, after all."

"*Was* the Emperor," Stephen said cheerfully.

The Frenchman's shoulders stiffened, and then he inclined his head. "I stand corrected."

When they descended from the carriage, they rejoined Sir Giles and made their way to an exhibition of paintings depicting the various stages of Bonaparte's military career. Georgiana studied a marble and bronze bust of the French general before moving on to cases filled with weapons.

"How the English love to gloat in victory." Monsieur Alphonse glanced rather contemptuously at a case of Napoleonic knick-knacks, including a saddle, a sword, and a pair of steel duelling pistols inlaid with gold. "Bullock travelled to Paris to buy these artefacts from the Emperor's servants and friends, all to satiate the desire of the British people who love to glory in his defeat."

"The spoils of war..." Georgiana murmured sympathetically.

Sir Giles strolled over and studied the contents of the case. "These pistols seem custom-made to fit a boy's hands," he said.

"It is rumoured that the Emperor gave them as a gift to his young son," Monsieur Alphonse said. "They are beautifully made, although I prefer the small sword. Pistols lack the finesse necessary in an *affaire d'honneur*." He gave a slight bow in Sir Giles's direction. "I believe you favour the small sword as well, Tavistock. You are often at Signor Fazio's rooms."

"It is good to keep one's wrist in practice," Sir Giles said coolly.

"It is, indeed," the Frenchman replied. "One never knows when one might be called upon to defend one's honour."

Georgiana frowned. "Duels are outlawed in this country."

Monsieur Alphonse shrugged. "Amongst gentlemen, they are still the best way to exact satisfaction."

"Well, I think they are barbarous," she said.

Sir Giles smiled wryly. "Man's layer of civilization is very thin, Miss Linfield. Our passions are not always contained."

"Reason—not passion—should dictate our actions. A much

more sensible path, don't you agree?"

Sir Giles studied her, a small smile curling his lips. "And are you always sensible, Miss Linfield?"

Her cheeks warmed under his blue gaze, and she hurriedly turned to Monsieur Alphonse. "Have you any idea where William Bullock found the duelling pistols, monsieur?"

His lips thinned. "In all probability, at either the Malmaison or the St Cloud chateaux, Bonaparte's imperial residences. Bullock has made a fortune from this exhibition, but rumours abound that he is seeking a buyer for the entire collection."

"It is a good thing then that we came today to see it," Georgiana said lightly. "Thank you for inviting us, *monsieur*."

He bowed. "It is my pleasure, *mademoiselle*. As always." He went on to relate an amusing tale about a friend who had vowed never to return to Bullock's after seeing a boa constrictor wrapped around a tree in the animal enclosure.

Georgiana listened attentively to his conversation, interspersing the odd remark, all the while acutely aware of Sir Giles. He had moved away and was observing the contents of a nearby case.

Eventually, the Frenchman drew a watch from his pocket. "I am afraid we must depart now, as I have another engagement. You did not properly examine the butterflies due to my sister's impatience to see the carriage. *Mille pardons, mademoiselle*."

"It is no matter, *monsieur*. My brother and I will look at them on our way out."

Stephen shook his head. "I'm meeting Aldwell in half an hour. We shall have to return another day."

"Oh! That's a pity."

Sir Giles joined them. "Allow me to drive you home in my curricle, Miss Linfield. I have no pressing engagements."

She quickly shook her head. "Thank you, sir, but I couldn't possibly impose on you in that manner."

"It is no imposition at all."

"Do go with Sir Giles," Stephen urged. "I needn't drive you home then. I'm going to be late as it is."

*Botheration!* She could not avoid accepting the baronet's escort without appearing churlish. "Thank you, Sir Giles. You are very kind to offer."

Stephen took his leave, and Georgiana said a polite farewell to

Mademoiselle Alphonse before turning to the Frenchman, a smile pinned on her face.

He bowed over her hand, raising it to his lips. "I must thank you for a most enchanting morning, *mademoiselle*."

Embarrassment lit a fire in her cheeks. For gentlemen to kiss ladies on the hand was no longer customary. Perhaps the rules were different on the Continent, but even so, the Frenchman had just made a bold statement in front of Sir Giles.

"Tavistock," he murmured, with a brief inclination of his head.

Sir Giles nodded coolly in response, and then brother and sister walked away.

After a moment of pregnant silence, Georgiana and Sir Giles both spoke at once: "I cannot..."

"Are you..."

"Ladies first." Sir Giles offered her his arm.

Georgiana placed her hand on his sleeve. "I cannot stay for long. My mother will expect me home shortly. Besides, I am not entirely sure if it is proper for me to be here alone with you."

He raised his brows. "You are suddenly concerned about the proprieties, Miss Linfield?"

She flushed at the amused expression in his eyes. "After our last encounter, I would be a fool not to be concerned."

He laughed, and Georgiana stared straight ahead as he led her back to the room where the insects were on display.

They examined the specimens in silence, and then she glanced up. Their gazes locked, and she hurriedly looked back at the glass case. A giant moth, which must measure all of nine inches across the wings, suddenly caught her eye. "Is that an Atlas moth?"

"Yes. It is a native of the East Indies and South America. I have one in my collection."

"Do you intend to ever return to South America?"

"Perhaps. One day. The continent is unsettled at the moment with talk of revolution in Brazil."

"Oh." She stared at the insects for a moment longer. "I would like to return home now."

"Running away, Miss Linfield?"

"Stephen should not have left me here with you, unchaperoned."

"You haven't answered my question."

"I'm no coward, Sir Giles." She crossed her arms and met his gaze with defiance.

"And yet here you are, seemingly encouraging Alphonse's suit." The amusement in his eyes had vanished.

She swallowed. How was she supposed to answer that? "I...my intentions regarding matrimony have nothing to do with you, sir."

He gave a formal bow. "Forgive me, Miss Linfield. I had begun to hope they had everything to do with me."

She stared at him, at a loss for words. How could she be so drawn to Sir Giles while having an equally strong desire to keep him at a distance? She liked her life to be as neatly arranged as the museums she set so efficiently in order. But his presence threw everything into disarray.

Reason should be the basis upon which to make important decisions about life. But thanks to his nasty habit of prodding her feelings—rather like she had inadvertently poked at that wasps' nest the other day—reason seemed to vanish when she was in his vicinity.

Those stinging attackers had swarmed out against her, swamping her rationality and leaving her vulnerable, exposed, and in pain. Georgiana feared her emotions, once released, might be every bit as dangerous.

She could not allow that to happen.

# CHAPTER TWENTY

On the drive back to Berkeley Square, Georgiana gazed at the bustling streets. She had grown quite accustomed to living in the Metropolis and the "merry, merry cries of famous London town!"

In the small village of Ashton near Linfield Court, the only melodies filling the air were the scraping sounds produced by blind fiddlers, accompanied by women singers who occasionally passed through.

As a child, she had been fascinated by these musicians. When she walked to the village with her governess, she had always looked for them, begging pennies from Miss Barratt to give in return for the entertainment they provided.

London, in contrast, was full of street music. Every corner seemed filled with ballad singers and bands. She had seen an unusual sight the other day—a hare, released from its box, used its forefeet to quaintly beat the time on a drum while its master played and sung.

Flower sellers carried fresh blooms in baskets and carts, and hawkers of fine herbs such as rosemary, sage, and lavender called out their wares as they walked along. And then there were the men selling herrings, mackerel, pies, and tarts, raising their voices high in a bid to attract customers.

When they drove into Berkeley Square, Sir Giles handed the reins to his groom before descending from the curricle to assist her. He held her hands briefly as her feet touched the ground, and then he released her and proffered his arm.

Georgiana walked silently beside him to the front door, where he bid her farewell. She smiled somewhat formally.

He studied her for a long moment. "I have tried to understand how you think, *mon papillon*, but I am afraid I am making little progress."

She looked away. How to change the subject? She cleared her throat. "Mama told me your mother is French, but you speak English without a French intonation."

"My mother spoke to me in French as a child, but my governess ensured I spoke English without a trace of an accent. She was a stickler for such things."

"Is it difficult to have a dual heritage?"

"At times. I am strongly aware of my French lineage, but I see England as my homeland."

"Monsieur Alphonse was born in England, yet he hasn't embraced our customs at all."

"No." A faint line appeared between his brows. "He hasn't."

He knocked on the front door, and when it swung open, Georgiana immediately stepped inside. "Thank you for driving me home, Sir Giles."

A wry smile played about his lips as he searched her face, but he only bowed and walked away.

Watching him go, Georgiana experienced a moment of inexplicable sadness...an aching certainty that she had lost something valuable today. But she wasn't sure exactly what.

She spent a rare evening at Linfield House, a welcome change after the frenetic activity of the past few months. After dinner, her father turned to her with a smile. "Would you care to walk to Covent Garden market with me tomorrow, my dear? Of course, it will be a very early start as we need to leave at six o'clock, but it will be worth it to see the fruit and flowers in their perfection at the start of the day. In my mind, it is the best sight London has to offer."

"I should like that, Papa. Thank you for inviting me. I have heard so much about the market, and am eager to see it."

So, the next day, while the rest of the family still slept, Georgiana rose and made a hasty toilet. She descended the stairs to her father, awaiting her in the hall.

"Good morning, my love." He patted her on the shoulder. "I

think it is best if we walk. The exercise will do us good, and it is only a mile or so, after all."

Georgiana was shocked to see several dirty, unkempt women roaming the streets, an air of desperation clinging to them like the worn-out cloaks they clutched around bony shoulders. As she followed her father into the bustling market, she caught her breath at the disparity between the wretched people she had just seen and the beautiful blooms on display.

She swallowed a lump in her throat. Too often in life, harsh reality and loveliness were juxtaposed in just such a way.

A large number of tables held a vast quantity of fruit and vegetables. Georgina stared in amazement. "Do the vendors manage to sell all this produce, Papa?"

"Indeed. Before noon, they will dispose of it all. The vegetables in London are of an excellent standard due to the quality of the soil and the large amounts of manure available. And with a population of a million, this quantity of food is necessary."

He bought a pot plant as well as some flowers for the drawing room. When one of the flower sellers asked if he wanted a basket, he shook his head and indicated that Peter, their footman, who stood a few feet behind them, would carry their purchases home.

After the footman departed, Georgiana's father turned to her. "Would you care to walk on to Regent's Park, my love? There are some splendid gardens nearby, with rows of lettuces and beds of cucumbers I would like to show you."

She nodded and fell into step beside her father. They walked in the direction of the park.

He glanced down at her. "I have been thinking about our conversation the other day, my dear, and I must say it has weighed heavily on my mind."

She frowned. "Our conversation?"

"About Monsieur Alphonse."

"Oh."

"You seem set in the belief that your mama and I would welcome your departure to another country. I must ask...why do you think so?"

She raised her shoulders. "It is only that I have always been such a trial to you both."

"You truly think that?"

"I have never been cast in the mould of a dutiful daughter like Harriet is. I fear I am a disappointment to you."

"You could never be that, Georgiana." His brow lowered as he began walking again. "Perhaps we have been stricter in our guidance of you as we have been concerned about your waywardness—and wilfulness—at times, but that does not mean we esteem you any less than your sister."

Georgiana stared straight ahead.

"You do know that, my dear?"

Georgiana's innate honesty required nothing less than what she considered the truth. "We all know that Harriet is your favourite."

He drew to a halt. "I don't understand why you think that. I share many interests with you. Indeed, I imagine very few fathers and daughters have so much common ground."

She shook her head. "Just because you share an interest with someone does not mean you share a...a harmony of mind with them. For you, that accord of mind is reserved for Harriet, even though she detests insects. I have always found that somewhat ironic."

He remained silent for a long moment. "I am saddened you believe that. Can you tell me why?"

She swallowed the knot in her throat. "Harriet has never had to do anything to earn your attention, Papa. You give it to her freely. But even though I have tried so hard to enter into your interests, the only conversation you reserve for me is the exchange of factual information about your natural history museum."

"I am afraid I have failed you, my love." He released a heavy sigh. "Harriet has always seemed particularly vulnerable, especially since you and Stephen have had one another to lean on. You presented a strong, united front. That strength, coupled with the fact that Harriet is the only one of my children with no interest in scientific pursuits, caused me to make an effort over the years to include her in family life. But somehow, along the way, it seems I managed to make you feel that you held a lesser value in my eyes." He rubbed the back of his neck. "That isn't the case at all, Georgiana. The fact of the matter is, one does not feel the need to affirm something that appears strong. Surely you must see that?"

"Yes, but still, I always felt that you were more sympathetic towards Harriet."

"I suppose I was. But that isn't because I love you any less. You and Stephen persisted in teasing her when you were children, and more often than not, I felt it was my duty to step in and come to her defence. Your strength made you appear invulnerable, and because you have always had more masculine interests, I suppose I treated you more like a boy than a girl, not realising that beneath the toughness of your exterior, you have your own vulnerabilities."

She sniffed. "Rather like a garden snail."

He chuckled. "Exactly like a garden snail, leaving a splendid silvery trail in its wake. Because you do, you know."

"Leave a trail?" She wrinkled her nose.

"Indeed. You force through obstacles, creating calm from chaos. An admirable quality indeed, but it does give people the impression you are a fighter."

"I suppose I fight for order," she said slowly. "The result of my battle gives me a sense of satisfaction."

"And it shows in your work. But it would be well to bear in mind that you cannot order everything in this world. It isn't possible."

Her father's words resonated in her mind. Her need to create an organised life for herself meant she had always paid more heed to reason than to her heart. And although she had thought herself resigned to playing second fiddle in her father's affections, today her emotions had risen up from the depths of her being. They had swamped her rationality to the point she could no longer deny the pain she had harboured for so many years. Deeply distressed, she experienced an instinctive impulse to clamp down on her feelings, and thereby regain a sense of calm in her life.

Instead, her thoughts turned to a novel Harriet had given her for her seventeenth birthday, titled *Sense and Sensibility*. She had identified immediately with the sensible older sister, Elinor Dashwood. Secretly, Georgiana despised the more romantical younger sister, Marianne, who allowed herself to fall into a decline over a failed love affair.

And yet...she pressed her lips together. Perhaps she wasn't as rational as she liked to think. She certainly had not shown a great deal of self-control around Sir Giles in recent days. On the contrary, when she was with him, she yearned to throw caution to the winds, wishing nothing more than to succumb to the tumult of emotion he aroused in her breast—feelings that had nothing to do with logic and everything to do with longing.

For the first time in her life, some unrecognizable part of her wanted to discard her carefully thought-out plan for her life and give in to the unknown. And it was terrifying.

# CHAPTER TWENTY-ONE

When father and daughter returned to Linfield House, Taylor informed Georgiana that Rothbury awaited her in the drawing room. She joined him with a quick step and bid him good morning in a cheerful voice.

"I am glad you have returned, Georgie." He turned away from the window. "I was about to give up on you."

"Papa and I went out for a walk."

"So Mama said." He crossed the room towards her. "Sit down, my dear. I've come to tell you what I discovered at Blackwall yesterday."

"Oh...yes?" She sat on a nearby armchair and leaned forward.

"The shipyard workers are constructing a vessel intended for smuggling."

"So Monsieur Alphonse isn't involved in a plot to rescue Napoleon? He is just a common smuggler?"

Rothbury rubbed his chin. "We don't know. He may be involved in smuggling activities to raise the wind as he is in financial difficulties. But he could have more sinister motives for building a vessel like this, particularly as Dr O'Meara is also involved in the scheme. We'll have to wait and see."

"Would you like me to persist in my inquiries? I am not making much progress at present, although Monsieur Alphonse did say he is resentful of how the English glory in Bonaparte's defeat."

Rothbury's eyes narrowed. "He said that in so many words?"

"Yes. He seemed personally affronted by what he referred to

as English gloating."

"Hmm. Barry O'Meara openly supports Bonaparte, but Alphonse has never done so. We suspect him only due to his association with O'Meara." He drummed his fingers on a nearby sofa table. "Fenmore has extended an invitation to Alphonse to visit Fenmore Park, and he has accepted. You may find that drawing information out of him at a country house party will be easier than in London."

"Indeed. It will be a much more informal environment."

He gave a faint sigh. "I am still not entirely at ease about your involvement in all of this."

"I'll be careful not to say anything which could give rise to suspicion."

"I'm more concerned about your safety, my dear. That is of the utmost importance." He hesitated, and then shook his head. "As long as you don't come up with any more hare-brained schemes that require you to dress as a boy."

She smiled. "It paid off in the end, though. Now you know Monsieur Alphonse and Dr O'Meara are working together."

"Yes. Hopefully, more will come to light as our agents observe the building of this ship. Fenmore has appointed a couple of men who will keep an eye on things at the shipyard. Any suspicious activity will be reported directly to him."

She raised her brows. "Surely building a vessel for smuggling is deemed as suspicious activity?"

"Yes, but smuggling is not our concern. Keeping Bonaparte on St Helena is."

Later that day, Georgiana's father informed her that Monsieur Alphonse had called and requested permission to pay his addresses to her. He'd told the Frenchman that he would not allow such an audience until Georgiana turned eighteen. "For I know your heart isn't set on marriage this year, my love, and after Rothbury told me of your eagerness to join him and Cassy on their next expedition, I agreed it would be best to put off all your suitors until after your birthday."

"Thank you, Papa."

"I hope you are no longer considering Alphonse in such a light?"

"I am not. Rothbury told me he is on the lookout for a rich

wife as he is in financial difficulties at present."

His brow creased. "I wasn't aware of that. He certainly does not give that impression."

"I have often thought that mankind has more in common with insects than we realise," Georgina said thoughtfully. "Our appearance can often be deceptive, especially when we wish to blend into our surroundings."

He gave a rich chuckle. "So speaks a true biologist."

The next afternoon, Georgiana and Cassy were walking in Hyde Park when they met Lord and Lady Fenmore. After exchanging greetings, they discussed the upcoming house party, now only a fortnight away at Fenmore Park. Georgiana had just asked Lady Fenmore about the notable sights in the county when a man with dark hair and a high forehead approached them.

After a moment's hesitation, Lord Fenmore introduced him to Cassy and Georgiana as Colonel Maceroni, a diplomat he had met in Naples several years ago. He then turned aside to engage the newcomer in further conversation.

Lady Fenmore began discussing the various entertainments she was planning. "I am praying the weather will be good so that we can arrange lawn games and visits to the local sights. There is nothing worse than being cooped up indoors all day during a gathering of this nature."

"Perhaps we could also go on a few butterfly hunting expeditions?" Georgiana asked.

"Yes, indeed, my dear. Several butterfly enthusiasts will be in attendance. I am sure Sir Giles will set something up."

Georgiana's stomach performed a somersault. "Sir Giles will be there?"

"I prevailed upon him several weeks ago to accept my invitation, and as he is my husband's favourite cousin, he was obliged to indulge me." Her eyes twinkled. "Usually, he avoids house parties like the plague." She shook her head but smiled indulgently. "That one is in no hurry to settle down, no matter how many eligible ladies are thrust in his path."

Colonel Maceroni took his leave of Lord Fenmore, and with a friendly smile and a nod, her ladyship moved away on her husband's arm.

When they were out of earshot, Georgiana turned to Cassy,

her eyes narrowed. "You did not tell me Sir Giles had been invited."

"I thought Rothbury had mentioned it to you."

"He didn't."

"Oh." Her sister-in-law walked on a few steps and then drew to a halt. "If you don't wish to see him, dearest, I am sure you will be able to cry off from the house party. Lady Fenmore will understand."

Georgiana shook her head. "It isn't possible."

"You truly dislike Sir Giles?" Cassy hesitated. "Perhaps I am mistaken, but I gained the impression the other day at Lord Hanssen's picnic that you were rather partial to his company."

"That man puts me out of all patience. He always has an answer. To everything. It grows tiresome after a while."

Cassy merely smiled, and then, after a short silence, she began speaking about their forthcoming journey to the Continent. Georgiana listened in growing excitement. An opportunity like this only came around once in a lifetime. Nothing—and no one—was going to prevent her from taking it.

The next evening, Georgiana attended Mrs Witherington's rout. Her mother had just moved away to speak to an acquaintance when the colonel she'd met in the Park approached her. "Miss Linfield! How charming to see you again," he said, bowing.

"Good evening, Colonel Maceroni."

"I am delighted you remember me after such a rushed meeting. You are a relation of Lord Rothbury, I believe?"

"I am his sister."

"So I heard. I met Lord Rothbury when I was journeying from Tivoli to Naples along the mountain paths of the Apennines some years ago. I also accompanied him to Mount Vesuvius, where we made a collection of the different strata of lava using our chisels and hammers. Is your brother still such a keen geologist?"

"He is. In fact, I shall be accompanying him to Italy later this year on an expedition."

"How delightful! I hope you enjoy travelling to my adopted land. I have Italian relatives and spent some time in Rome as a youth."

"We plan to visit Rome as well as several other towns and cities. Are you familiar with the rest of the country, sir?"

He bowed his head. "I travelled throughout Italy with an Englishman on his Grand Tour. Before descending to Capua and Naples, we were privileged to pass through Palestrina, Cori, Arpino, and Monte Cassino."

"Monte Cassino is a monastery, if I recall correctly? I have been reading as many books as I can find about Italy."

"Indeed. When we arrived there, we saw a massive thigh bone on display purportedly belonging to St Christopher." His smile seemed not much more than the baring of teeth. "More likely, it was the bone of an elephant or mammoth. Relics such as these are popular in Italy, but they are of doubtful authenticity, and it is commonplace for churches to display the body parts of various saints."

She pulled a face. "It sounds rather gruesome."

He laughed. "It is merely part of local tradition. Italy is a beautiful land, but when I resided there, I missed England so much that I introduced archery and cricket to the Neapolitan Court in a bid to ward off homesickness."

Her brow creased in puzzlement. "The Neapolitan Court?"

"Indeed. I once served as an *aide-de-camp* to the King of Naples."

Georgiana's mother returned at that moment, with Sir Giles at her side, but then immediately moved away to speak to an acquaintance.

Sir Giles greeted Colonel Maceroni coolly, and when the diplomat left a short while later, he turned to her with a slight frown. "I am surprised you are acquainted with Colonel Maceroni. He is something of an adventurer."

"I met him in Hyde Park yesterday when I was with Lord and Lady Fenmore. He told me he is acquainted with Rothbury."

"Well, I would prefer you not to associate with him. He fraternises with men of dubious character."

She pressed her lips together. "I am certain Lord Fenmore would not have introduced him to me, Sir Giles, if he did not believe the colonel a suitable person for me to know."

"Not necessarily. Fenmore mixes in diplomatic circles, and sometimes it can be difficult not to acknowledge an acquaintance. You were walking in the Park, you say?"

When she nodded, he rubbed his jaw. "My cousin must have

had his reasons for performing the introduction. I'll speak to him."

"You will do nothing of the sort, Sir Giles. It isn't your place."

He raised an eyebrow. "I shall speak to Rothbury then, and *he* can have a word with Fenmore."

She released an impatient breath. "I don't want you to speak to anyone. Not to Lord Fenmore and certainly not to my brother. What has the colonel done that you object to him being introduced to me?"

Sir Giles nodded at a passing acquaintance before returning his attention to her. "A few years ago, he used information supplied by a soldier who had once been in service to Bonaparte on St Helena to write a pamphlet condemning his treatment on the island. Several editions have been published since 1817, and these claims of Bonaparte's ill-usage have caused a deal of trouble for the British government."

Georgiana bit her lip. Supporters of Napoleon seemed to be around every corner. "I appreciate your concern, Sir Giles, but I am not a helpless female, unable to recognise danger when it confronts me. I can take care of myself."

"I am doubtful of that when you think nothing of venturing out into the streets dressed as a youth." He raised an eyebrow. "Do you ever plan to tell me why you did that?"

"As I said, my secret involves someone else, so I cannot disclose it."

He considered her in silence for a long moment. "I cannot force you to reveal it, *ma chérie*, but I want you to know that should you ever need my help, you have only to ask. You understand?"

"Thank you." She swallowed. "That is kind of you."

"Kindness is not my primary motivation." His voice was rather grim.

"What is?"

"Oh, I think you know."

She blushed under his scrutiny. But then her mother came back, and she turned to listen to her joyous account of an unexpected reunion with a childhood friend, who had come quite unexpectedly to the rout this evening.

Sir Giles took his leave, and Georgiana tried to put her disturbing conversation with him out of her mind. But she couldn't prevent herself from staring after him in dismay as he walked away.

She liked it far too much when he called her his *chérie*.

# CHAPTER TWENTY-TWO

An invitation arrived at Linfield House for a dinner party Lady Fenmore was holding at her home in Grosvenor Square.

"I have suggested to Mama that we pick you up in our carriage as she has another engagement that evening," Cassy told Georgiana when they met for a walk later that day. "Lady Fenmore has invited all the guests who will be at Fenmore Park to dine so that we can become better acquainted with one another before we gather for the house party. Stephen is joining us?"

Georgiana nodded. "His good friend Henry Aldwell will accompany his sister and his parents to Fenmore Park, so he is reconciled to the idea. At first, he was reluctant to attend as he is itching to return home to resume his fieldwork."

"He will have a splendid time. House parties such as these allow one a great deal of personal freedom, you know."

"Mama was unsure about sending us to Fenmore Park without her, but she is eager to return home after so many months in London, and she trusts you will provide adequate chaperonage for me."

"It sounds like a weighty chore when you put it like that." Cassy pulled a face. "I hope I'm up to the task."

"I'll be very well-behaved, never fear." Georgiana laughed.

"Thank you, dearest. I feel rather young to be a chaperon, truth be told." She placed her arm through Georgiana's as they strolled along. "After the house party, we plan to take you back to Linfield Court so you can pack everything you need, and then we'll travel on to Rothbury Park to prepare for our expedition."

"I cannot believe my dream is about to become a reality." Georgiana clasped her hands. "At the beginning of the year, I was in the doldrums about the prospect of coming to London, but it has worked out remarkably well. You have helped me develop my drawing skills, I sorted out Cousin Howard's museum, and I've been privileged to see some marvellous insect collections. I thought my world was shrinking when in fact, it has opened up."

"Oh, just wait, Georgie. Travelling abroad will open it up even more. It broadens the mind and thrills the senses in a way I cannot explain." Cassy tilted her head to one side. "In some ways, it is like falling in love. You enter a brand new country, where you begin to see things differently."

"You are fortunate that marrying Rothbury opened up your life," Georgiana said slowly. "Marriage usually narrows a woman's world. Monsieur Alphonse told me the other day that Englishmen are tied to their land like sturdy old oaks and that once they marry and have children, they sink their roots and never go anywhere. I am inclined to agree with him."

Cassy pursed her lips. "Monsieur Alphonse strikes me as somewhat contemptuous of the English. I wouldn't take what he says to heart."

"But, don't you see there is a grain of truth in what he says? I can't see Rothbury travelling far and wide once you have children."

"Maybe not when the children are young. But when you share a spirit of adventure with someone, life becomes a romance in itself, and you needn't travel to find enrichment of your mind and heart. You find it wherever you are."

"I didn't realise you were so sentimental, Cassy."

"I am just stating the truth as I see it." She hesitated. "When you are seeking a husband, it is so important to find the companion of your heart. Don't marry for any other reason, dearest. You may well be satisfied for a short period with the things he can provide, but after a while, living in intimacy with someone you don't love will become a penance. Only love can plaster over cracks created by the small, irritating habits we all have."

The ring of truth in her sister-in-law's words gave Georgiana pause. Although she had always dismissed romantical ideas as foolish, she saw now that her more pragmatic approach to marriage lacked heart and was perhaps even somewhat shallow.

She had set up her future husband as some sort of adversary who needed to be tamed rather than a human being it was possible to hurt. This nameless person appeared invulnerable to her, imbued with the invincibility of the stronger sex. But Cassy's words made her wonder if, by ignoring his humanity, she hadn't also been ignoring her own. No man, after all, was an island. Nor was any woman, no matter how independent she might be. It was a sobering thought.

The day of the dinner party dawned, and Georgiana awoke to a flutter of anticipation, which she tried unsuccessfully to ignore. Sir Giles had been out of Town for the past week, but she had overheard Lady Fenmore telling Cassy at a rout they attended that he would be back in time for the special gathering.

The Fenmores lived in an imposing mansion on the far side of the Square across from Rothbury House. When their party entered the hall that evening, they were led upstairs to an elegant drawing room where several guests had already gathered.

Lord and Lady Fenmore welcomed them warmly before speaking to the Aldwells, who arrived on their heels. As they moved further into the room, a young gentleman greeted Rothbury.

"Murchison!" her brother said. "I didn't realise you were in London."

"Mrs Murchison and I are only here for a short visit before we travel on to Fenmore Park." He inclined his head towards a lady, probably about thirty years of age, who had stopped to speak to someone. She joined them a short while later, and Rothbury performed the necessary introductions.

"I met Mr and Mrs Murchison in 1816 when I was touring France, the Alps, and Italy," Rothbury said. "Mrs Murchison has an interest in science, and her particular field of study is geology. After we met, we discovered that Murchison served in the army with Fenmore."

Cassy smiled at Mrs Murchison. "How charming to meet another lady who has an interest in geology."

"Indeed, Lady Rothbury. There aren't many of us, are there?" Mrs Murchison laughed.

Georgiana frowned. Her name seemed very familiar. Then she realised that this must be the lady Monsieur Alphonse had told her about the other day. She glanced around to see if the Frenchman had arrived yet, and her gaze came to rest on Sir Giles, standing in conversation with Lord Hanssen and the Balfour sisters, two ethereally fair young ladies who were particular friends of Miss Hamilton. They were laughing at something Sir Giles had just said, and Georgiana turned abruptly away to listen to Mrs Murchison, who was speaking about her stay in Rome.

A short while later, Monsieur Alphonse approached her, and she walked into the dining room on his arm. The table had been beautifully set, with an epergne filled with flowers in the centre. Lady Fenmore directed the seating of her guests as they entered the room, and Georgiana took the place she indicated in front of the epergne between Monsieur Alphonse and Sir Giles.

Georgiana's eyes met Lord Fenmore's fleetingly, and he gave a slight inclination of his head. He evidently wished for her to engage in private conversation with Monsieur Alphonse tonight, but she did not relish doing so with Sir Giles on her other side.

However, she did not have much choice in the matter. Etiquette demanded that she converse with both gentlemen during the meal. The first course consisted of dishes of fried and boiled fish with accompanying sauces and white and brown soup in tureens on either side of the epergne.

During this course, the conversation flowed to the left of Lady Fenmore, which meant Georgiana was obliged to speak to Monsieur Alphonse, who served her politely from the various dishes within his reach. "I hope I shall be able to take you butterfly hunting at Fenmore Park, *mademoiselle*," he said, offering her some fried fish.

"I should like that." Georgiana helped herself to a small portion.

After placing the dish back on the table, he went on: "A close friend of mine, Colonel Maceroni, told me he met you the other day."

Georgiana froze as she raised her fork to her mouth. "Indeed. He spoke to me about his travels to Italy. He seems to have led an intriguing life."

"*Oui*. Bonaparte awarded him the Légion d'Honneur for his

services to the republican cause. He was a great favourite, as well, of The Dandy King."

Georgiana frowned. "The Dandy King?"

"That was the name given to Joachim Murat, whom Napoleon installed on the throne in Naples. It was due to his taste in elaborate uniforms, *vous savez*." He poured her a glass of wine. "Colonel Maceroni has recently returned to England and has hopes of meeting some of his old acquaintances, including your good brother, with whom he became acquainted in Italy."

"I am sure Rothbury would be pleased to see him again, *monsieur*. I believe they share an interest in geology."

"*Oui.* It is always a good thing to see old friends." His voice was smooth. "When I told him I would be attending a dinner party with you this evening, he asked that you remember him to Lord Rothbury."

"Yes, of course I shall do so."

"*Merci, mademoiselle.*"

The plates and tablecloth were removed, and fresh linen and china laid for the second course, which consisted of a selection of stewed and roasted meat dishes placed on each end of the table. In addition, a plate of chicken and a decorated ham were set on either side of the epergne. Two footmen then deftly arranged various covered dishes at the four corners of the table before returning to their stations at a sideboard.

Lady Fenmore turned to speak to the guest on her right, thus turning the table, and conversation began to flow in the other direction. Sir Giles offered Georgiana some stewed rump steaks, and she had just helped herself to some vegetables, presented by a footman, when the baronet said in a low voice: "How are your caterpillars, ma'am?"

The reserve she had been attempting to maintain melted away under the warmth of his smile. "Very well, thank you, Sir Giles. Last night one of them formed a pale green chrysalis."

"Within a fortnight, it should emerge from its pupal case."

She tucked a stray curl behind one ear. "I cannot wait to see it."

"Rothbury tells me he is taking you to Fenmore Park the day after tomorrow." He picked up his wine glass. "Will your parents be travelling to Fenmore Park at a later date?"

"No. They plan to stay in London for a few more weeks before returning to Linfield Court."

"I see." His brows drew slightly together.

"Lady Fenmore told me you would probably arrange a butterfly hunting expedition at Fenmore Park."

"If there is enough interest, I'll most certainly make up a party."

"I am sure there will be. Both Stephen and Monsieur Alphonse will want to join us."

An arrested look appeared in his eyes. "Alphonse will be in attendance?"

"Didn't Lord Fenmore tell you he had invited him? Everyone here tonight will be at the house party. Lady Fenmore arranged this dinner so we could all become better acquainted with one another. But I suppose she didn't inform you of this evening's purpose as you have been out of Town."

"Indeed."

The epergne was taken off the table when the second course was removed, giving Georgiana a clear view of Miss Hamilton, who gazed across the table at Sir Giles.

The direction of the conversation changed again with the third course, and Georgiana turned once more to Monsieur Alphonse. She spoke to the baronet again only when a glass dish containing rosewater passed around the table.

Dipping the corner of her napkin into the liquid, she refreshed her fingers as Sir Giles offered her a slice of Savoy cake. She politely declined his offer and studied the selection of grapes, pineapples, peaches, and berries on display before popping a raspberry into her mouth.

Sir Giles engaged her in conversation for the next few minutes, but Georgiana gained the impression he was miles away. Indeed, a heavy frown descended upon his brow when she rose from the table to leave the dining room with the other ladies a short while later.

Something was amiss.

# CHAPTER TWENTY-THREE

Giles waited until everyone had taken their leave, and Lady
Fenmore had made her excuses and disappeared upstairs before
turning to Fenmore. "I am surprised you've invited Alphonse to
Fenmore Park."

His cousin merely inclined his head. "Indeed."

"Can you elaborate on your reasons for doing so? I assume it
has something to do with your work for the Government?"

"Let us just say that we are keeping an eye on him."

"I'm not surprised. He is a devilishly ugly customer."

Fenmore studied him thoughtfully. "You were at Eton together, weren't you?"

"Yes."

"Did he make his political views known as a boy?"

Giles leaned against the drawing-room wall, folding his arms.
"I gained the impression he was very conflicted about his position
in English society. He was born here, you know, but he spoke
English with a French accent as his family mixed mostly with
other French *émigrés*." He frowned. "He didn't fit in at school, and
he suffered for it. In turn, he tried to make me suffer. I wasn't
treated in quite the same way, you see, as I didn't sound French."
He gave a faint sigh. "Although I was victimised at Eton for my
dual heritage, it was not to the same degree as Alphonse. I'm sure
he resented that."

"Did you gain the impression he supported Bonaparte?"

"He would never have dared say anything of the sort while we were at war with France. And Alphonse comes from aristocratic lineage. Yet I wouldn't be surprised if he did and does support him, even if only because Napoleon is Britain's enemy." He hesitated. "Boney inspires extreme loyalty in his men...and a sense of connection. That connection would be attractive to someone who has never belonged in the land of his birth."

"Indeed," his cousin said again.

Giles straightened. "I must take my leave. But I hope you will advise me if you need assistance in your investigation."

"I shall. And if you discover anything of interest concerning Alphonse's political connections, don't hesitate to tell me."

"I won't. I only hope he doesn't spoil your house party."

"I know." He gave a wry smile. "Lady Fenmore did not wish to invite him. But duty must prevail at times."

The following day, Giles walked to Linfield House in the hope of obtaining an interview with Sir Barnaby. He was admitted to the library, where the older man, seated at a table, was writing a letter.

Sir Barnaby smiled as he set his quill to one side. "Sir Giles."

"Good morning, sir. I trust I haven't called at an inopportune time?"

"No, no." He waved at the leather armchair in front of his desk. "Pray be seated."

Giles lowered himself onto the seat. "I won't take up too much of your time, sir. I have come to ask for your permission to pay my addresses to your daughter."

Sir Barnaby leaned back, tapping his fingers on the wooden arms of his chair as he studied him thoughtfully. "I believe you would be an excellent match for Georgiana. However..." He puffed out his cheeks. "She isn't quite ready for marriage yet. Given this fact, I have decided it will be best to wait until she is eighteen before I allow anyone to pay their addresses to her."

Giles frowned. "When is Miss Linfield's birthday?"

"It is actually in three days. But I'm not sure she will be ready to make such a commitment for a while yet." He sighed. "Georgiana is restless and not at all inclined to settle down. She was only meant to come out next year, but her sister married earlier than expected, and we decided to bring Georgiana's *début* forward by a year. I am not entirely sure it was the best decision, although I believe she has become more reconciled to the idea of matrimony since we came to London."

"You will not object then if I pay my addresses to her on her birthday?"

He hesitated. "I have stated that I will not accept any offers for Georgiana's hand until she turns eighteen as I wanted to defer the matter of her marriage until next year. However, you are welcome to offer for her if you wish to. I only hope she will accept you."

Giles frowned as he left Linfield House a short while later and made his way home. He had hoped for a slightly less negative reception, but once he and Georgiana were able to spend long stretches of time in one another's company, he would be better able to read her mind and heart. And although Sir Barnaby had not been particularly encouraging, Georgiana would not, in all probability, confide in her father about such things.

He found interacting with her in Town quite frustrating, given all the social restrictions that were in place. But many of those barriers would be lifted when they arrived at Fenmore Park for the house party, and he would finally be able to communicate with her without the formality necessary in London. And although he wasn't quite sure where he stood with her, she wasn't indifferent to him. He was certain of it.

That kiss had shouted silent secrets into his soul.

~

When Rothbury popped in the next day while Georgiana was directing the packing of her belongings, she told him about Colonel Maceroni's desire to see him.

"I am surprised." Her brother raised his eyebrows. "I saw very little of the colonel in Italy, but I suppose he is hoping to gather some allies about him now that he has been charged with treachery."

"Treachery? But why?"

"Oh, it is some diplomatic contretemps. Maceroni is a keen republican and has only recently returned to England after living abroad for a number of years."

She shrugged. "Well, Monsieur Alphonse seemed eager for the two of you to become reacquainted. Perhaps he believes you will be able to assist his friend."

"It must be that. But claiming acquaintanceship after so many years is an act of desperation. I barely know the fellow."

Rothbury and Cassy came to fetch her the following day in the Rothbury family travelling carriage, picked out in yellow, with a coronet of pearls and leaves positioned above the coat of arms. The baggage and servants would follow in another coach, while Stephen had decided to drive to Fenmore Park in their father's curricle.

The journey took only three hours, and Georgiana looked around in delight as they entered the gates of Fenmore Park and progressed down the winding drive. Acres of woodland stretched to her left while a herd of fallow deer grazed near a beautiful lake to the right.

A yew tree walk, parallel to the driveway, linked a succession of individual garden enclosures, including an ornamental shrubbery and a flower garden. It all quite took Georgiana's breath away.

They swept around the final bend in the road, and a stately four-storeyed house constructed of red brick stone came into view. A cornice with curved and triangular pediments stretched across the front of the building, throwing the skyline into sharp relief. French windows on the ground floor integrated the house and garden in a most inviting way.

When they reached the end of the driveway, a footman opened the carriage door, and Georgiana gazed in awe at the splendid lawns stretching towards the lake in the distance. She took a moment to breathe in the flower-scented air as she stepped down from the coach before following Rothbury and Cassy towards the grand entrance of the house.

The butler led them to a drawing room. Before sitting on a satinwood armchair, Georgiana glanced up in amazement at the ornate coved ceiling, coffered with rosettes and friezes in an intricate floral design.

Lady Fenmore entered the room and greeted them in her usual warm fashion, and then a footman led Georgiana up a carved, winding staircase towards her allocated bedchamber. She glanced around at the charmingly decorated room as she stepped inside. A vase of white roses adorned the mantelpiece. Blue chintz bedcovers matched the curtains, drawn back from the windows to reveal a view of magnificent grounds.

She left her bedchamber a short while later and spotted Cassy walking ahead of her down the corridor. She hurried to catch up. The house was so large she could easily become lost trying to traverse the series of interlinking passages. "Thank goodness you're also going downstairs, Cassy. You can lead me to the hall."

Her sister-in-law came to a halt. "It can be a little confusing. I remember feeling quite lost on my first visit."

"I thought Linfield Court was large, but Fenmore Park seems enormous."

They made their way downstairs.

"Would you like to walk in the gardens?" Cassy asked as they entered the hall. "Rothbury and Fenmore have some business to discuss, and it would be pleasant to get some fresh air. I'm feeling rather tired today."

"I'd like that. Are we the first guests to arrive?"

Cassy nodded. "Rothbury wanted to arrive early as his business with Fenmore is quite urgent."

They strolled over the lawns towards an Italian garden consisting of an orangery at one end and a diagonal stairway, with statues standing to attention on each step, at the other. A large fountain, buttressed by four white stone mermaids, bubbled peacefully in the centre of the enclosure beside an iron garden seat, set temptingly to one side.

"What a beautiful place," Georgiana said as she sat down. "A wonderful retreat from the world."

Cassy seated herself on the bench beside Georgiana. "House parties can become a little tiresome after a while, so it will be pleasant to have a place to escape to."

Georgiana laughed. "Yes. But what if the houseguests all have the same idea at the same time?"

Her sister-in-law chuckled. "We will be dodging one another in and out of the enclosure, no doubt."

They left the Italian garden fifteen minutes later and had crossed the lawn to the ornamental shrubbery when Sir Giles stepped out of the front door and walked towards them.

Georgiana drew to an abrupt halt and then began moving again, this time more slowly. Her heart raced, and an odd tingling sensation spread up the length of her spine. *I wish I didn't react to Sir Giles like this.*

He smiled as he greeted them, and after inquiring politely about their journey, he turned towards Georgiana. "I hope to arrange that butterfly-hunting expedition for tomorrow afternoon, if it fits in with Lady Fenmore's plans."

"That would be lovely, Sir Giles. Stephen and I brought our nets."

Cassy smiled. "I trust you had a good journey, sir?"

"I did, thank you, Lady Rothbury," he replied. "I sent my baggage on ahead and drove here in my curricle. I hope the fine weather lasts."

Georgiana grimaced. "So do I. Being cooped up indoors with a group of strangers is not something I'd enjoy."

His eyes gleamed as he offered her his arm. She placed her hand on his sleeve, and her cheeks warmed when he covered her fingers briefly with his.

"It is another matter entirely to be cooped up indoors with friends," he murmured. "And I hope you do number some friends among the guests?"

Georgiana's face heated even more after remembering her firm assertion that they could never be friends. "Um...yes. Yes, I do, Sir Giles."

"I believe it is your birthday tomorrow?" he said in a low voice when Cassy stepped away to admire some roses.

"So it is. Going on a butterfly hunt will be the most wonderful birthday present. I cannot thank you enough."

"I am glad it is within my power to give you such a gift, *ma chérie*. Your happiness is of supreme importance to me, you know."

She gazed into his eyes, completely lost, and she knew then— she loved him, and had for some time. She longed to hurry away and hug this knowledge to herself, but was forced to participate in a mundane conversation about gardening as they slowly traversed the ornamental shrubbery before making their way back to the house.

Georgiana mumbled an excuse the moment they entered the hall and rushed upstairs to her bedchamber. Flinging herself onto her bed, she stared wide-eyed at the canopy overhead.

How could she have been so obtuse? For months she had pushed aside her very real attraction to Giles, convincing herself it was a mere superficial awareness of his good looks. But slowly, steadily, he had pushed through her walls until she couldn't keep them up any longer. And today, the last remaining bricks had crumbled away.

Deep emotion had always made her uncomfortable, so she tended to shy away from it, focusing instead on the physical and cerebral realms. Now, however, she couldn't deny that her heart had awakened to the point that her happiness was now entirely dependent on another human being.

Giles had made it clear he wanted to marry her. And although she had always dismissed love as sentimental foolishness, she realised now that she had been the foolish one. How could she ever have believed she would be content with a husband who would do her bidding? Only the distinctly unbiddable Sir Giles could show her that her idea of wedded bliss was sadly flawed.

The look in his eyes today had been unmistakable, and she basked in pure joy for a moment before the dire reality of her situation began to sink in. She was committed to seeking out information from Monsieur Alphonse for the duration of this house party, and she was therefore not at liberty to reveal the true nature of her feelings for Giles.

She absolutely must talk to Rothbury.

# Chapter Twenty-Four

The rest of the houseguests trickled in throughout the day. When the Murchisons arrived, Georgiana joined Cassy and Mrs Murchison on another walk around the grounds. This time, her sister-in-law led them toward a ha-ha that separated the garden from a nearby river. Cassy opened a gate onto a stone bridge, and as Georgiana and Mrs Murchison passed through, she said, "Do tell us more about your travels, Mrs Murchison. Are there any places you recommend we visit in Italy?"

The older lady smiled. "Where do I begin? We left England in the spring of 1816 and only returned from our sojourn in Italy last summer. Rome, of course, is of particular cultural significance, but I particularly enjoyed my stay in Genoa."

"Did you study Italian, ma'am?" Georgiana asked.

"I did. It is a beautiful language."

"If you have any of your sketches with you, I should dearly like to see them," Cassy said. "Rothbury told me the other day that Paul Sandby was your drawing master. His watercolour paintings are beautifully executed."

Mrs Murchison inclined her head. "He was an excellent instructor. My particular interest is in sketching landscapes with unusual geological features."

Georgiana glanced from Cassy to Mrs Murchison. "You are both fortunate to have husbands who take you travelling."

"Indeed," Mrs Murchison said. "Many soldiers, however, are travellers at heart."

Georgiana knit her brows. "I sometimes wonder whether possessions and responsibilities do not chain us unnecessarily to our places of birth. If we had more freedom, we could fully explore the world, but our duties tend to bind us to our homes."

Mrs Murchison studied her thoughtfully. "That is frequently true. But I do think we can shape our lives according to how we should like to live them."

"Women are bound by their husband's wishes, to a lesser or greater degree," Georgiana said.

"Indeed." Mrs Murchison nodded. "That is why flexibility of the mind is so important in a spouse. If a man is eager to learn about the world around him, he will not be rigid in his thinking and will, more than likely, be pleased to accommodate his wife in her ambitions. At least, I have found that to be the case."

"As have I," said Cassy quietly. "A man of intelligence will nurture your hopes and dreams. as he wishes to make you happy."

Mrs Murchison started to speak about their mode of travel through Italy, and Georgiana's attention wandered from the conversation. Monsieur Alphonse had appeared to display admirable qualities when she met him and was seemingly supportive of her scientific endeavours and personal freedom. And yet, he had not been at all sincere in his intentions. He had merely told her what she wanted to hear, as he desired access to her fortune.

Meanwhile, Giles, who had appeared so rigid in his thinking when she first encountered him, had shown he wasn't the intransigent man she imagined him to be. She found it strange how one's initial impressions of people could be so wrong.

Or perhaps she was merely guilty of the sin of wishful thinking. Her interest in natural history and travel had assumed such vast importance that she allowed these desires to dominate her thinking. So much so, in fact, that she had latched onto the first man who indicated he might fulfil them, without considering that he could be manipulating her for his own ends.

When there was a pause in the conversation, Georgiana turned to Mrs Murchison. "Monsieur Alphonse mentioned that he met you in France, ma'am."

"Indeed. He spent many hours talking to my husband about his interest in entomology and his travels abroad."

"He has a theory that Englishmen are less inclined to travel once they marry." Pausing, Georgiana shook her head, making curly strands dance around her face. "But Mr Murchison disproves that completely."

The older woman shook her head. "I wouldn't pay too much heed to Monsieur Alphonse's opinions, my dear. He said some harsh things about the English when we met him, which I found rather shocking, truth be told. But I imagine he only showed his disdain in such an open fashion because Mr Murchison is Scottish and not English."

Georgiana's brow creased. "I find it strange that he detests the land he has chosen to live in."

"Perhaps the problem is that it *isn't* his land of choice. I gained the distinct impression when we conversed with him that he would prefer to make a life in France one day. Circumstances must exist which compel him to remain here."

They turned and began to make their way slowly back to the house. Georgiana glanced around at the serene grounds and took in a lungful of fresh air. Nothing compared to country living. Despite her severe misgivings about the role she had committed to play during the next two weeks, her spirits lifted. She was in the most beautiful surroundings, and the man she loved would be nearby for the entirety of the house party. She couldn't ask for much more.

She just needed to get through the next fortnight.

Only Giles, Georgiana, and Stephen committed themselves to the field excursion the following day. Cassy had planned to join their party, but she excused herself as she wasn't feeling her best. "I hope I am not coming down with something," she said, with a crease between her brows. "I feel utterly exhausted again today."

"Should we put off our expedition until you feel better?" Georgiana studied her sister-in-law's pale face with concern. "It will be a pity if you have to miss out."

"I wouldn't hear of it, dearest. I know it is the exact way you would like to spend your birthday." Her eyes twinkled. "Have you asked Miss Hamilton to come along?"

A bubble of laughter escaped Georgiana. "I would never be so cruel. She might feel obliged to accept."

"And the Balfour sisters?"

"Lady Fenmore extended the invitation to Miss Balfour and

Miss Susannah, but they do not have suitable footwear. And Monsieur Alphonse made some excuse as to why he couldn't join us, but I believe it is merely because he and Sir Giles do not get on."

Cassy tilted her head. "I believe they were at school together and have never seen eye to eye. Edward alluded to it the other day."

"I didn't know that," Georgiana said slowly. "It explains a few things."

After a light luncheon, they left the house, laden with butterfly nets, collecting boxes, a repair set consisting of a clasp knife, as well as needles and thread to fix any netting torn by briars or thorns—an all-too-frequent occurrence on trips such as these.

After walking over a stone bridge, they made their way across the fields, where Stephen picked up his pace. "I want to see if I can find some musk beetles in those willow trees up ahead. I'll see you later."

Very soon, her brother was a small figure in the distance, and then he disappeared completely out of sight. Sir Giles turned to face her, smiling. "I would have preferred a more private setting, but I do not wish to wait a moment longer."

The tender light in his eyes was unmistakable, and Georgiana's heart fluttered as he took her hands in his. "When we met, *ma chérie*, I was determined not to marry for at least a few more years as I believed matrimony would tie me down and prevent me from travelling the world. But now..." He drew her hand to his lips. "Now, I cannot imagine doing so without you at my side. I spoke to your father before I left London, and he told me you were resistant to the idea of matrimony. But when I saw you yesterday..." The glow in his eyes intensified. "It gave me hope that you do, in fact, return my regard. My dearest Georgiana, would you make me the happiest man alive by accepting my hand in marriage?"

Joy and dismay warred in her breast. She had not expected Giles to declare himself so soon, certainly not before she had spoken to Rothbury. Unfortunately, she hadn't managed to have a private word with her older brother, as he had remained upstairs with Cassy for most of the morning. This meant she wasn't at liberty to tell Giles as yet about her part in the investigation...

She drew in a shaking breath. "I am afraid I cannot give you my answer now due to reasons I am not at liberty to disclose.

Would...would you please ask me again at a later date?"

"I had hoped..." He carefully searched her face and then released her hands. "If you don't know your heart by now, Georgiana, why would you magically know it at a later date? If you consider this a kind way of turning me down, I would prefer the cold, hard truth."

She twisted her fingers together. "I am not able to reveal why I am asking you to postpone your proposal, at least not at the moment. Unfortunately, I am under an...an obligation which makes it impossible for me to speak frankly with you..." She trailed off at the incredulous expression in his eyes.

"This becomes stranger and stranger. What could possibly prevent you from speaking your mind to me? You have always done so in the past."

"I am aware of that. But..." She breathed out slowly. "I cannot say more at present. I can only ask for your patience—and your trust."

He gazed at her for a long, agonising moment. "Very well. I'll wait. But answer me one thing."

"Yes?" The muscles in her shoulders tensed.

"Has this anything to do with your ridiculous masquerade the other day? You said you couldn't reveal your reason for dressing up as a boy as it involved someone else. Are you in some sort of trouble?"

"Not...not precisely."

He kneaded the back of his neck. "Very well. You are evidently in a difficult position. But whatever it is preventing you from speaking, I want you to know that I love you and will do anything to keep you safe. Do you understand?"

She nodded, unable to say a word through the constriction in her throat. If only she were free to confide in him. She opened her mouth in a further attempt to reassure him, but Stephen came bounding back towards them before she could say anything.

"You will never believe what I've just seen!" he called out, unmistakable joy in his voice. "A Purple Emperor, flying above the trees... Come and have a look at it. It's truly spectacular."

They hastened after him, and when they reached the forest, Georgiana stopped to gaze up at the beautiful spectacle. The size of a small bat, the butterfly passed at high speed through the woodland canopy.

"What an amazing creature," she breathed.

"They are very difficult to catch. It is a good thing Sir Giles found those larvae."

"Indeed," she agreed, and then lifted her gaze to Giles's. "I cannot wait for my butterfly to emerge from its chrysalis. It's the most exciting prospect."

"It is, isn't it?" he murmured, looking down at her.

As their eyes met, Georgiana remembered their conversation from many months ago, when he had compared her to a caterpillar. She had been so indignant at what she perceived as an insulting comparison. But perhaps he hadn't been so far off the mark. She had certainly undergone a change in heart over the past six months, or maybe it was more accurate to say it was a *changeover* of heart.

For that's what it was like to fall in love.

# CHAPTER TWENTY-FIVE

Georgiana lowered her head and closed her eyes for a moment when Rothbury did not come down to dinner that evening. Evidently, Cassy was still indisposed, and they both remained upstairs. And the following day, when Georgiana visited her sister-in-law in her bedchamber, Cassy informed her that she would not be going on the excursion Lady Fenmore had planned to the Roman remains of Silchester.

"Would you like me to stay with you?" Georgiana asked, sitting on the edge of the bed.

Cassy shook her head. "I wouldn't hear of it, dearest. Stephen can drive you to Silchester in his curricle, and Mrs Murchison has kindly agreed to act as your chaperon in my stead."

"I would be happy to stay with you."

"No, no. It will be so dull for you here, Georgie. You must go. It sounds like an intriguing place."

"Well, if you are sure..."

"I shall have Edward for company, so I'll be perfectly content."

Georgiana stood. "Would you tell him I'd like to speak to him upon our return?"

"Yes, of course. Now you had better hurry; otherwise, you'll keep everyone waiting."

After fetching her bonnet and shawl, Georgiana met Stephen in the hall, and they made their way outside to his waiting curricle. Giles was nowhere to be seen, so perhaps he had no plans to join the excursion today. Her heart sank at the horrid thought, and she frowned as she climbed into the passenger seat. If her beloved failed to join them today, she must still find enjoyment in the outing. Otherwise, she was on a slippery slope to discontentment...

The scenery on the way to the Roman remains was beautiful. However, the road eventually became too rough to traverse, and the convoy of carriages halted for them to proceed the rest of the way on foot.

Lady Fenmore explained that the ruins were hidden amid some woodland as they strolled through the labyrinth of trees. And, indeed, no hint of the ancient site was visible until Georgiana, following her host and hostess through a tangle of branches, came suddenly upon some crumbling walls.

She was studying the outline of the one-time city when Mrs Murchison approached her. "A fascinating place, is it not?"

"Indeed. Do you know anything about its history?"

"A little. When I learned we were to visit the ruins, I found a history of Silchester in the library and did some reading. Historians say this was a principal Roman Station due to its size, the manner in which the walls were constructed, and the many Roman roads that branch off from it. Its walls measure nearly two miles in circumference and twenty-four feet in thickness."

Giles came through the trees just as Georgiana turned to follow Mrs Murchison along the bank that ran beside the wall. "I thought you weren't coming!" she said with a small gasp.

"I was delayed." He regarded her quizzically. "Did you miss me, Georgie?"

She pressed her lips together and jutted her chin in the direction of Mrs Murchison's back. He laughed and walked silently beside her until they reached the Roman Amphitheatre.

Mrs Murchison drew to a halt beside the steep bank covered with a grove of trees. "This is where the gladiators once exhibited their athletic abilities," she said. "They participated in wrestling matches as well as other feats of strength."

"How enthralling that wild beasts once roamed this very ground," Georgiana said, gazing around.

"I don't envy the poor men who had to fight them off." Mrs Murchison's voice was dry. "The beasts were brought in here to battle each other, and this was also the place of public executions, where criminals were condemned to fight with the wild animals."

Georgiana shivered. She could almost hear the roar of the lions and the shouts of the spectators echoing through the surrounding woods. "The Romans must have been a brutal people. I'm glad we live in a more civilised age."

"Sometimes I wonder…how much more civilised are we, really?" Giles said quietly.

She was about to respond when Monsieur Alphonse stepped into the enclosure. "Miss Linfield!" He bowed. "There are some beautiful butterflies in the woods. Would you care to view them with me?"

Mrs Murchison gave a brisk nod. "*We* would be delighted to look at them, wouldn't we, Miss Linfield?"

A flash of annoyance crossed Monsieur Alphonse's face, but then he smiled and bowed again. "*Bien sûr, madame.*"

As they moved away from the arena towards the woods, Giles offered Georgiana his arm just as Monsieur Alphonse proffered his. Georgiana glanced somewhat helplessly from one man to the other. Her mother had told her once that a gentleman could take two ladies upon his arms, but under no circumstances should a lady ever take the arms of two gentlemen.

Mrs Murchison laughed. "Perhaps you could alternate in escorting Miss Linfield, gentlemen?"

Monsieur Alphonse bowed in Sir Giles's direction. "You were first, I believe, Tavistock."

Georgiana gave a friendly nod in Monsieur Alphonse's direction as she placed her hand on Giles's arm. They crossed the uneven ground towards the woodland, where Stephen stood gazing up at the trees.

"Seen anything of interest?" Georgiana asked.

"A Silver-washed Fritillary. Look…" He pointed at a large orange and black butterfly, fluttering high.

"Well spotted. You must have a look at the amphitheatre, Stephen. Mrs Murchison has been telling us about the history of the Roman remains."

"I should like to. I once heard a legend that giants used to live in Silchester."

"I read about that in the book I found in the library," Mrs Murchison said. "The story of the giants who once lived here isn't quite what it seems."

"Pray tell us more." Georgiana gave the older woman an encouraging smile.

Mrs Murchison's brow puckered. "The word 'gigas' has an interesting origin, being a Greek word which the Romans borrowed. Old English, in turn, took its name for 'giant' from Latin. However, for the Romans, a giant signified a man of great stature as well as a person accomplished in war. Princes and military heroes were termed 'Gigantes' therefore, and Silchester, being a military station, was, of course, occupied by high-ranking men, including soldiers, famous for their skill and bravery in war. So when we hear tales in England of places once inhabited by giants, the Romans were not speaking of any unusually tall inhabitants but men who were famous in their profession of arms."

Stephen grinned. "In that context, Bonaparte would be classified as a giant of a man, even though he is so short."

"It is a myth perpetuated by the British that Bonaparte is short. I have met the Emperor, and he is, in fact, of average height." Monsieur Alphonse's voice was stiff.

Georgiana's mouth dropped open. "You've met Napoleon, *monsieur*?"

"Merely in passing when I travelled abroad." He frowned. "I am not well-acquainted with the Emperor."

A strained silence followed, and Georgiana began speaking about the grand Summer Ball to be held next week at Fenmore Park. However, the gentlemen did not evince much interest in the subject. She was relieved when Mrs Murchison started a discussion about the history of the Roman Empire. Giles pressed her arm a short while later, and they wandered off together along a path through the trees, which eventually led to a small clearing.

A sudden rustle of leaves broke the stillness, and Giles put his finger to his lips as a stag with magnificent antlers stepped into the glade. The handsome creature studied them alertly as if challenging them for trespassing on his domain. Then his large ears twitched, and he darted away into the trees.

Georgiana quoted softly: "'My beloved is like a roe or a young hart... My beloved spake, and said unto me, Rise up, my love, my fair one, and come away... For, lo, the winter is past, the rain is over and gone; the flowers appear on the earth; the time of the singing of birds is come..."'"

"Beautiful verses, *ma chérie*."

"I appreciate lovely words, although you probably wouldn't expect that from me." Her voice was slightly defensive.

"Why do you believe that?"

"I have never been romantical."

"Perhaps not." He studied her thoughtfully. "But you are a connoisseur of beauty in the natural world. It is likely, therefore, that you would appreciate beauty in other forms."

She stared up at him, transfixed by his gaze before a breaking twig recalled her to her surroundings. She peered over Giles's shoulder to see Monsieur Alphonse coming through the trees.

A challenging smile curled his lips as he observed Giles, and then he turned to study Georgiana. "May I escort you back to the ruins, Mademoiselle Linfield? I believe the servants are setting up a picnic under a tree."

"Yes, of course, *monsieur*."

She stepped away, but Giles retained her hand, bringing it slowly to his lips. When he eventually released her, Georgiana walked over to Monsieur Alphonse, whose smile had now twisted into a sneer.

Tension thrummed in the air before Georgiana said in a bright voice: "How lovely that Lady Fenmore has arranged a picnic. I am rather hungry."

Mrs Murchison still stood at the end of the path, talking to Stephen. When Georgiana and Monsieur Alphonse reached them, they all made their way out of the wood towards a massive oak tree on a knoll. Beneath its branches, the Fenmore servants had set up tables laden with a splendid repast, as well as a few chairs.

Georgiana gazed at the vast array of food which included a joint of cold roast beef, two roast ducks, a splendid-looking ham, pies, cheese, rolls, and a basket of salad along with bottles of stewed fruit, a couple of cheesecakes, tarts, a blancmange in a mould and a large plum cake.

She accepted a glass of lemonade from a passing footman before engaging Miss Aldwell, who sat on one of the chairs, in polite conversation. A few minutes later, Giles brought Georgiana a plate of food and some cutlery. She thanked him for his kindness just as Monsieur Alphonse came up to her, bearing yet another plate of food.

When he noticed she had already been served, he turned to Miss Aldwell with a quick bow. "How eager we are to attend to the charming ladies of this party. For you, *mademoiselle*."

Georgiana gave a quick prayer of thanks that the other girl did not seem to realise Monsieur Alphonse had not initially intended the plate for her. This expedition was becoming more and more fraught. Fortunately, the gentlemen moved away a short while later, which gave her a brief respite from the unease holding her in its grip.

If only she could accept Giles's proposal. But she wasn't free to do so yet, and Monsieur Alphonse's behaviour troubled her. Giles had kissed her hand in front of him, which had not improved Alphonse's mood. That little gesture had probably seemed like a direct challenge to him, particularly since Monsieur Alphonse had pressed his lips to Georgiana's hand in a similar fashion at Bullock's Museum the other day. It was as if the two men were jockeying for position in her affections.

However, it was Giles who had won her heart. And although she could not show her preference for him to the assembled company, she found it impossible not to treat him accordingly when they were on their own.

After the picnic, Georgiana and the other guests walked past a small church and a farmhouse, the only two structures within the ancient walls.

"These buildings are about 250 years old," Lady Fenmore told her when they stopped to look at the brick church. "The Earl of Blessington is the present owner of this site, and I live in hope he will one day bring to the surface some of the antiquities buried beneath the ground."

Her ladyship sighed as they walked on. "I am afraid, though, that the farmer who lives here has no interest in preserving history." She pointed at the farmhouse door, where the shaft of a Roman column had been made into a horse-block. "I shudder to see to what use he has put that ancient column. He is so busy with his own concerns that he does not stop to think that this place once bustled with Roman soldiers during the fourth century."

Georgiana studied the column doubtfully. "I suppose it does work rather well as a horse-block. But to be surrounded by antiquities and to have so little regard for them is a very sad thing."

"It isn't only him, I'm afraid. I have heard that the stones from these walls are frequently taken to mend the public road."

Georgiana gazed around. "History seeps out of every stone in this place. One would think the people living here would want to preserve it for posterity."

"Not everyone has the gift of foresight. And perhaps they fail to see its intrinsic value because it is right under their noses."

"It is odd how we resist seeing the value of our surroundings, dismissing them as commonplace merely because they are familiar to us," Georgiana said slowly.

As the words left her mouth, she stilled. Perhaps she was just as guilty of doing that. Although she had grown up in a lovely part of England, she had never taken much heed of its beauty. Instead, she had become fixated on travelling abroad to discover the beautiful places that could be found elsewhere.

Human beings were contrary creatures.

# CHAPTER TWENTY-SIX

When they returned to the house later that afternoon, Georgiana sought out Rothbury in the library. "Would you care to walk in the gardens with me, Edward? I have something I need to discuss with you."

"Yes, of course, Georgie." He moved away from the window where he stood. "I have been meaning to speak to you too."

They left the house together and strolled across the lawns in the direction of the ornamental lake. The day was warm, and Georgiana was grateful for the shade when they came to a halt under the old oak tree at the end of the garden.

She gazed out at the vast expanse of water before turning to her brother. "I discovered something today that you may find of interest. Monsieur Alphonse admitted he had met Bonaparte when he was travelling abroad."

He gave a quick frown. "Did he indeed? I shall be sure to let Fenmore know. You are helping us tremendously, my dear."

"I am pleased to be able to do so. But I confess that I am in something of a quandary." She hesitated. "You see, Sir Giles proposed to me yesterday, but I had to put him off due to my involvement in the investigation."

Rothbury's eyebrows shot up. "What excellent news, Georgie. But unexpected after all your protestations. You wish to marry him?"

"I do."

"Hmmm." He rubbed his jaw. "The timing of Giles's offer

could not be worse."

"I know." She hesitated. "Would it be possible to speak to him on my behalf? I dislike keeping him in the dark like this."

"Yes, of course. But it complicates matters, particularly as Alphonse and Giles have never got on. Giles won't like your involvement in the investigation at all."

"Perhaps you could give him the plain facts of the matter, and then at least he will understand why I couldn't give him an answer?"

"That is only fair," he said slowly. "I did not intend for this to impact your life negatively, which it is beginning to do." His expression lightened somewhat. "I find it highly amusing that Cassy was right all along. You *are* in love with my cousin."

Georgiana lifted her chin. "Don't sound so smug about it."

He grinned. "Giles is an excellent chap. I am pleased you finally recognised that. And, frankly, I'm relieved I won't need to disappoint you as we may no longer be going abroad." He paused for a moment. "You see, Cassy has just realised she could be with child. She has been feeling a trifle pulled recently, and this morning, she cast up her accounts."

"Oh!" She clasped her hands. "I'm sorry Cassy isn't feeling well, but what splendid news that she may be pregnant. I am delighted for you both."

"Thank you, my dear. It is early days yet, though." He pulled out his watch. "I must return. Rest assured, I shall speak to Giles, and once I have done so, I'll let you know."

She smiled her thanks as they walked back to the house. They parted in the hall, and Georgiana made her way upstairs to her bedchamber to change, feeling somehow lighter. She would be able to tell Giles everything in her heart soon. It couldn't come quickly enough for her.

~

Giles came downstairs some time before dinner and came upon Rothbury outside the double doors of the Salon. His cousin immediately asked him for a private word.

"Yes, of course," Giles said. "Should we step into the library?"

When they entered the spacious apartment just down the corridor, Giles closed the door behind him and looked at his cousin inquiringly. "Is anything amiss?"

"No." Rothbury leaned against the back of a mahogany table. "Although you will probably think differently. I hear from my sister that congratulations are soon to be in order."

"Georgiana has spoken to you?"

"She sought me out this afternoon." Rothbury paused for a moment. "I asked a favour of her in London, which has placed her in a difficult position. It has to do with Pierre Alphonse."

The muscles in Giles's shoulders tensed. "I know Fenmore is investigating Alphonse. But how is Georgiana involved?"

"Alphonse, as you know, has been dangling after her for the last few months. Recently I discovered he is in damned low water—from my tailor, of all people. But, in order to keep his creditors at bay, he has been putting it about that he is to be married to Georgiana, curse his impudence."

"I suspected as much from various rumours which have been circulating in the clubs," Giles said slowly.

"Indeed. I told Georgiana about the rumours Alphonse was spreading, as she had ignored an earlier warning I'd given her father about Alphonse's lack of suitability as a husband."

"She regarded him in such a serious light?"

"Yes. But only because she nurtured hopes that he would take her on field trips should they marry. She has been fixated on the idea for several years now. So when Alphonse hinted that he would take her abroad on his entomological expeditions, she began to look more favourably on his suit. That was before she realised her affections lay in *your* direction, of course."

Giles's mouth set in a straight line, but he merely nodded for Rothbury to continue.

"Fenmore informed me that the Government has been investigating Alphonse as a possible conspirator in a plot to rescue Bonaparte from St Helena. He proposed that Georgiana should assist us in our investigations as Alphonse is more likely to speak to a lady he is enamoured of than to any of the secret agents who have been investigating the plot. I broached Fenmore's suggestion with Georgiana, and she agreed to help us. Thus far, her aid has been invaluable."

"I see. Is that why she dressed up as a boy the other day?"

"Yes. She was on a drive with Alphonse the other day when

he stopped to speak to Barry O'Meara, who acted as Bonaparte's doctor on St Helena until last year. Georgiana got wind of a proposed meeting at Blackwall Yard and went there dressed in Stephen's clothes to investigate further."

"What did she discover?"

"O'Meara and Alphonse met an unknown man at the Yard, and now we are waiting to see what they'll do next. We trust that Georgiana will be able to find out something more about their plans during the next fortnight. However, I have warned her not to take any more risks."

"I see," Giles said again.

"Georgiana asked me to tell you about the investigation. I had sworn her to silence as we wanted as few people as possible to know about it. So, if you could wait until the end of the house party to announce your betrothal, that would help us enormously." He grinned. "It is a relief that you and Georgiana will be making a match of it, truth be told, as I may need to thwart her dreams of travel once again. Cassy might be with child."

"That is splendid news, Rothbury. My congratulations to you both." Giles studied his cousin for a long moment. "Miss Linfield was planning on joining you on your journey, you say?"

"I suggested she travel with us to make up for her disappointment at the discovery of Alphonse's perfidy. She leapt at the chance."

Giles glanced at the clock on the wall. "We had better leave now if we don't wish to be late for dinner."

Rothbury preceded him through the doorway. "If you could keep an eye on Georgiana during our stay, it would set my mind at rest."

"Yes, of course," Giles murmured as he followed his cousin out of the library. However, when he entered the Salon and spotted Georgiana amongst the assembled guests, he could barely summon a smile in response to the warm look she sent him.

He felt as if he had been kicked in the stomach.

~

Georgiana's forehead creased as she surreptitiously studied Giles from across the room. His acknowledgement had seemed very distant. But perhaps it was understandable as she had placed him in a very difficult position.

The guests began making their way across the saloon to a connecting door that led to the enormous dining room. Georgiana took her place between Henry Aldwell and Monsieur Alphonse and maintained a civil conversation with the two gentlemen for the duration of the drawn-out meal.

The entire time, however, she was acutely aware of Giles, seated across from her between the Balfour sisters. He appeared to be keeping the two ladies very well entertained, and Georgiana clamped down on the fierce jealousy which sprang up in her as Miss Susannah gave a peal of laughter in response to something he said.

The rules of etiquette dictated that Sir Giles speak to the two ladies on either side of him during dinner. No doubt he was just being polite.

However, she revised her opinion the next day when the house guests visited the ruins of Reading Abbey, founded by Henry I, in 1121. Stephen drove her to the ancient royal monastery, and it soon became clear that Giles was avoiding her. He did not talk to her unless it became strictly necessary, and when their gazes accidentally met, he looked straight through her.

When their party stopped at The George for refreshments afterwards, Georgiana approached Rothbury to ask if he had spoken to Giles.

He glanced across the taproom at his cousin. "I took him aside before dinner last night."

"Oh! Thank you. That must be why he's keeping his distance today."

"No doubt. He is fully aware of the gravity of the situation."

Georgiana gave a sigh of relief. Giles was, in all probability, only complying with Rothbury's wishes. Still, she could not help but feel anxious. Something about Giles's manner today bothered her. He did not seem merely distant; he appeared angry with her. And he was paying far too much attention to Miss Hamilton and those Balfour sisters.

He may not wish it to become known that he had proposed to Georgiana, but surely he need not go to such lengths to keep the other ladies entertained? If she had to listen to one more of their bright, tinkling laughs today, she had no doubt she would scream.

As Georgiana turned away from Rothbury, she spotted a familiar face in the doorway. It was the tall man she had seen in the shipyard. Within a minute, however, he had disappeared, and Georgiana turned back to her brother. "He's here, Edward! The man who met Monsieur Alphonse and Dr O'Meara at Blackwall Yard."

Edward frowned. "Where?"

"He just left. He was in the doorway."

"You are certain it's the same man?"

"I recognised him instantly due to his great height and his weathered features. When I saw him at Blackwall Yard, it struck me that he must spend a lot of time out of doors."

Edward glanced around. "It's a pity we can't search for him now. This is a busy coaching inn, so perhaps he is passing through."

"Or he could be meeting Monsieur Alphonse?"

Rothbury nodded. "I thought of that. Can you see Alphonse?"

"He's standing near the fireplace."

"If he separates from our party, we shall know he has planned a meeting."

And sure enough, a short while later, Monsieur Alphonse exited the taproom after informing Lady Fenmore, who stood nearby, that he would make his own way back to Fenmore Park.

When Georgiana resumed her seat in Stephen's curricle a short while later, Giles climbed into his vehicle alone, which gave her a small grain of comfort.

On the way back to Fenmore Park, they stopped at Wilder's Folly, situated on Nunhide Hill. Georgiana and Stephen walked briskly up the hill to the tower with its castellated top. She puffed a little as they approached the brick structure, with its open arcade on the ground level and Gothic-arched windows on the two floors above.

They climbed up the external timber staircase and entered a painted room on the first floor with glazed ogive windows. After briefly exploring the circular chamber, Georgiana left Stephen and made her way to the flat roof at the top, which provided splendid views of the surrounding countryside.

Giles was already on the viewing platform with Miss Hamilton and the Balfour sisters. After glancing in their direction,

Georgiana moved a short distance away and was grateful when Lady Fenmore joined her a few minutes later. "This folly has a most romantic history," she said with a smile as she leant on the castellated edge. "It was built in 1769 by Henry Wilder of Sulham House during his courtship of Joan Thoyt, who lived nearby at Sulhamstead House. He built it so it could be seen from both their homes."

Georgiana smiled. "What a wonderful symbol of his love."

"It is indeed," Miss Hamilton said as she approached them on Giles's arm. "Gentlemen can be so romantic when they are in love, do you not think so, Sir Giles?" She cast an innocent look up at him.

He bowed his head but did not respond, and a few minutes later, Georgiana murmured an excuse and headed down the stairs. At the bottom, she stood to one side, hoping to see Stephen. The sooner they returned to Fenmore Park, the better.

Giles came down the stairs at that moment and, on an impulse, Georgiana approached him. "Would you care to walk with me a little way? I have something of a particular nature I would like to say to you."

He studied her for a minute and then proffered his arm. Georgiana rested her hand on it, feeling suddenly better. Perhaps he was merely ill at ease due to the very odd position she had placed him in.

They walked a short distance down the hill, and then Georgiana halted and turned to face him. "I know this isn't the best place to have a private conversation, but Rothbury informed me earlier that he told you about the investigation into Monsieur Alphonse."

"Yes. What he had to say was most enlightening." His expression was inscrutable.

"I am relieved to be able to speak to you frankly about it." She drew in a breath. "Although we cannot show our attachment to one another in public yet, I... I want you to know that I love you and should dearly like to become your wife."

His jaw hardened as he studied her upturned face. "I assume this is because your first two opportunities to travel the world have fallen through, Miss Linfield?"

She stared up at him. "What do you mean?"

"Rothbury told me last night that before you discovered Alphonse was a fortune hunter, you seriously considered marrying him as he promised to take you travelling with him."

Georgiana opened her mouth, but before she could respond, he went on: "To make up for your disappointment over Alphonse, Rothbury invited you to join him on *his* next trip. But that journey is also now in doubt due to Lady Rothbury's pregnancy."

"Er...yes." Her throat was suddenly very dry. "But you have misunderstood..."

"Have I?" His lips twisted. "You expect me to believe that your sudden decision to accept my offer of marriage is not a last resort to fulfil your dreams of travelling abroad?"

Georgiana's heart turned over at the hurt in his eyes. "I...I did weigh up all the prospects of matrimony that were available to me this Season. But that was *before* I realised I wished to marry you."

"I see. And I suppose it is mere chance that you agreed to marry me only *after* your first two opportunities to travel slipped away?"

A sense of helplessness gripped her as if she were in a dream, where she was desperate to move, but her limbs remained fixed and immovable. "I know it must look like that, Giles. But...but I only realised my sincere regard for you a couple of days ago when you arrived at Fenmore Park."

"How very convenient for you."

Georgiana bit the inside of her cheek so hard she tasted the metallic tang of blood in her mouth. She was about to attempt a further explanation when Stephen approached them. "Are you ready to return to Fenmore Park, Georgie?"

She hesitated as she met Giles's unflinching gaze, and then she turned around and followed her twin slowly down the hill. When she reached the bottom, she looked over her shoulder. Sir Giles stood motionless where she had left him, his shoulders set in an uncompromising line.

Georgiana was grateful for Stephen's silence on the journey back as she stared unseeingly at the passing scenery. Examining the situation from Giles's point of view, she could see how damning her behaviour must appear. She had made it clear to him from the very beginning that she wasn't looking for a love match but rather a husband who would accommodate her scientific ambitions.

Indeed, that was all she had believed she wanted until Giles had stirred such unexpected—and unwanted—feelings inside her. She had fought her attraction to him for months, keeping doggedly to the path she had laid out for herself, ignoring her deeper emotions in an attempt to maintain some sort of control over her life.

And now, when she had finally acknowledged her love for him, he did not believe it was sincere.

She couldn't blame him. She must appear a cold, heartless sort of person to him. Circumstances and timing did not help, having conspired disastrously to make it seem as if she had agreed to marry Giles only because her other plans for the future had not come to fruition.

One tear slipped out of the corner of her eye and then another and another until they streamed down her cheeks in a torrent. She kept her face averted from Stephen in the hope he would not notice, but after a while, he shoved a handkerchief onto her lap. "Use that," he said gruffly. "And if you need to talk..."

Georgiana sniffled into the linen square she had embroidered for his last birthday. "It...it's too painful to speak about."

"It must be. I haven't seen you cry like this since we were ten, and old Bonny died."

She took a shuddering breath. "She *was* a lovely pony."

"She was indeed," he agreed gently.

Georgiana sniffled into the handkerchief all the way to Fenmore Park. When they arrived, she sent a watery smile in her brother's direction before hurrying inside and up the stairs to her bedchamber, where she gave in to yet another storm of weeping.

Stephen was right. She hadn't cried like this since her beloved first pony had died. The same sense of grief and loss overwhelmed her now. When she had no more tears to cry, she stared up at the bed's canopy with burning eyes, awake in her nightmare of immobility.

# CHAPTER TWENTY-SEVEN

Giles stared grimly at Stephen Linfield's retreating carriage. Georgiana must think him a fool if she thought he truly believed her assertion that she loved him. She had only given thought to marry him once her other plans came to nought—it was as plain as a pikestaff. What stung the most was that she had considered Alphonse in such a light. Giles and the Frenchman were as unlike each other as two men could be. Yet Georgiana had seriously considered accepting the other man's proposal. Knowing that sunk her even lower in his estimation.

Miss Hamilton came to a halt beside him. "Would you be so kind as to give me your arm, Sir Giles? This hill is so steep I am scared I'll take a tumble."

He offered her his arm immediately and listened with half an ear to her lively conversation as they made their way down the incline. She had come in Lady Fenmore's coach, and now, as they walked past it, she sighed. "How I wish I could travel home in the open air. My cousin's coach is rather stuffy."

"Would you like to drive back to Fenmore Park in my curricle?"

"Oh, yes, Sir Giles! That would be delightful. I shall ask John-coachman to tell Diana."

She hurried over to the driver and spoke to him briefly before returning to Sir Giles's side. He helped her up into his vehicle, listening politely as she expounded at some length about her plans for the summer. "I plan to travel to Brighton to visit my aunt in a few weeks. My cousin mentioned you have a house there, Sir Giles?"

"I do."

"How wonderful." She dimpled up at him. "I do like the seaside air."

"You seem to have a penchant for fresh air, Miss Hamilton."

She studied him rather doubtfully. "I do?"

"You have just informed me that you like travelling in the open air."

"Oh, yes, yes, of course. It is utterly delightful. And very good for one's health, my aunt tells me."

Giles just prevented himself from sighing. *Ingénues* did not appeal to him in the least.

Back at Fenmore Park, he helped Miss Hamilton down from the curricle before driving around to the stables. He handed the reins over to his groom and frowned as he prepared to descend from the driver's seat.

What believable excuse would free him of this house party with the least amount of insult to his host and hostess? He had to get away.

～

The next few days passed in a blur for Georgiana. She went through the motions of behaving like a well-mannered houseguest, but it took some effort to maintain the polite façade. Sir Giles kept well out of her way most of the time while Monsieur Alphonse paid determined court to her. And although she attempted time and again to bring the conversation around to the Frenchman's political persuasions, he avoided any mention of them.

Cassy was unwell every morning, and it soon became apparent that she must be with child. As her sister-in-law was meant to act as her chaperon, Georgiana used her indisposition as an excuse to remain upstairs for a good part of every morning.

"Dearest, I don't wish for you to be restrained by my sickness," Cassy said eventually. "Why don't you seek out the company of the other ladies?"

Georgiana gave a slight shrug. "Because I don't want to?"

"And why is that?"

"The Balfour sisters and Miss Hamilton are as thick as thieves. I feel a little as if I am intruding when in their company. And when she isn't playing lawn games, Miss Aldwell spends most of her time working on her embroidery in the drawing room." She pulled a face.

"Perhaps you should practise the pianoforte then, Georgie? You may well be called upon to play one evening."

She let out a long sigh. "I suppose so."

So, after requesting Lady Fenmore's permission, Georgiana retreated to the Music Room every morning, where she played her instrument of choice. And somehow, making beautiful music soothed her troubled soul, calming her in a way that nothing else seemed to.

She was playing her favourite Beethoven symphony one morning when the door opened, and Sir Giles walked into the room. She hit a false note and stood up immediately, searching his face for any hint of softening.

"Miss Linfield," he said formally. "As I was coming this way, Lady Rothbury asked me to request your presence in her bed-chamber."

His face was set in rigid lines, and she let out a breath of dis-appointment. Nothing had changed. "Thank you, Sir Giles," she said as she resumed her seat.

He gave a brief nod and disappeared out of the doorway, and after a minute, Georgiana rose once more and left the room. Her heart ached. How could they have come to such a pass? The easy understanding that had existed between them had evaporated, and Sir Giles looked at her now as if she were a stranger. A stranger he did not trust.

She knocked on Cassy's door, and when her sister-in-law bid her enter, Georgiana slipped into her bedchamber. She looked a great deal better now than she had earlier in the day. "Are you feeling more the thing, Cassy? Sir Giles gave me your message."

"I saw him in the hall on my way back from taking the air." She studied Georgiana with concern. "Is anything the matter, dearest? I received the impression that Sir Giles did not wish to deliver my message to you even though Rothbury told me a few days ago that you are all but betrothed."

Georgiana turned away. "Matters are somewhat complicated.

Has Rothbury told you the whole?"

"Merely that you need to wait until the end of the house party to announce your betrothal as Lord Fenmore wants you to make some important inquiries of Monsieur Alphonse."

Georgiana met her sister-in-law's gaze. "Indeed. Rothbury asked me not to say anything to anyone, not even Stephen, so when Sir Giles proposed the day we arrived, I wasn't at liberty to accept his proposal. I asked Rothbury to speak to him, which he did, but when I told Sir Giles I wanted to marry him when we were at the Folly, he was furious with me as he believes I only accepted him as I wish to travel the world and can no longer do so due to your pregnancy."

"Oh, no, Georgie!"

Georgiana clenched her fingers together. "Rothbury also told Sir Giles that I considered marrying Monsieur Alphonse before I discovered he was a fortune hunter. And, I confess, I did contemplate marrying him for a brief while as he hinted he would take me abroad, but I never felt comfortable with the idea."

Cassy shook her head. "That husband of mine. He has never been a master of subtlety, and during courtship, subtlety is very often needed. My sincere apologies, Georgie." A crease appeared between her brows. "I know Fenmore and Edward are working closely with the Government and that they are not free to speak about their work. So I didn't press Edward for any details when he told me you were involved in the inquiry into Monsieur Alphonse. If it is causing you so much trouble, though, surely you can be released from your promise to assist them? Then you can try to clear up this misunderstanding."

Georgiana grimaced. "Unfortunately, it is also a matter of trust. Sir Giles interpreted the facts he was given negatively instead of giving me the benefit of the doubt. If he can be so easily swayed in his thinking, then maybe he doesn't truly love me."

Cassy studied her sympathetically. "Hopefully, he will come around. Emotions can run high during courtship when you are still getting to know one another. And Edward told me a while ago that Sir Giles and Monsieur Alphonse have been at odds since their school days. It must have stung that you considered Monsieur Alphonse as a suitor. Perhaps Sir Giles's pride is hurt."

"Perhaps."

Cassy pressed her arm. "Things have a way of working out, dearest, so don't repine. I hate to see you in the suds like this." Her expression brightened. "Let us speak of something more pleasant. Did you bring a new gown along for the Summer Ball?"

"Mama ordered one for me from Madame Bouchet."

"I am sure you will look delightful in it. Sir Giles will probably take one look at you and forget everything that has passed."

Georgiana sent up a prayer that her sister-in-law would be right. But she did not feel particularly optimistic as she dressed for the ball later that week, even though her gown of transparent white gauze, bordered by white satin and chenille and worn over a white satin slip, was a truly striking creation.

Kirby set a headdress of a high wreath of fancy flowers in her hair before arranging a few loose ringlets at the side of her face. Georgiana then fastened the emerald pendant her parents had given her as an early eighteenth birthday present around her neck before dabbing on her favourite orange-blossom scent and leaving her bedchamber.

She made her way to the ballroom on the second floor. The houseguests had dined early, but Sir Giles had been nowhere in sight, and she wondered if he would even put in an appearance this evening. He had made himself very scarce over the last few days.

Lord and Lady Fenmore stood on the second-floor landing near the entrance to the ballroom, welcoming their guests who had started to arrive in a steady stream. Georgiana proceeded through the double doors into a mirrored room decorated with gilt ornament in the French style of Louis XV. A huge cut-glass chandelier, two-tier lustres on the mantelpiece, and branches of candles on tripods in the corners of the room lit up the ample space, and Georgiana glanced around in amazement. How pretty!

Beautiful floral chalk patterns adorned the floor, and a splendid arrangement of flowers and greenery spilled from the fireplace that dominated the far end of the room.

Cassy and Rothbury came up to her then, and she conversed with them until the room filled up, and the musicians, established on a raised dais at the end of the room, began to play. Monsieur Alphonse approached Georgiana to ask her for the first dance. However, before he led her away, Rothbury said coolly, "I believe you dined recently with an acquaintance at The George, Alphonse. Do they provide good fare?"

Monsieur Alphonse froze for an infinitesimal second before saying, "The Whitebait Suppers at The George are excellent. I frequently dine there."

Rothbury's brows rose. "I meant The George in Reading, not The George in Blackwall." His voice was gentle.

Monsieur Alphonse's lips tightened. "*Mais oui.* I misunderstood. The food and wine are indeed excellent."

He smiled rather thinly at Rothbury before leading Georgiana away. His expression seemed somewhat preoccupied, but the faint line between his brows disappeared as he bowed in response to her curtsey, and the dance got under way.

He spoke in his usual lively fashion as they moved down the line, but his manner appeared a little more forced than usual. Perhaps he was berating himself for his blunder. Although many gentlemen attended the Whitehall Suppers in Blackwall, it was doubtful Monsieur Alphonse would want anyone to know he frequented the area if he was building an illicit sailing vessel there.

Georgiana was never without a partner for the duration of the ball, but Sir Giles, who arrived late, did not come near her. And, to make his snub even worse, he stood up with all the other single ladies of the house party.

When he danced with Miss Hamilton a second time, a core of misery froze in Georgiana's chest. Miss Hamilton smiled radiantly up at him as they waltzed by, and he appeared to be charmed by her presence. Perhaps the air of fragility the other lady exuded made him feel heroic.

From what Georgiana had observed, gentlemen liked to feel that they were the champions of their ladies. Although Miss Hamilton disliked insects, Sir Giles would not, in all probability, hold this against her. On the contrary, it might even work in her favour to win his affection. Her sister Harriet, after all, was terrified of the creatures, and she had married Lord Wentford, a renowned entomologist.

Oliver had not been in the least put off by Harriet's fear. Instead, it had aroused his protective instincts, and he had become more and more enamoured of her.

Perhaps Sir Giles was starting to feel the same way about Miss

Hamilton.

Georgiana swallowed the knot in her throat. Whatever the truth of the matter, one thing was clear: Sir Giles had written her off.

# CHAPTER TWENTY-EIGHT

Despite Giles's outwardly attentive air, he hardly heard a word Miss Hamilton said as she chattered away. He cursed the day he agreed to attend this house party. And he couldn't simply depart with a flimsy excuse as Lady Fenmore had invited exactly five single ladies and five single gentlemen. He would upset her numbers if he left early.

That he had not wanted to ask Miss Hamilton to waltz increased his irritation. The young woman had come up to Lady Fenmore, with whom he was conversing, just before the first strains of the dance sounded, and his cousin's wife had looked at them expectantly and said with a laugh: "Somehow it seems wrong, Sir Giles, that you are standing here talking to me."

He had felt compelled to ask Miss Hamilton to dance with him a second time, and now, as they circled the room together, he wished her at Jericho. She had a habit of speaking at great length about absolutely nothing, and he had never enjoyed this kind of inconsequential conversation.

"We went on a shopping expedition to Reading this morning, and I must say that the shops in London are far superior. Miss Balfour couldn't find the correct shade of pink ribbon to trim her gown, and she was vastly disappointed." She cast him a coy glance. "I do believe everyone from Fenmore Park was in Reading this morning except you, sir. We met up with the Aldwells and the Murchisons and walked past Monsieur Alphonse, but he did not see us. He was speaking to a foreign-looking gentleman Miss

Balfour recognised from a rout she attended in London. A Colonel Macaroon or something of the sort."

"Perhaps it was Colonel Maceroni?" Giles asked.

"That must be it. I did think it rather odd that he had the name of a cake."

They waltzed past Georgiana, who was dancing with Hanssen, and Giles's jaw tightened. His friend had approached him the day before to ask if he could pay more particular attention to Georgiana. "I don't wish to poach on your preserves, old chap," he'd said. "But I have noticed you haven't been much in Miss Linfield's company these past few days."

Giles had informed Hanssen that he was no longer pursuing her, and it made no difference to him. But seeing them together tonight, he realised, rather grimly, that it made a definite difference.

Georgiana looked exquisite in her shimmering white ball gown; time and again, he found his gaze drawn back to her. Although determined to avoid the matrimonial net into which he had so nearly fallen, it dawned on him now that he might be irrevocably committed. Georgiana could claim with complete justification that they were a betrothed couple as Giles had proposed to her, and she had accepted his offer. Never mind the fact that he had undergone a complete change of heart since his proposal.

*Or had he?*

He gave a faint sigh. Something about Georgiana Linfield made him behave in a regrettably contrary manner. No doubt it had something to do with the fact that she shared his interests. Meeting a woman so knowledgeable in his field, to whom he could speak with such ease, had been a novelty. But that should not have made him lose his head as he had.

Perhaps it all came down to the fact that she was so damned lovely. Giles could not put her out of his mind, no matter how hard he tried to convince himself he was better off without her.

When he left the ballroom a short while later, Georgiana stood on the landing outside. She inclined her head stiffly, her eyes enormous in her white face as she stared up at him. Her lips parted as if she were about to speak, but then she clamped them together and moved away with a regal nod.

Giles followed her down the corridor, frowning deeply. By not asking her to dance with him this evening, he had snubbed her in front of the other single ladies of this confounded house party. That breach in good manners would not go unnoticed, especially as he had paid such particular attention to Georgiana in London.

But he could not have borne the utter torture of holding her in his arms tonight. He found it difficult enough to observe her from a polite distance every day. He raked his fingers through his hair. No matter that he desperately needed to get away and clear his mind…he couldn't leave for a few days yet.

A damnable situation, indeed!

To his profound relief, however, Giles's wish to leave the house party was granted the very next day. He received an urgent communication from London stating that his house had been burgled. After expressing his regrets to Lady Fenmore and promising he would return, if at all possible, he headed back to Town in his curricle, leaving his valet and most of his baggage behind.

When he arrived in Upper Grosvenor Street, Sydney met him in the hall, his brow creased in concern. "I locked up just as I always do, Sir Giles. However, when I entered the book-room this morning, I found it in complete disarray. Nothing has been touched, as I believed you would want to see the state in which I discovered the room."

Giles's eyes narrowed as he stepped inside and looked around. Nearly all his leather store-boxes had been taken down from the shelves and placed on a mahogany table in the centre of the room. They were all open. Yet, after a careful examination, he ascertained that none of his butterflies had been taken.

He stared into space and then did a careful re-examination of each box. They appeared untouched, but when he came to his collection of South American butterflies, he noticed that the cork-lined setting board on which the specimens were pinned was not entirely straight. Someone had dislodged it. But why? He carefully removed the board and studied the empty cavity behind it before setting it back in place.

If his South American butterfly collection had been taken, he would have immediately suspected Captain Tom Johnson. Before he started working for the Admiralty, Johnson had been a notorious smuggler. Giles felt certain the man would have no qualms about resorting to criminal methods to acquire something he wanted.

Of course, the captain could have been interrupted during the theft. He might have heard a noise and fled before he succeeded in removing the butterflies from the store-box. But why not just take the box with him, then?

Giles frowned. The best thing he could do was take his store-boxes somewhere safe while he completed his investigation. None of the windows had been broken, so the burglar must have bribed one of his servants to gain access to the house. He'd be foolish to leave his collections here in case the thief returned.

With Sydney's help, he packed his store-boxes into his coach and drove around to his godfather's home. The older man was reading in his library, and upon hearing Giles's news, he immediately consented to the boxes being brought inside. When they had been neatly stacked in the corner of the library, he waved at a leather armchair. "Sit down, dear boy. Do you suppose that Johnson chap is behind this?"

"He may well be." Giles took his seat. "The only box which looked as if it had been tampered with was my South American butterfly collection. And both Johnson and Alphonse expressed an interest in buying it."

"You don't suspect Alphonse?"

"He is staying at Fenmore Park at the moment, so it cannot be him." Giles tapped his fingers on the arm of his chair. "When the Flies were on display at the Linnean Society, they disappeared for a short while. The Librarian found them on a chair at the back of the room and returned them to the display table. Johnson admitted when he called that he had seen the specimens at the Society and that the Librarian had taken him to task for handling them. Perhaps he attempted to remove them that evening."

His godfather's forehead wrinkled. "But surely he wouldn't have admitted this to you if he planned to steal them?"

Giles's lips twisted. "Johnson? He's a brazen fellow if ever there was one. Telling me such a thing straight to my face would probably amuse him." He paused for a moment. "I shall go to the Society's House and make some inquiries. Perhaps the Librarian will remember something about that evening which can throw some light on things."

"An excellent idea. It is concerning that someone would go to so much trouble to steal your collection."

"Indeed. I won't rest easy until I find the culprit."

His godfather leaned back in his chair. "Were you sorry to leave Fenmore Park?"

"Not in the least. I dislike gatherings of that nature."

"Even though Georgiana is there?"

"I am not sure of your meaning, sir." Giles spoke stiffly.

"I have eyes in my head, boy. That you are enamoured of my young cousin is plain as a pikestaff." He chuckled. "I am glad I was proved wrong. I told Georgiana many months ago that you were far too restless to settle down."

"It seems that Miss Linfield and I share the same failings. Her father told me the same thing about her the other day."

His godfather smiled. "Then you are excellently suited to a life of travel together."

"Unfortunately, Miss Linfield values travelling above all else. I don't think it matters to her who takes her."

"You truly believe that?"

"She has made it clear that her scientific ambitions are of primary importance to her."

The older man raised his brows. "And have yours not been of primary importance to you all these years? You, however, have had the opportunity to fulfil them while Georgiana has had to cope with the restrictions of having been born a female. I don't see why you should hold her to a different standard than you hold yourself."

Giles rose to his feet. "Georgiana considered marrying Alphonse because he promised to take her abroad with him."

"Ah. There's the rub." His godfather's smile was wry. "But...correct me if I'm wrong, of course...I thought the entire purpose of a Season was for a young lady to weigh the positive and negative characteristics of each gentleman who pays court to her before deciding who to marry."

When Giles made no reply, he continued: "I told Georgiana I had changed my Will in her favour so she would have the means to go abroad one day, even if she decided to remain a spinster. I am sure Stephen would be willing to escort her on their travels when they are older. An eccentric arrangement, perhaps, but as she would be travelling with her brother, it would be deemed acceptable." He shrugged. "Georgiana does not need to marry to fulfil her dreams, Giles."

His godfather's words stunned him. He had been mortified when he learned from Rothbury that Georgiana had considered Alphonse's suit as a possible way in which to fulfil her desire to travel abroad. Such an arrangement seemed to make a mockery of the love Giles felt for her. Stung, he had instantly swung back to his earlier opinion of her as a cold, calculating woman without a conscience.

But his godfather's neutral assessment showed the truth of the matter. Georgiana was merely trying to find her way in the world, and she had the right, as did he, to assess the choices open to her before deciding on the kind of life she wanted to live.

He had not given her that right. Instead, he'd placed her into society's restrictive cage. Georgiana's uniqueness was the major reason he'd fallen in love with her. But that same uniqueness had caught him off guard, challenging the way he had been brought up to see a woman's place in the world—as inherently secondary to his.

Georgiana was no milk-and-water Miss, content to allow others to direct the course of her existence. On the contrary, she wanted to participate fully in life on her own terms. She also valued honesty, which was why she had not denied her consideration of Alphonse as a suitor or that she planned to travel abroad with the Rothburys before Lady Rothbury fell pregnant.

She had given him the truth with no bark on it, not softening the facts, and he had found it difficult to accept, particularly as he had always been so courted and flattered by other young ladies. He groaned silently. Why, he had turned into a conceited oaf! Perhaps only Georgiana, with her *joie de vivre* and complete lack of dissimulation, could have pierced the arrogant mantle he had assumed.

Giles set his mouth in a straight line. He had his work cut out to win her back, especially after he had ignored her so pointedly at the Summer Ball. But he was accustomed to going to the ends of the world to achieve his dreams. That's what he did.

# CHAPTER TWENTY-NINE

Giles took his leave of his godfather and drove to the House of the Linnean Society, where he asked to speak to the Secretary about the attendance of Captain Tom Johnson at the meeting earlier in the year.

"Let me find the register-book," the Secretary murmured. He left the room and returned with the Clerk. "As you know, any member of the Society has the right to bring a stranger to every general meeting of the Society," the Secretary stated. "The name of the stranger is entered into the register-book as well as the minute-book, along with the name of the member who introduced him."

He paged through the register-book until he found the entry he sought. "Captain Johnson was the guest of Mr Pierre Alphonse that evening, Sir Giles, and Mr Alphonse was therefore responsible for the Captain's conduct during the meeting. I must say, I was disappointed that Mr Alphonse did not inform his guest that touching the exhibits is not allowed."

"Indeed," Giles said quietly.

He thanked the Secretary before taking his leave and climbing into his curricle. However, as he set his horses in motion, he frowned. He had seen Captain Johnson the night his paper had been read aloud, but he had not spoken to him. And he had certainly not known that Johnson had come as the guest of Pierre Alphonse. The two men did not move in the same circles. How did they even know each other?

What was even stranger was that they had approached him separately to buy his South American butterfly collection. His eyes narrowed. What kind of connection could Alphonse have to Johnson? The captain had a reputation for being a charming turncoat, having filled the roles of both smuggler and revenue man over the years. During the war years, he had been employed by the Admiralty to develop weapons, but it was well-known that he had worked for the French government as well at one time.

Giles frowned. Was it possible that Johnson, with his naval background and his expert seamanship skills, was the unknown man Alphonse had gone to meet at Blackwall Yard? Rescuing Napoleon from St Helena was just the sort of scheme to appeal to an adventurer like him. The captain's sudden interest in entomology, however, seemed distinctly out of character.

He drove his curricle around to the mews and left his team with his groom before entering his house. His frown deepened as he strode up the stairs. When he travelled to the Americas, he encountered many followers of Bonaparte, as the former Emperor supported the continent's bid to gain independence from Spain and Portugal.

Giles had met a group of French officers during his travels, and they had been vocal about their wish to see the Little Corporal, as they affectionately called him, rescued from the island.

Aware of the officers' hostility towards the English, Giles had spoken to them at first in his native tongue. Only later in the evening, after the brandy had flowed freely for quite some time, had he revealed that he lived in England.

Their initial antagonism at the news had quickly dissipated after they asked him if he was acquainted with their friend, Pierre Alphonse. When he told them he had been at school with Alphonse, they became excessively friendly. The Frenchmen had plied him with even more brandy and expressed such an interest in his work as an entomologist that he had shown them his butterfly collection. He drew to a sudden halt on the landing and groaned. *He had shown them his collection.*

Everything made sense now. Sometime during the evening, they must have placed some sort of communication for Alphonse in the cavity behind the setting board. That was why Alphonse and Johnson had both approached him. They weren't interested in the Flies. They wanted what those officers had concealed in that store-box. What they did not know, however, was that Giles had created a duplicate collection of specimens and that the butterflies he had shown the soldiers that night had been from his second collection. The collection he had given Georgiana.

He released a harsh breath. Georgiana had told him the day he arrived at Fenmore Park that she was taking the butterflies on to Linfield Court, where she planned to display them in her father's museum. If she mentioned that to Alphonse...

He strode to the bell and pulled it. When a footman came upstairs, he instructed him to send word to the stables to bring his curricle around immediately as he would be returning to Fenmore Park.

After retrieving his case of duelling swords, Giles left the house and climbed into the driving-seat, staring grimly ahead. What if he was too late?

⁓

Georgiana breakfasted in bed the next morning and only learned of Giles's departure when she bumped into Rothbury in the hall.

"Another burglary?" She crinkled her nose. "It seems to be a common occurrence in our part of London. Did Mama tell you about our burglary at Linfield House?"

"She did. Although she said only your room was disturbed."

"Yes. Nothing was taken, fortunately. The new footman disappeared that same night, so in all likelihood, he was the culprit." She peered up at him. "Do you know if Sir Giles intends to return?"

"I'm afraid I don't. He left very early this morning before I could speak to him."

Georgiana pasted a smile on her face. "How is Cassy feeling today?"

"A little fatigued. She had hoped to walk in the grounds with Mrs Murchison this afternoon, but she may not be up to it. Perhaps you could go in Cassy's stead?"

"Yes, of course. I should like that. Thank you."

After luncheon, Georgiana met Mrs Murchison in the garden. She'd dressed in her most hardy gown and shoes as she knew the older lady was a strong walker and would probably wish to go quite far. They were crossing the well-kept lawns to the ha-ha when Monsieur Alphonse approached them from the opposite direction.

"*Madame, mademoiselle...*" He glanced at Georgiana's sensibly shod feet. "You are going out for a walk?"

"Indeed," Mrs Murchison said amiably. "We plan to go beyond the river and climb to the top of the hill to take in the view."

He fell into step beside them. "If I may accompany you, *mesdames?*"

"Yes, of course," Mrs Murchison said. "I must warn you, however, that we like to walk briskly."

He inclined his head. "Such energetic ladies as you are." They came to the gate that separated the garden from the bridge, and he gallantly opened it for them. "You are planning on looking for butterflies today, Mademoiselle Linfield?"

Georgiana smiled. "I am always looking for butterflies. But I don't have my net with me today."

After crossing the bridge, they veered off to the left, over the fields. When Mrs Murchison stopped to observe a particularly beautiful cornflower, Monsieur Alphonse spoke again: "Did Sir Giles inform you that your scientific illustrations were praised at the Linnean Society, *mademoiselle?*"

"He did. I am delighted that my first serious attempt at scientific illustration was so well-received."

"One would not guess that it was your first attempt. The drawings are of exceptional quality."

"Thank you, *monsieur*."

"You kept those specimens with you for quite some time, did you not?"

"Indeed. I did not wish to rush such painstaking work."

He flicked a spot of fluff off his coat. "Did you, by any chance, remove the butterflies from the store-box to study them more closely?"

Georgiana stared at him. "No, I would never do that. I'd be afraid of damaging them."

"*Bien sûr.*" He met her gaze. "I am merely interested in the artist's methods, *vous savez.*"

"You should rather ask Mrs Murchison about that. She has a great deal more experience as an artist than I do." She shrugged.

"Indeed, I was fortunate Sir Giles had the collection in duplicate. Otherwise, I never would have finished those drawings in time."

He stopped walking. "Sir Giles has two collections of South American butterflies?"

"Why, yes! He used the other collection to write his paper."

"I was not aware of that."

Mrs Murchison came back to them then. "You are speaking about your South American butterflies, Miss Linfield? When I told Mr Murchison about the collection, he asked if he could see it."

"Yes, of course, ma'am. I should be delighted to show it to him."

Monsieur Alphonse stood still. "*Your* butterfly collection, Miss Linfield?"

Georgiana felt the heat rising in her cheeks. "Sir Giles gave me his second collection."

"*Vraiment?*"

"To...to...thank me for doing the illustrations for him."

Mrs Murchison chuckled. "A most charming and romantical gesture, if I may say so, my dear."

Georgiana smiled rather awkwardly before hastily changing the subject. They walked to the top of the hill and spent some time looking out at the beautiful prospect of Fenmore Park, with its woods, lake, and surrounding fields dotted with sheep. Eventually, they found the path once more and began walking downhill.

Monsieur Alphonse dominated the conversation on their return. Georgiana and Mrs Murchison walked in silence, interspersing the odd remark here and there. When the Frenchman eventually took his leave of them, Mrs Murchison turned to Georgiana with a wry smile. "Not quite the outing I was planning, my dear."

"Perhaps we could meet again tomorrow," Georgiana said. "You have such an extensive knowledge of plants that I would dearly like to go on another ramble with you. I know a lot more about animals than plants, I'm afraid."

"That would be delightful, Miss Linfield, particularly as Lady Rothbury is indisposed at the moment. My mother is a talented florist and botanist and taught me everything I know. I never fail to take advantage of an opportunity to explore somewhere new. But I am afraid my enthusiasm for walking is not shared by everyone in this party."

"Perhaps it helps that I have sensible shoes. I don't think the other ladies brought theirs."

"I doubt they possess anything so practical."

"Or unfashionable." Georgiana laughed. "But I never put fashion before fauna and flora."

Mrs Murchison's eyes twinkled. "What self-respecting lady biologist ever would?"

They entered the house then, and Georgiana made her way slowly up the stairs to her room. Sinking onto the bed, she stared absently into space. The walk had distracted her from her troubles, but now her thoughts returned inexorably to Giles and his sudden departure.

While he was at Fenmore Park, they might still have found their way back to each other. But now, the real possibility existed that he would not return. Instead, he might decide to go abroad once more, and she would never see him again. Her heart squeezed at the dreadful thought, the very air in her lungs cutting off as she struggled to draw in a breath.

Before she had fallen in love with Giles, she hadn't understood how Marianne Dashwood had almost died of a broken heart. She believed Jane Austen had exaggerated that part of the story. But now…now she fully grasped how grief and unhappiness could affect a person's physical well-being to the point of them fading forlornly away.

Although she had walked to the top of a hill and back again today, it had taken more effort than she would ordinarily expend on such an excursion. Her usual vitality was sorely lacking, almost certainly due to her low spirits.

That Georgiana was always full of boundless, untiring energy had become a standing family joke. But now, for the first time in her life, she knew how it felt to be tired.

So terribly, terribly tired.

# Chapter Thirty

Georgiana entered the Salon before dinner that evening and looked around at the assembled gathering. Finally, she approached the Murchisons, who stood near the window.

"We were just speaking about your butterfly collection, Miss Linfield," Mrs Murchison said with a smile. "Would it be possible for you to bring it to the drawing room later to show it to Mr Murchison?"

"Yes, of course, ma'am. But let me fetch it for you now. I am not feeling quite the thing and wish to retire to my bedchamber directly after we have dined."

"I am sorry to hear that." The older woman's forehead creased with concern. "You *are* looking a little pale. Perhaps we walked too far today?"

She shook her head. "I haven't been sleeping very well. I am sure an early night will set me to rights."

"I do hope so, my dear."

Georgiana left the Salon and walked back up the stairs. When she reached her bedchamber, she found the door slightly ajar. Frowning, she pushed it open and stepped inside. Kirby must not have closed it properly.

She stilled, alarm skittering through her like a stone thrown fitfully across the surface of a pond. Monsieur Alphonse stood at the table near the window. He had opened her store-box, which she had left there, and was in the process of removing the setting-board.

She advanced a few steps into the room. "What do you think you're doing?"

He froze, but after a moment, he turned around. "I am merely having a closer look at your Flies, *mademoiselle*."

"In my bedchamber?" Her eyes narrowed. "I am not such a fool as to believe that."

"You weren't meant to come upstairs until much later." His voice held no inflexion. "*C'est dommage.*"

He came rapidly towards her, and Georgiana, seeing the flinty expression in his eyes, opened her mouth to scream.

~

Giles made the journey in under three hours, arriving at Fenmore Park just before dinner. After making discreet inquiries of the butler, he ascertained that Georgiana had already come downstairs and was in the Salon.

Relieved that she was safe from Alphonse, at least for the moment, he made his way up to his bedchamber. Perhaps he had been a fool to feel such a sense of urgency to return, but Alphonse could be dangerous when crossed. Now that Giles was back, he would warn Georgiana not to mention her butterfly collection to the Frenchman. And, at the first available opportunity, he would investigate what lay hidden beneath that setting board.

He rang for his valet, who assisted him into his evening clothes with record speed. As he left, Giles said with a smile, "Thank you, Pennyworth. I know how much that must have pained you."

His valet sniffed. "More than you know, Sir Giles, more than you know."

Giles chuckled as he made his way down the stairs. He greeted the Fenmores, who stood near the door of the Salon, and then looked around for Georgiana. She was nowhere to be seen, and after thoroughly inspecting the room, Giles noticed Alphonse was also missing from the gathering. The hairs on the back of his neck began to prickle as he walked across to Lady Rothbury, who was in conversation with the Murchisons.

After a few pleasantries, he said quietly: "I am looking for Miss Linfield. Have you seen her?"

Mrs Murchison nodded. "Why, yes, Sir Giles. Miss Linfield was just here, but she left to fetch her butterfly collection. Mr

Murchison is desirous of seeing it."

A pulse throbbed in Giles's temple, but he did not betray his disquiet. Instead, with an apologetic smile in the Murchisons' direction, he murmured, "A word, if I may, Lady Rothbury?"

He moved a short distance away as Lady Rothbury said in an urgent undertone: "Is anything the matter, Sir Giles?"

"I am concerned Georgiana may be in imminent danger. Could you come with me to her bedchamber?"

"Yes, of course."

They left the drawing room immediately, with Lady Rothbury leading the way up the stairs. She knocked softly on Georgiana's bedchamber door and entered the room, leaving Giles waiting impatiently in the passage. Upon hearing a muffled shriek, he rushed inside, cursing himself for not insisting he enter the room first, propriety be damned.

Alphonse held Georgiana's wrists in one hand while his other arm was wrapped around her waist. Her cheeks were ghostly white as she glanced wildly in their direction.

"What's going on?" Giles said softly.

Alphonse smirked. "I fear you have discovered our secret, Tavistock. We are in love, you understand. And sometimes..." He lifted his shoulders. "Passion can overwhelm us mere mortals, *vous savez*."

Georgiana gasped and jerked free of him. "That is a complete and utter lie, Monsieur Alphonse. How dare you say that?"

"Because it is the truth, *mademoiselle*. But you will, of course, deny it in order to preserve your reputation."

"I deny it because it is a complete falsehood! You do believe me, don't you, Giles?" Her gaze was beseeching. "I found him in my bedchamber when I came upstairs to fetch my butterfly collection."

Giles covered the short distance between them, taking her shaking hands in his. "Of course I believe you, *ma chère*." Then, turning to Alphonse, his tone hardened: "Do you choose swords or pistols? You have attempted to besmirch Miss Linfield's good name, and as her future husband, I demand satisfaction."

Alphonse stilled for a minute and then bowed. "Why, swords, of course." He turned to Georgiana and said with a mocking little smile: "How well you conceal your affections, *mademoiselle*. I thought..." His lips twisted into a sneer. "But it appears you have been playing your own game, *n'est-ce pas*?" He turned back to Giles. "My duelling swords are in my abode in London."

"It is no matter. I have mine with me, if you would care to inspect them?" He walked to the door and held it open. "Lady Rothbury...if you and Miss Linfield would please leave."

Georgiana ran up to him. "Can't you settle this in some other way, Giles? You may be injured or...or worse..." Her voice dropped to a whisper. "Please don't fight him." Her eyes welled up, a single tear rolling down her cheek.

He wiped it away gently. "There is no other way, *mon amour*."

She let out a shaking breath, and then Lady Rothbury took her arm and led her away.

When the door shut behind them, Giles turned back to Alphonse. "I propose we repair to the fencing room and settle this between us here and now. I don't want a hint of scandal attaching itself to my future wife's name."

"It is unconventional not to have seconds. But I prefer discretion as well." He bowed ironically. "I believe this is the first time we have ever agreed upon anything, *mon vieux*."

The fencing room was on the same floor as Giles's bedchamber, and after he had retrieved his duelling swords from the wardrobe, he walked in silence beside Alphonse to the end of the corridor.

Late evening light poured in through the skylights and windows when they entered the spacious apartment, ensuring excellent visibility for their upcoming encounter. While Alphonse inspected the weapons, Giles stripped off his coat and waistcoat and removed his shoes to stand in his stockinged feet.

"They appear evenly matched." Alphonse placed the swords on a table in the corner of the room before stripping down himself. Then he took the weapons across to Giles and bowed, handing him a sword. "At your service, Tavistock."

"*En garde*!" Giles gave him the briefest of salutes, and then steel met steel as their blades scraped together. They circled one another at first, and then Alphonse gave an unexpected advance-lunge. Giles counter-attacked, and the Frenchman continued on the offensive with a counter-riposte.

Alphonse, though much shorter than Giles, was far more agile.

So light was he on his feet that he almost danced around his opponent. Giles was more efficient in the use of his strength, parrying the frequent attacks of his opponent with an unwavering resolve.

The fierce battle wore on and on, and Giles started breathing heavily, sweat beading on his forehead. The Frenchman attempted a feint, but Giles saw through the move and did not make the mistake of parrying.

Instead, he attempted his own feint immediately afterwards, and Alphonse fell into the trap. Seizing the opportunity, Giles's sword flashed below the other man's blade, and hard steel met yielding flesh. The Frenchman cried out and dropped his sword as a bloodstain spread slowly over his shirt.

"*Canaille.*" His voice was full of venom as he fell heavily to the floor.

The door burst open, and Georgiana rushed inside, clutching some cloths and a pair of scissors to her breast. "Giles!" Her gaze flew to Alphonse. "I heard a thump. I thought..."

Lady Rothbury followed her inside, her face pale. "Georgiana refused to stay away. Lady Fenmore took her on a tour of the house the other day, so she knew where to come." Her face paled even more when she set eyes on Alphonse. "Is he dead?" she whispered.

Giles placed his sword on the table. "No, he is merely in a faint." He studied the other man. "It isn't a deep cut, but the wound is bleeding profusely."

"Here." Georgiana gave him the items she held. "I thought these might be needed."

"Ministering angel." He gazed down at her before dropping a kiss on her mouth.

Her lips trembled. "May I help you bind up the wound? I am not at all squeamish as I used to tend to Stephen's cuts and scrapes when we were children."

"Thank you, *ma chère*, but no. I shall bind up the wound and take Alphonse back to his bedchamber."

"Damn you, Tavistock, you nearly killed me." The prone man came out of his swoon, already talking.

"It is a mere scratch." Giles turned back to Georgiana. "It will be best if you leave us now, as I have to remove his shirt."

"Yes, come, Georgie," Lady Rothbury said. "You must see that you cannot stay. Besides, Lady Fenmore will be wondering what has become of us."

"Please send her my excuses and make up some reason for Alphonse's absence, if you will," Giles said. "And tell Rothbury and Fenmore I shall speak to them later."

Lady Rothbury nodded and, taking Georgiana's arm, led her towards the door. Before they reached it, however, Georgiana broke free from her grasp and raced back to Giles.

Placing her hands on his chest, she reached up and pressed a kiss to his lips. "Please never frighten me like that again. I...I thought it was you who had fallen." She drew in a shaking breath. "It was the worst moment of my life."

He tilted her chin up as she blinked away a suspicious sheen of tears. "You should have more faith in me, my love." His voice was gentle.

"I know." She gave him a tremulous smile before running back to Lady Rothbury, who waited just beyond the door.

After the ladies left, Giles moved across to Alphonse. Ignoring the other man's gasp, he cut away his shirt sleeve with the pair of scissors. When he had swabbed the wound, he bound it tightly before stepping back and studying his workmanship. "That should do."

He helped Alphonse to a chair at the side of the room before walking across to the window. Then, after staring out at the rolling fields that stretched into the distance, he turned and said in a low voice: "Leave the country, Alphonse. That is my advice to you. The Government is investigating your plot to rescue Bonaparte."

The other man stared at him. "*Je ne peux pas le croire.*"

"Believe it." Giles frowned. "They have been watching you and O'Meara for months. You must leave England and never re-turn."

"Why are you warning me of this? Especially after..." He shrugged.

Giles leaned against the window frame, folding his arms. "Should we say for old times' sake?" he said curtly.

Alphonse scrutinised him. "You always kept your cards close to your chest. That was what caused me the most annoyance at school. While I suffered the jibes of the English boys, you appeared imperturbable. Uncaring, even."

"Oh, I cared, Alphonse." He straightened. "I cared."

"You never showed it."

"That would have only made the teasing worse. Showing a re-action was what they wanted from us."

"From 'us'..." His lips twisted. "That is all I ever wanted from *you*. Someone to take my side. But you never did."

Giles gave a faint sigh. "I was a frightened child. And when you drew attention to my French heritage, it made the taunting from the other boys worse."

"So you denied it. You acted a part that wasn't real."

"But it was real," Giles said quietly. "I was brought up an Eng-lishman. I wasn't playing a part. You wouldn't accept that, though."

"No." He sighed. "It was easier to ignore."

"Let me assist you to your room now. Time is of the essence."

"*Merci*." Monsieur Alphonse rose to his feet before saying, once again, as he hesitantly stretched out his hand: "*Merci*, Giles."

Giles grasped it briefly before giving Alphonse his arm to his bedchamber. When the Frenchman went inside, Giles walked to his own room to change. Before the night was up, Alphonse would undoubtedly head back to London, travelling by the light of the full moon. Now that he knew his game was up, he would not want to stay under the same roof as Rothbury and Fenmore.

~

Georgiana asked Cassy to make her excuses to Lady Fenmore as they walked back to her bedchamber. "I think I will just have a tray in my room tonight. I'm rather tired."

Her sister-in-law nodded sympathetically. "Of course, dearest. I shall ask Lady Fenmore to send up some dinner on a tray. Would you like me to stay with you?"

"No, no. I shall be quite all right. Thank you."

After ensuring the door was properly closed, Georgiana walked over to the store-box, which lay open on the table, and peered inside. Monsieur Alphonse had dislodged the setting-board. When Georgiana lifted it out, she found a leather pouch with a drawstring concealed in the cavity below.

She opened it carefully and pulled out two letters. One was

signed by a Captain Tom Johnson and had several annotations written on it, while the other was in French, addressed to Monsieur Alphonse. Georgiana placed the French message to one side and picked up Captain Johnson's letter. As she read it, her eyes widened in utter astonishment:

"I am an engineer and a man of inventive genius, and my expertise, which I now make available to you, will ensure that we influence the destinies of nations.

"On the payment of £40,000, I shall venture to build you two submarine ships propelled by steam engines. These vessels, the *Eagle* and the *Etna*, will sail upon the seas and then sink themselves into their depths to rescue the emperor Napoleon from the fangs of his jailor, Sir Hudson Lowe.

"The ships, equipped with twenty torpedoes, thirty seamen, and four engineers, will be stationed at a convenient distance from the rock at St Helena, abreast of Longwood House. They will lie at anchor at a cable's length from each other, the smaller one lying close to the rock.

"This smaller ship will be provided with a mechanical chair, capable of containing one person on the seat, and a standing footboard, so that the person at the back can regulate the ascent or descent. Attached to this chair will be a patent whale-line, two thousand and fifty feet long.

"The vessels will be submerged during the day, and at night they will approach the surface. I shall go on shore dressed as a coachman and obtain my introduction to His Imperial Majesty, whom I shall provide with a groom's livery similar to my own. Thus disguised, we shall hide in the coach house until an opportune moment when I shall place Napoleon in the mechanical chair and lower him with a corresponding weight on the other side. Then, upon safely reaching the bottom, we shall make sail and steer for the United States."

Georgiana read through the communication again and then glanced at the letter addressed to Monsieur Alphonse, containing further information about the plot. After placing all the pages back in the leather pouch, she hid it at the back of her wardrobe. Although she doubted Monsieur Alphonse would return to her bedchamber tonight, she wasn't going to take any chances.

If only she could see Giles. But he was fully occupied with

tending to the Frenchman, and even if she went downstairs later, it was unlikely she would be able to speak to Giles privately as he first needed to talk to Rothbury and Lord Fenmore.

She would have to wait until tomorrow when they would hopefully be able to slip away together.

# CHAPTER THIRTY-ONE

Georgiana woke the following day, dressed quickly, and removed the leather pouch from its hiding place before going to Cassy's bedchamber. More often than not, Rothbury stayed upstairs and had breakfast with her in the mornings, so it was as good a time as any to hand over the letters to him.

Cassy bid her enter. Rothbury sat in the armchair beside her bed. He rose to his feet as Georgiana entered the room, and she smiled at him before approaching her sister-in-law, who was propped against some bed pillows. "How are you feeling today, Cassy?"

"Better now, thank you." Her cheeks were pale. "Rothbury has taken to requesting tea and toast for me the minute I wake up, as I feel less nauseated after a meal."

Georgiana turned to Rothbury, who had observed them in silence. Now he spoke. "I believe you and Cassy shared some adventures last night."

Her lips curved into a wry smile. "You could put it that way."

"I can't believe this all happened while I was downstairs in the Salon."

"I cannot believe it either." She shook her head. "I never expected two gentlemen to ever fight a duel over me."

"Indeed," he said. "Giles explained the whole to me last night. And while we were in the library, Alphonse left Fenmore Park."

Georgiana blinked. "Even though he is injured?"

"He is aware of the trouble he is in." His gaze rested on the pouch in Georgiana's hand. "Are those the papers Giles mentioned?"

"Yes." She handed the small leather bag to him. "There are two letters—one in English and the other in French."

He opened the pouch and removed the pages. "Well, well," he said as he perused the letters. "So this is what they are building at Blackwall Yard. Dr O'Meara is mentioned by name in the letter to Alphonse, and Maceroni, who met Alphonse in Reading a few days ago, has also been seen at the shipyard." He looked up. "They are all in this plot together."

"At least the Government can put a stop to it now," Georgiana said.

"Indeed. And we wouldn't have managed without your help. Thank you, my dear."

"It is my pleasure. I am delighted to have played even a small part in preventing another war."

Rothbury returned his attention to the letters. "I must say it is a very far-fetched scheme. But Johnson claims to know the American engineer, Robert Fulton, who invented the Nautilus, so perhaps he does know how to build such a vessel."

"The Nautilus?" Georgiana frowned.

"A submersible craft, built in 1800 in France under a grant from Bonaparte."

"Oh." Her brow creased. "It seems a very strange plot, but I understand why the British government is taking it seriously. It would be dreadful if Napoleon also managed to escape from St Helena." She glanced at Cassy, who seemed tired, before looking back at her brother. "I'll leave you now. I just wanted to hand the papers into your safekeeping."

"Thank you, my dear. And congratulations on your engagement. We are delighted that you have decided to marry Giles."

She smiled at him. "I have never been so happy. And now, if you will excuse me, I haven't spoken to my betrothed since last night!"

She closed the door and headed downstairs to the Breakfast Room, where Giles was already seated at the table between Lady Fenmore and Lady Aldwell. He rose from his chair, and the look in his eyes as they met hers was so tender that her heart nearly burst forth from within her.

He resumed his seat, and Georgiana took her place beside Stephen after a murmured greeting to the assembled guests. She crumbled a roll on her plate, but her usual hearty appetite had deserted her, and when Giles pushed back his chair a short while later and walked around the table, she set her napkin down as well and rose to her feet.

"Would you care to stroll in the gardens?" he asked in a low voice.

"Very much so."

She placed her hand on his proffered arm and glanced in a distracted fashion at Stephen, who was making some joking remark to Giles. Then they left the room and crossed into the hall and out the front door. The strange mists shrouding her brain began to dissipate as she breathed in the summer-scented air, filled with the fragrance of flowers and freshly-trimmed grass and budding hope.

So much hope.

They walked in silence across the lawns until they reached the Italian Garden, where Giles led her to the ornamental garden seat beside the fountain. Georgiana was about to sit down when he took her hands in his and pulled her slowly into his arms.

For a moment, as she gazed up at him, the only sounds were of early morning birdsong and bubbling water, and then Giles said in a rough voice, "*Mon coeur*," and his lips met hers in a kiss of such intensity that it burned the remaining mists away.

Georgiana's hands were crushed between their bodies, but after a few hard tugs, she pulled them free and flung her arms around his neck. "I love you so much," she breathed when he eventually drew back. "So very, very much."

"*Mon cher coeur*," he murmured, leading her towards the bench and pulling her down onto his lap. He rested his chin on top of her head. "I like this. *C'est très agréable.*"

She turned to look at him. "You have always sounded like an Englishman, Giles. Yet now..."

He pulled her closer. "My mother tongue is linked to my heart, *ma chérie*. I cannot help but speak it when I am in love."

She brushed her fingers across his cheek. "*C'est très charmant.*"

"The very words that describe you, sweetheart."

He leaned back against the bench, taking her with him, and

they sat in silence for a few minutes, his arms around her waist. "Would you like to travel to France on our wedding trip?" he said eventually.

She twisted around in his lap, meeting his gaze. "Oh, yes! More than anything, Giles!"

"Excellent. We should make the most of our travels when we can. Before we know it, we might be settled at home like the Rothburys."

When she failed to respond, he said quietly, "Would you mind that very much, Georgie?"

Her lips curved softly. "Lady Fenmore told me the other day about the tower Henry Wilder built for his lady love. It seems that a life of domesticity can be spiced with both love and adventure. When the Wilders climbed to the top of that tower, it must have felt as if they were looking out over the entire world together."

"You do know they ended up having eleven children?"

"What?" She blinked.

"Indeed. And there is always the possibility we could follow a similar path once we marry." A crease appeared between his brows. "I don't want you to become bitter one day if your dreams of travel are thwarted by domestic concerns."

She remained silent for a moment. "I've been giving this a great deal of thought as I have been concerned about it too. But I have realised that I don't need to travel the world to study biology. The diversity of the natural world is so rich that I can never exhaust its wonders. England is as full of marvellous creatures as any other nation, and my work will always bring me joy even if I never get the chance to travel to foreign lands." She raised her hand to his cheek. "And when I am with you, my love, somehow I don't feel restless. I am happy to be where you are."

He kissed her lingeringly once more. "Shall we go butterfly hunting today, *chérie*?"

"I'd love to."

He glanced up at the cloudless sky. "Let us leave now, then, before it gets too warm."

They returned to the house, and Georgiana hurried up the stairs to change into a more suitable gown. Then, after Kirby had helped her into a walking dress of Cambric muslin, she slipped on her shoes and walked across to the window to look out at the splendid view. Somehow everything had turned miraculously around, and she couldn't quite grasp it as yet. How strange to have gone from the depths of despair one day to the heights of joy the next.

As she turned around, her gaze came to rest on the box on her bedside table containing the Purple Emperor larvae, now all in their pupal cases except for one, which had started to emerge from its chrysalis earlier this morning. She took a step closer and drew in a sharp breath.

The most beautiful butterfly lay inside.

Picking up the container, she hurried down the stairs to the hall where Giles awaited her. "Look!"

He took the box from her hands and glanced inside, giving a silent whistle. "A magnificent specimen, Georgie. That colour..."

She gazed at the iridescent purple of the butterfly's perfect wings. Truly, it was majestic.

"He is too beautiful to be pinned," Giles murmured. He raised a questioning gaze to hers. "Should we release it into the woods?"

"Yes," she said softly. "Such a creature was never meant to be kept in a box."

They walked along the winding drive until they came to some thick oak woodland some distance away. Giles carefully removed the butterfly, and when he let it go, it soared to the very tops of the trees.

"Purple Emperors actually live in the domain of birds," Giles said as he gazed up at it. "I sometimes think they are more bird than butterfly. They were made to fly high."

She placed her arm through his as the glorious creature fluttered out of sight, and then they walked on, stopping every now and then to observe the splendours of the natural world.

Georgiana had been instinctively drawn to Giles from the very beginning, and she hadn't quite understood why. But perhaps it had something to do with the immense value he placed on personal freedom. Someone who had such respect for his own liberty of mind and sovereignty of action would never want to trap anyone else in a cage. So many women were treated thus in their society, but Giles had made it clear he wanted her to fly free.

And that, more than anything, made Georgiana's heart soar.

A jutting-out root caused her to stumble, and she held on to her beloved's arm a little tighter as she regained her balance. Giles dropped his net to steady her with both hands and then turned her to face him.

Leaning down, he placed a soft, gentle kiss on her lips…like the faintest whisper of a butterfly's wing. Then he deepened the kiss, and Georgiana's hands crept up to rest near the heart of the man who loved her.

# Author's Note

## Charlotte Murchison

Charlotte Hugonin was born on 18 April 1788. Her parents were General Francis Hugonin and Charlotte (nee Edgar), a skilled florist and botanist.

Charlotte met her future husband Roderick Murchison in the early summer of 1815 and married him a few months later. She was interested in studying science, and during the first years of her marriage, she travelled extensively with her husband, teaching him about natural history. He, however, did not share her interests until much later in his life. In Roderick's words:

> "I...gave myself up recklessly but jovially to a fox-hunting life. It was during the years 1818-22 (three in the north country, and two seasons in Melton Mowbray) that my wife was always striving to interest me in something more intellectual than the case, and began to teach herself mineralogy and conchology..."

In 1824, the Murchisons moved to London. Encouraged by his wife, Roderick attended geology and chemistry lectures. His first paper for the Geological Society of London was titled "Geological Sketch of the North Western Extremity of Sussex, and the Adjoining Parts of Hants and Surrey" [published in the *Transactions of the Geological Society of London*, series 2, vol 2 pp97-107].

Charlotte suffered from recurring bouts of malarial fever. It is believed that she first fell ill in Italy in 1817, but this did not prevent her from accompanying her husband on his geological travels in later years.

By the 1860s, Charlotte's health had deteriorated, but she still supported her husband's work and assisted him with his scientific papers. She also was a talented illustrator.

Charlotte Murchison died on 9 February 1869.

Source: The Geological Society (geolsoc.org.uk)

# THE PLOT TO RESCUE NAPOLEON

When Napoleon Bonaparte was exiled to St Helena, he was heavily guarded, with ships continually patrolling the remote island in the South Atlantic.

Nonetheless, his supporters came up with various plots to rescue him using yachts, steamboats and even balloons. The strangest plot of all involved the use of a submarine.

Captain Tom Johnson, born in 1772, maintained that he was offered £40,000 from supporters of Napoleon to build a submarine to rescue Napoleon from exile on St Helena.

The British government took these plots to rescue Napoleon very seriously and implemented several preventative measures to stop them from coming to pass.

Colonel Francis Maceroni and Dr Barry O'Meara were both supporters of Napoleon and petitioned for his release from the island.

Further reading: https://www.cairn.info/revue-napoleonica-la-revue-2011-2-page-11.htm and https://www.smithsonianmag.com/history/the-secret-plot-to-rescue-napoleon-by-submarine-1194764/

# ABOUT THE AUTHOR

Alissa Baxter wrote her first Regency romance during her long university holidays. After travelling the world, she settled down to write her second Regency novel, which was inspired by her time living on a country estate in England.

Alissa then published two chick lit novels, *The Truth About Clicking Send and Receive* (previously published as *Send and Receive*) and *The Truth About Cats and Bees* (previously published as *The Blog Affair*).

Many years later, Alissa returned to her favourite period with her Linfield Ladies Series, a trio of Regency romances that feature women in trend-setting roles who fall in love with men who embrace their trailblazing ways... at least eventually.

Alissa currently lives in Johannesburg with her husband and two sons. She is a member of The Beau Monde - Regency Fiction Writers. Her website is www.alissabaxter.com.

# Acknowledgements

*The Aurelian Legacy: British Butterflies and Their Collectors* by Michael A. Salmon, Peter Marren, Basil Harley

*Scenes and Stories of a Clergyman in Debt* Vol. 2 of 3: Written During His Confinement in the Debtors' Prisons

*The History and Antiquities of Silchester, in Hampshire*, Third Edition

*Maria's first visit to London* by Elizabeth Sandham

*Letters to a Young Lady: on a Variety of Useful and Interesting Subjects: calculated to improve the heart, to form the manners, and enlighten the understanding* by Rev. John Bennett (published in 1798).

Beta Readers:
Pauline M. Ross
Mimi Noble

And many thanks to my excellent editor, Delia Latham.

# DEAR READER

If you enjoyed reading *The Baronet's Lady Biologist*, I would appreciate it if you would help others enjoy this book, too. Here are some of the ways you can help spread the word:

**Lend it**. This book is lending enabled so please share it with a friend.

**Recommend it**. Help other readers find this book by recommending it to friends, readers' groups, book clubs, and discussion forums.

**Share it.** Let other readers know you've read the book by positing a note to your social media account and/or your Goodreads account.

**Review it.** Please tell others why you liked this book by reviewing it on your favorite ebook site.

Everything you do to help others learn about my book is greatly appreciated!

*Alissa Baxter*

CPSIA information can be obtained
at www.ICGtesting.com
Printed in the USA
BVHW041757160223
658686BV00012B/269